Singer Island

A NOVEL

DAN HOLOHAN

2nd Edition

"And where we lived, they would all come to land on this one stretch of electric line. They'd sit next to one another, like beads on a rosary. My father told me that's how they pray; that if I listened carefully I could hear all those Hail Marys and Our Fathers in the cooing. He said they were praying for a safe place."

- Clare

1

The seashell was about the size of a girl's toenail, colored the lightest bronze and rainbowed three times with ivory. It was simple and perfect and he stooped to pick it up, being careful not to bend the wrong way. He didn't need back problems now that he was done.

Charlie Molloy straightened up and reached into the shell with his pinkie. Got as much of the sand out of it as he could. He'd rinse the rest when he got back to the apartment he and Donna had for the whole month of February here on Singer Island in Florida. He was wearing sneakers and didn't want to go too near the water; otherwise he would have used the surf.

The standing seabirds turned their backs to him and faced the light breeze as he trudged the sand. They were like daily commuters, looking down the track for an overdue train. It was good to be here, away from the snow and the crowds. Seventy degrees, with a robin's egg sky. Could be warmer, but he'd take it.

Charlie was doing everything that he was supposed to be doing today, now that he was finally done. Walk the beach awhile, and when he had enough of that, go sit with

Donna again and maybe read more Thomas Hardy. Or maybe they'd go for a drink. Retirement was still too new for him to just go and sit on the beach and read all day. She was able to do that. She could always do that, and she loved the sun, but he needed to move right now, even if it meant going nowhere in particular.

This beach was fun-house sloped down by the surf, which made the going tough on his ankles and knees, but up above, where the sand was flatter, it was also deep, and he didn't like walking there because it was reminding him of those last years at work.

He had traveled a lot in airplanes and cars, and he slept in questionable hotel beds in rooms where he never noticed the pictures on the walls or the colors of the wallpaper. He hated those little bars of soap that were small enough to disappear up your ass if you weren't careful, and the TVs that took five seconds to move from one channel to the next.

Some of the hotels, the cheaper ones (and he had stayed in plenty of those) smelled like a nasty mop. The clerks would sometimes give him a handicap room, even though he wasn't handicapped. He'd ask for an ordinary room, but those were all gone, so he'd be stuck with the damn too-high toilet that always messed with the trigonometry of his internal plumbing. In the old days, he'd be able to put his feet on the phone book and the Yellow Pages when he got a too-high toilet. That gave him the proper angle to take care of business, but what hotel has phone books and Yellow Pages in their rooms these days? Gideon's Bible is too thin, and besides, they only give you one of those, if they give it at all anymore.

One time, he opened the door with the card key the desk clerk had just given him and there was a couple going at it on the bed like Cirque du Soleil was in charge of the event. The woman screamed. The man snapped his head sideways, barked a curse. Charlie apologized, shut the door softly, and waited for the very slow elevator to take him back to the desk, four floors down. He looked down at his companions: one carry-on bag, and one briefcase. The woman kept screaming.

"There's a couple in the room you gave me," he said to (by his nametag) Mr. Deepro Patel.

Mr. Patel checked his computer and sing-songed, "Four-thirty? No, sir. That room is empty and clean. Very empty. Very clean. The computer says so. See?" He turned the screen so Charlie could see. "The computer is correct. See?"

"Well then I suppose what just happened didn't really happen. The screwing and the screaming? Okay, I'll just go back up there and join them in bed. Do you sell Vaseline in your gift shop, Mr. Patel?"

"Vaseline? No, we don't have a gift shop. I'm very sorry, sir. Very, very sorry. There is a CVS not far from here, though." Sing-song.

"Do you know if they sell Panax Ginseng? I'll also need some of that if I'm going be part of a household of three."

"Panax Ginseng? I don't understand, sir."

"It's a natural herb. It helps with the, well, you know." Charlie points at his crotch. "Little Chucky may need some help if there's another guy in the sack. I'm sure you can understand."

"I'm getting confused, sir."

"I was joking, Mr. Patel. I'm very tired. May I please have a different room?"

"If you insist, sir, I will accommodate you, but there is nothing wrong with four-thirty. Nothing at all. Very empty. Very clean. The computer says so. See?" Sing-song.

"I humbly insist, Mr. Patel. Thank you."

Mr. Patel gives him a handicap room.

He had appointments all day long and the people at the companies he visited were fussy about time. It hadn't always been that way. When he was younger, before there was an Internet, Charlie would visit the people and bring them news they couldn't get anywhere other than at the trade shows, or by calling the company for a catalog. The people were happy to see Charlie in those days because he brought not only news of the products, but also industry gossip. He kept their catalogs up to date and shared what he had heard. He got very good at telling stories, and even better at listening, and he closed sales because they liked him. People buy from people they like, and Charlie liked people.

Whenever Charlie visited a customer, he would talk to everyone equally. He ignored no one. He'd learn their names. He'd admire the objects on their desks, and the photos taped to the grey cubicle walls. He'd ask about their kids and the trophies. He noticed and appreciated everything, and he'd always work his way around to what their favorite pastry was.

And as soon as he left that office, he'd draw a map of the place, showing each desk. He'd write the name of the person at each desk, and all that he had learned about him or her. The next time he visited, he'd stop at a local bakery and buy the pastries each person liked. He'd study his map before he went in so he'd get all the names and the pastries right, and all the other details fresh in his mind, and then he'd go to work. And the people loved Charlie for this. He cared about them. He really did. What a guy.

But people grow older and they retire, and the Internet arrived, and now, what's new is as close as a click, and thanks to social media, so is the gossip. He still had his stories and his office maps, and his list of their favorite pastries, and his listening was never better, but the younger people that were coming into the business these days had little time for Charlie and his old-fashioned ways. And some of the companies were now billing their time by the hour, the way law firms do, and that left even less room for what Charlie was good at, which was The Chat. He still tried his best, but it wasn't working as well as it once did.

He was glad to be finally done.

The sand was slowing him and now it made him think of the dream.

His responsibilities back then often woke him from shallow sleep. A blizzard was approaching from the West, or thunderstorms were rising with the urgent gestures of The Weather Channel guy. He'd worry about how he was going to make this trip. What if something happens? What's his back-up plan?

In his dream, he'd be at some airport, already through security, and waiting to board the completely full flight. People were crowding each other. It was sweaty. There were constant garbled announcements he had to strain to hear. Kids were running and whining, stepping on people's feet, and parents were just staring at their smart phones and letting the kids do whatever the hell they wanted to do. Young men with splayed legs and rapper sneers were each taking up three seats. They didn't care.

Carry-on luggage and opened lunch bags were taking up the other seats. He wished he was somewhere else, anywhere else, and in his dream, he would look around for the bar, but then he would notice that his catalogs were missing, or he'd suddenly realize that he was naked because he had forgotten to pack his clothes.

He'd panic in his dream and try to rush back to his house to make things right, but his house was always impossibly far away in his dream, and he had to run past people and circumstances that beat him down and slowed him, as the sand on Singer Island was slowing him now. In his dream, his daughter, or his wife, or his granddaughter would appear, each with an emergency. They needed him to fix it, and right now. Or a stranger would send him off on some crazy tangent that pulled him deeper into his dream and a tossing panic.

He'd wake like he was breaking the surface of a dark ocean, breathless with despair, and disgusted with himself for allowing it to happen again. He knew that none of this was real, but still. He'd mutter as Donna breathed softly beside him, curled and small under the quilt. It's not *real*, he'd say. Not *real*. Stop it. He'd push off the sweat-wet sheets and toss his legs over the side of their bed. Sit for a time. Smooth the pillow quietly and try lying on his other side. It's not really happening, he'd think. You're okay. Change the channel. This is *not* real.

But his dream, it just laughed at him. It would return.

He ran in sand many times in the dream. He had grown up on Long Island and he knew sand, and how it was beautiful and timeless, but also ruthlessly grasping. It could burn his bare feet in the heat of the summer. It could break down his knees and his ankles when he walked in its deepness, and it couldn't care less about him. He knew that. He had learned that. It was a part of nature, and it was dead.

He was so glad to be done. Ravenous young people, with ambition as sharp as knives, had appeared in his company a few years back. Each had an engineering degree, a paper Charlie had never earned. They were all about the Internet and social media, and they spent most of their time staring at screens and tapping, rather than talking and listening to people who were in the same room with them. They forgot people's names, or never bothered to really hear them in the first place. They knew little of actual face-to-face relationships, or of pastries. The company paid these youngsters less than they paid him, but only because they were kids and a company can take advantage of kids for a time. They all do.

And they circled Charlie like vampires, these kids. If he was gone, his salary and his benefits would be up for grabs. They wanted to suck the life right out of him. He saw that in their eyes, and in the smirks they exchanged when he was trying to explain to them about the way it used to be, and how good it all was when relationships really mattered, and about The Chat, and about the pastries. But it was like talking to the dead. Their eyes emptied and went dull when he walked into their cubicles.

And then Mr. Ho Kim showed up.

Mr. Ho Kim was born in Flushing, NY, right in the shadow of the old Shea Stadium. Many South Koreans began coming to the U.S. in the '80s and what came to be called Koreatown had quickly spread eastward along

Northern Boulevard in Flushing. Before long, it reached right into the tony North Shore of Nassau County. Mr. Ho Kim was 28 years old, and now he was Charlie's big boss. He just showed up one day as the General Manager of the whole shebang. He had graduated from Harvard, and then stacked a joint major in Marketing and Operations Management from Wharton on top of that. Smart fella and he had a rocket up his ass. The company needed a turnaround specialist, and not being able to afford an older superstar, they recruited Mr. Ho Kim, just out of school.

And here he was.

Charlie was in his cubicle when he first met Mr. Ho Kim. They shook hands and Charlie smiled down at him. Mr. Ho Kim is noodle thin in a grey Brooks Brothers suit and shiny-red power tie. He measures a hair less than five feet tall. He could be a jockey, or share clothes with Donna, if he went that way.

Charlie was fascinated by the cold handshake and the smallness of Mr. Ho Kim's right hand. It was like holding a tiny bag of frozen baby carrots.

"Hi, Charlie." Queens in his voice. "I'm Mr. Ho Kim."

"Hi, Ho," Charlie said, and then, realizing the Lone Ranger aspect of that greeting, guffawed in his new boss' face. At least he didn't get Silver the horse involved.

"Good one, Charlie. Please call me *Mr. Kim.*" Thirty-one-degree Fahrenheit stare. Charlie thought he just heard a thermostat click somewhere.

"So tell me, Charlie. What exactly do you *do* for us?" That hit Charlie like a punch in the gut. He had been with the company for nearly his entire adult life. You'd think this guy would know what he did for them.

But he was new, right? A kid fresh out of college, just trying to find his way by talking to an older, wiser, company man, someone with real-world experience. Hey, they don't teach *everything* in college, right? Charlie figured he'd cut this book-smart kid some slack.

The problem, however, was that Charlie had never developed an elevator speech about what he did. He just *did*. No one at the company had ever asked him this question. What exactly do you *do* for us? Hey, they were supposed to know, right? This was like those drug commercials where they say you should tell your doctor about your medical condition. But isn't your doctor supposed to tell *you* about your medical condition?

Mr. Ho Kim is staring up at Charlie and waiting. He glances at his watch. It's a nice watch. He smoothes an iPhone out of his trouser pocket, thumbs it, glances down at the screen, and puts it back in his pocket. Looks up at Charlie again. Waits.

"Well, I love my job, Mr. Kim. I always have. I guess you could say that I travel a lot. I'm away from my wife,

Donna, much of the time. She understands but it's never easy. I know it's necessary, though, and I'm okay with that. I love this job."

Mr. Ho Kim is listening, but also glancing around, like he's decided something already and now has better things to do. He takes the iPhone out of his pocket again. Thumbs it. Reads a text while Charlie continues to talk. Answers the text. Charlie stops talking. Mr. Ho Kim looks up, annoyed. "Please *continue*," he says.

"But you were texting," Charlie says.

"Continue." He continues to text.

"I keep their catalogs up to date," Charlie says. "I bring my customers news about what we're doing, and show them the products. Answer all their questions. And if I can't answer right away I tell them that I'll get back to them, and when. And I always do. Oh, and I close a lot of sales. I also chat with them. That's so important, even though there's not as much chat these days as there was in the old days, but I do my best to get it going. It's important. It's all about relationships, Mr. Kim. I've been at this for a long time."

"That's interesting, Charlie," Mr. Ho Kim says, checking the iPhone again. Facebook this time. Charlie waits. Waits.

"You like the Mets?" Mr. Ho Kim asks without looking up. Charlie has a Mets cap hanging on his coat hook.

"You bet I do."

"I dress appropriately for work, Charlie. I don't think this is the place for baseball uniforms, do you?" Mr. Ho Kim slides the iPhone back into his pocket.

"I guess not."

"That's good, Charlie. Thanks for understanding that image matters in business." Mr. Ho Kim shoots his cuffs. Nice cufflinks. He touches his trouser pocket, checking to be sure the iPhone is still there. "And that's interesting, what you've been doing for us. Very interesting. Thank you for sharing those thoughts with me, Charlie. Now I need to tell you about a program we'll be instituting in the coming weeks. It's called Kaizen. Ever hear of it?"

"No. Is it like meditation or something? Zen?"

"*Kaizen*, Charlie. It's a Japanese word that means change for the better. It's what we'll be doing here in the coming days. We'll be changing for the better. We'll be striving for perfection. How do you feel about perfection, Charlie?"

"Well, no one's perfect," Charlie laughs, and then wonders why he did.

"This *funny* to you, Charlie?"

Some of the air just left the room.

"Well, it's just the thought of chasing something you'll probably never be able to catch. *Nobody's* perfect. I mean, what's the point? It's like a dog chasing its tail. It's silly." He chuckles. Can't help himself. He wonders what sort of dog Mr. Kim would own. Probably a pit bull.

"The *point* is the journey, Charlie. And the *belief* that perfection is possible within an organization such as ours. That's change for the better." Jack Nicholson smile.

"Some things never change, Mr. Kim, but we've always tried to do the best we can with what we've got. I believe in that. Do the best you can with what you've got."

"You're old-school, aren't you, Charlie?" Mr. Ho Kim glances at his watch. Charlie considers the question and the iPhone is out again. Facebook.

"I guess you could say that," Charlie says. "I've been at this job for a very long time. My customers like me."

Mr. Ho Kim's head snaps up. "*Our* customers, Charlie." He jabs the iPhone at Charlie, like a revolver. "You may be visiting them, but they're *our* customers. They belong to *all* of us. Not *you*. The *group*, Charlie. The *company*. And we must all work together to change for the better, to improve so that we may serve *our* customers better, to strive for perfection so that this company prospers. Do you understand that, Charlie?"

He keeps pointing the iPhone. Why is he pointing the iPhone?

"Do you want this company to prosper? *Do you?*"

"Yes, Mr. Kim." (Maybe a Rottweiler?)

"That's *good*, Charlie. Now please tell me three things that you do right now that help this company prosper. Three things. *Quickly.*" Mr. Ho Kim snaps his fingers three times, looks back at his iPhone.

"Well, when I visit *our* customers, I always arrive with pastries. I've learned what each of our customers likes, and I bring those. I keep maps of their offices and I think they really appreciate that."

"Maps? What? To find their offices? Don't you know where they're located? Do you not have GPS? Is that too new-school for you, Charlie? GPS?"

"No, Mr. Kim. I mean maps of where their desks are within their offices, and who sits at which desk. To remember their names, and the names of their kids, and the trophies they've won for bowling, and baseball, and other things that matter to them. And their favorite pastries. I *really* listen. People come and go, and I keep up with all of that, and with the changes that are going on with people. That's why they like me. That's why they buy from me. You can't buy maps like that. Mr. Kim. You have to make them. It takes time and you have to care about the people."

"Are you a *baker*, Charlie?"

"No, Mr. Kim, I'm not a baker." (Doberman?)

"That's good, Charlie, because you confuse me with this cake business." Mr. Ho Kim twitches his head quickly. Three times. Blinks. Touches his trouser pocket.

"We'll let that go for now, Charlie. But once again, can you tell me *three* things you do right now that help this company prosper?" Snaps his fingers again. Snap. Snap. Snap.

"Well, I respect their time," Charlie says after a moment.

"And *how*, Mr. Ho Kim returns with a vicious verbal backhand, "does that help this company *prosper*, Charlie? *How?*" He checks his watch.

"I'm not sure. I guess because I'm thinking about them. About their time, and how it's valuable to them. When you come right down to it, time is really all any of us has to offer."

"*Really*, Charlie? That's very deep. Very, very *deep*. Tell me something. Do you spend a lot of time in waiting rooms, Charlie? They keep you *waiting*, Charlie? Remember, that's all you *have*. *Time*, right? *Our* time." The iPhone is back in his hand.

"Sometimes I have to wait."

"Is that a *waste* for this company, Charlie? All your *waiting?*"

"I don't think so. I always get in. Sometimes it takes time, that's all. It's business. People are busy. I'm courteous toward them."

"And do you put the pastries on your expense reports, Charlie?" he shifts. "I'm curious." He's thumbing the iPhone again.

"Uh, yes. I do. Yes."

"I see."

"Now, wait a minute," Charlie says. "I've *always* done that. It helps sales. It's *always* gone through with Accounting's approval. I include all my receipts."

"Receipts? For cake?"

"Yes."

"You mean like crumb buns? Receipts for *crumb buns?*"

"Well, some of the people prefer Danishes. Mostly cheese. Others like apple turnovers. It varies with the city, but yes, there are some crumb-bun people. I keep good notes. It's all on my maps."

"And you spend time waiting on line in bakeries, buying pastries with company money when you could be selling our products and helping our company become perfect? This is not Kaizen, Charlie. This is not being a team player. Team players play for the *team*, not for the bakeries of America. We need to change for the better, Charlie."

"But it works for me, Mr. Kim."

"Oh, is it all about *you*, Charlie? Or is it about the *team?*" iPhone back in the trousers.

"I was talking about the pastries and how they help me communicate with people."

"Do you understand social networking, Charlie? *That's* how people communicate nowadays. Facebook. Twitter. Pinterest. Instagram. LinkedIn. This is how we do things nowadays, not by eating fattening cake together." The iPhone appears again.

"I guess I'm just old-school, Mr. Kim. I don't do computers too well. I send personal notes in my own handwriting. People appreciate that. It's how I do my job. I've always done it that way."

"Do you do have a *phone*, Charlie?"

"Yes, I have an iPhone. Like yours." Charlie fumbles for it in his pocket. Holds it out.

"And what do you do with your iPhone in that childish New York Mets case to help the company become perfect, Charlie? That iPhone is a computer, isn't it?"

Charlie looks at his iPhone like it's something he's seeing for the first time. Childish? He looks back at Mr. Ho Kim who is again looking at his own iPhone. Charlie doesn't have an answer to this question. He's never thought about the iPhone as a computer. He has it because flip phones went out of style. The iPhone tells him stories, and it's pretty easy to use. He has it because he has to have a phone. He bought the case because he's a Mets fan. Now he's confused.

"Thoughts, Charlie?" Mr. Ho Kim's hand is down at his side. He's snapping his fingers slowly. *"Thoughts? Hmm?"*

"I think that *people* matter, sir. And I think college is great, even though I never went. But I also know for sure that you don't learn *everything* in college, and I know that nobody in this world is perfect, or ever will be. I know that life is about relationships, and I know this company isn't perfect and never will be. That's reality, Mr. Kim, and I've *lived* it. I've been here since you were a little boy, Mr. Kim." Charlie holds his hand out, palm down and level with the top of Mr. Kim's head.

Mr. Ho Kim stares at the hand. The thermostat clicks again. "Goodbye, Charlie." He spins on his heel and leaves, taking short, quick steps, iPhone in hand. (Chihuahua?)

"Bye, Ho," Charlie whispers to his back. "Bye, Ho. It's off to work we go."

But not for long.

Charlie had known Frank Moore, his sales manager, for a bunch of years. Frank wasn't a traveling man; he had seven kids and his wife needed him to stay close to home. He coached kids' soccer and was a good guy to share a drink or two with.

Frank wasn't good at hiding his emotions, though, and Charlie didn't like what he was seeing right now.

"I guess you heard there are some changes in the wind, Charlie."

"More than in the wind," Charlie says. "I think they've arrived."

"I know you've met Mr. Ho Kim," Frank says. "He mentioned he had a conversation with you about what you do. He doesn't approve of the pastries."

"Not everybody gets that," Charlie says. "It's what I do, though. You know that. It helps sales. Always has."

"I know, Charlie, but he *definitely* doesn't get it."

"So he wants me to stop buying them? He didn't say that to me. Not in so many words anyway."

"Well, he didn't say that to me either. What he said was that he wants you off the road and into Inside Sales, and right now."

"Are you serious? Those people aren't salespeople. They're order-takers. You know that. The phone rings; they answer it and take the order. I'm the one out there in the trenches doing the selling. I'm the one that creates those phone calls."

"I can't be holier than the church," Charlie. "He's the big boss now and I gotta go along with what he wants or I'll be looking for a new job. We're striving for perfection these days. You got the word on that. So did I."

"So he wants me on the phones?"

"Actually, he doesn't want you on the phones. He says you talk too much and you waste too much time. He wants you on a computer. You'll be processing orders starting tomorrow. Your trips are cancelled. Sorry."

"What? That makes no sense, Frank. How can the company afford to have me doing that? I'm making a salesman's salary?"

"Well that's the thing, Charlie. Once you make the move you'll be making what the computer guys make."

"But that's a lot less than what I make. That's what they pay the new kids. All they do is tap keyboards all day long. How am I supposed to live on that?"

"I don't know, Charlie. I'm just following orders here."

"And I don't know anything about computers, Frank. You know that. How am I supposed to work on computers?"

"I don't know, Charlie. I guess you could learn."

"Ah, c'mon, Frank. Is there another way? I don't want to give up the road. It's what I do. How can you do this to me, Frank?"

"I don't have a choice, Charlie. I *need* this job." Frank looks at his shoes. "What can I do, Charlie? It is what it is. I don't know what you said to him, but you made a bad impression on the man." Frank looks up. Just can't hide those emotions.

Charlie feels for him. "Maybe it's time for me to leave, Frank."

"That's your choice, Charlie. I'll miss you, but it's your call."

"I gave my heart and soul to this company, Frank. You know that. I did the best I could with what I've got. I always have."

"I know, and I'm sorry, Charlie. I'm just telling you what they're telling me. Please don't kill the messenger."

Frank got him a mediocre severance package, which he accepted after talking to Donna. He called it voluntary retirement and tried to hold onto the tatters of his pride. No gold watch. Just an anemic pension that may or may not work, followed by a small and unforgettable retirement party at his desk.

Curtis Hayden was one of the young engineers, but he seemed better than the others. He often asked Charlie questions about the old times, and about his sales techniques, especially about how he kept the maps of where his customers sat, and about the pastries they liked, their kids' names, all of what Charlie was good at doing with people.

The Chat.

Charlie always took the time to tell Curtis Hayden stories, and he really seemed interested. Maybe Charlie had been wrong about the young engineers.

On his last day, when Charlie was clearing out his desk, Curtis Hayden showed up with a surprise. It was a box of Twinkies. Charlie had mentioned that Twinkies, an old-school cake, were *his* favorite pastry.

Curtis Hayden spread out some paper towels and lined up the Twinkies in a vertical row. When that was done, he made another row, this one went from the bottom of the vertical row and off to the right side of Charlie's desk, forming a large letter L.

"How about that?" Curtis Hayden said. "*Appropriate*, don't you think? You know what L stands for, doncha, Charlie? I mean you of all people really *should*." He laughed, but not in a nice way.

And then the rest of the young engineers came into the cubicle. They'd been watching from around the corner and they were also laughing. Each of the young engineers had a thumb and forefinger on his forehead in the shape of an

L. They kept laughing and looking at each other. Smirking. They each grabbed a Twinkie. One said, "Stick yours up your ass on your way out, old man." He spat a laugh and left.

Charlie said nothing.

Curtis Hayden was the last to leave. "You won't be missed, old fool," he said. He took a bite of his Twinkie and spit it onto Charlie's desk. Tossed the rest onto the desk with it. Squashed it with his palm. Wiped his palm on the edge of the desk. Held out his hand. "Want to shake?"

Charlie said nothing.

"I guess not. Enjoy your *Twinkie*, loser."

And that was that.

Done.

And then there was a second shell, as beautiful as the first. He bent carefully, poked with a pinky, brushed away the rest of the sand and put the shell into the pocket of his shorts that didn't hold his iPhone. He didn't want to scratch the screen. The iPhone still mattered, even though he was finally done. It told him stories.

He looked down and saw more shells. He huffed a small laugh, shook his head, realizing that he had been inside of himself, looking out but not really *seeing*. Like he was in some anonymous, cheap hotel room. *The damn job.*

Stop it; you're done.

These shells were *everywhere*, and he suddenly realized that they were all of one species, each the remains of a tiny clam, the sort you'd want in a good chowder. This is not the way it is on Long Island, he thought. These tiny shells littered the dead sand like confetti, billions of them, and nearly all the same, but each a bit different in its own way, like snowflakes. He stooped and picked up more. He held one to his tongue and tasted it. Salt. And what? Calcium? He stopped and watched a cargo ship heading for the Intracoastal Waterway. He wondered what it was bringing. What a life that must be, working on a ship. A cloud moved and the sun blared down. Felt good.

When his pocket was full, he walked back to her. It took a while. He had walked further than he had thought he would. He missed her.

"You ready to go, Charlie?" Donna asks, stretching out of her beach chair, smooth and tan and confident. "Time to go?"

He nods and starts folding the two chairs. She bends easily, grabs the blue beach bag. She's blonde and Kristin Chenoweth tiny.

"There are beautiful shells here," he says. "They're all nearly the same. They're these tiny clams. Wait 'til you see them."

"That's nice. What do you want to do now?" Donna asks.

"I don't know. It's up to you."

"Let's go back to the place and we'll figure it out from there."

"Okay. Maybe we'll go get a drink?"

"Sure, we can do that, Charlie. Hey, are those shells in your pocket or are you just happy to see me?" She points. Jiggles her eyebrows like Groucho Marx.

Charlie laughs. "Shells. And I *am* happy to see you. I'm sorry I was gone for so long. It's hard for me to sit still. Thanks for putting up with me. I hope you weren't lonely."

"No. I'm never *really* alone, Charlie. You know that. What will you do with the shells?"

"I think I'll save them for Trista?"

Donna considers this for a moment. "Okay," she says.

When Charlie first met Donna, she was just 19 years old, and she had a pronounced lisp, which he loved because it made her that much more adorable. She also told stories that stopped abruptly in the middle. He'd wait for her to say more but she'd just giggle.

"Is that it?" he'd ask.

"Dathsit!" she'd lisp in her childlike way. His heart would melt as she leaned in to hug him. She smelled like a soft summer.

On their second date, he asked her what she wanted from life. It was a windy winter Saturday on Long Island and they were at the mall, having lunch at Burger-N-Brew. She told him that she just wanted to be happily married and have kids. This on a second date. Well, he had asked.

He looked at her and smiled. "That's *all* you want? Nothing else?"

"Nothing elths."

"You sure?" he said.

"Yep. Dathsit!"

And that *was* it. She was prayer brought to life. He couldn't wait for their next date.

The third led to a fourth, and then they were inseparable. Her lisp faded with the years, and she picked up a toughness that arrived with fury on the day their daughter, Abigail, was born. They had waited years and prayed for Abby. They had nearly given up when the good news finally arrived.

Donna's labor wasn't long, but neither she nor Charlie knew what to expect. They had taken a Lamaze class, and Charlie was there in the room with her, stroking her hair and trying to get her to do that ridiculous breathing. He puffed and blowed, which was what *she* was supposed to be doing, but the pains kept coming faster. She looked wide-eyed at Charlie and screamed.

"Come on, Donna. You can do it. Puff and blow. Come on. Puff! Blow!"

Charlie's lips were pursed and his cheeks were going like a bellows. "Come on, Donna. Come on." She was shrieking and sweating and writhing on the bed, ripping the sheets, making a hot, smelly mess of it all. He didn't know what else to do but to say, "Puff and blow, Donna. Please."

"Blow it out your *ASS!*" she hissed at him. Eyes like neon-green lasers.

No lisp whatsoever.

There was a small black-lacquered table in their rented-for-a-month, Singer Island apartment. He laid out a dozen of the shells on the table, pretty-side up, and used his iPhone to take a photo. It was perfect - beauty on black. He hit Send and the photo appeared on their daughter Abby's iPhone back on Long Island. Abby showed it to three-year-old Trista.

Chirp!

She asked if she can touch them. Isn't that sweet?

Tap, tap, tap.

Tell her I said soon. Everything okay?

Chirp!

Yeah, we're good, Daddy. Don't worry. Have fun.
You earned it.

When Abby was two years old, he held her sandy hands above her head and lifted her in and out of the surf at Tobay Beach on Long Island. It was a hot, humid Sunday afternoon in mid-July. The surf scooted in like piping plovers to tickle Abby's feet, and she squealed each time he lifted her. Her skin smelled like Coppertone and her laugh made him want to hold her forever, to pull her inside of him and protect her from all that was sharp in life.

A fishing boat was passing by and Abby said, "Daddy, can we walk to that boat?"

He smiled at how a child can believe that the Atlantic Ocean is only as deep as the top of her little foot.

"We'd need magic for that, Abby."

"Do you have magic, Daddy?"

"Sometimes."

She giggled.

The magic vanished 10 minutes later when, after she insisted that he let go of her hands, he did. He used the moment to rinse the sand from his own hands when a rogue wave appeared and knocked her down. She had turned her back on the ocean, as he had turned his back on her. She wanted to see if Donna was watching her be a big girl. She went down fast and hard and the undertow grabbed her and flipped her over twice. She screeched when she came up from under the water, gasping for breath. Charlie took two quick steps and pulled her from the surf. She screamed, *"Bad!"* Her eyes were terror-wide. She screeched, and pushed at his bare chest, and that ripped at his heart.

Bad *daddy*, he thought. *Bad.*

He carried her quickly back to the beach chairs and handed her shrieking down to Donna, who dried her with a blue beach towel and cooed over her. After a while, Abby calmed, but continued to stare at the ocean. She chewed her lower lip, and shivered. She now knew that the ocean didn't care about her. Not one bit. She knew.

Charlie walked the Singer Island beach the next morning, and this time with a plastic bag left over from his and Donna's trip to the grocery store. Milk for coffee, rolls, cold cuts, snacks, and, of course, wine. Now he was more careful with the shells he chose. Each was beautiful, but some more so than others. He began to look for patterns, knowing that the shells were all going home to Trista, and that she would look at each with a three-year-old's critical eye. How many rainbow stripes, Grandpa? How many browns? How many ripples? How white could a shell be? And some had holes, which made them perfect for necklaces. Can we make a beautiful necklace with ribbon? Can we make three of them? One for me and one for Mommy and one for Grandma? Can we count them all? Can we make believe the rug is a beach and dump them all out? Will you help me pick them up later, Grandpa?

He wanted to live long enough to see her again.

He wakes each morning before Donna does. He sits on the edge of their bed and marvels at how beautiful she still is, even after all these years. She sleeps with her small fist tucked under her chin, like she's trying to decide. She breathes quietly and her chest moves softly, like the surf on a late-spring morning when the wind is distracted and off somewhere else. He wonders how many more days there will be for them. And did they wait too long?

Darlin' you got to let me know.
Should I stay or should I go?

The words from that old song by The Clash were stuck in his head. It was playing in the bar when his friend Patrick (Don't call me Pat.) told him he was thinking about leaving Bertha, and this after 10 years of what they had always joked of as a mixed marriage - Irish and German. Napalm and dynamite.

They had all been friends for a year or so. Charlie knew Patrick through business; knew him before Bertha. He always smiled when he thought of her name, which she wouldn't catch up with for another 50 years. It had been her grandmother's name. It means "bright one," and Bertha does shine. She's is beautiful, like a distant granite mountain. He always kidded her about how she never seemed to change, never seemed to be any older. Forever lovely, forever strong.

She'd smile quietly and gaze off when he'd say that, like she was looking to be atop that granite mountain with someone. He could never tell what she was thinking, this quiet woman, but later, when she wasn't around, Patrick would say, "She likes it when you say shit like that to her. Likes it a *lot*."

"Do you say things like that to her?"

"Nah, we're married too long."

Patrick had lost the habit of romance.

If you say that you are mine,
I'll be there 'til the end of time.

Charlie was noticing the shells everywhere now on his beach walks. Some of their magic was gone now because of their sheer quantity. It was like a beauty pageant. So much gorgeous, all in one place. How do you decide which to choose?

The Clash played in his head as he chose this shell over that one. Should you stay or should you go, shell? Pageant winner or Miss Congeniality?

He had been married to Donna for a very long time. They had met and that was that. A blizzard of winter dating that turned into summer on the beach. She became his best friend and his lodestone, with her quiet, pulling strength, forever there to keep him centered when he needed it most. Like now, when he was terribly hurt and filled with doubt. Was he nothing more than just an old fool? Had the young engineers been right?

Had they?

He shook it off and thought again of Donna. Thought of how they once were. At first, there was the adorable lisp and the way she parted her blond hair down the middle.

The bright green eyes. The self-contained compactness of her. Her little feet. He thought The Beach Boys must have written their songs with Donna Doyle in mind. She was shy then, and tiny, and she looked up at the world from beneath long, light lashes. The wonder of her. He gasped at her beauty.

"What do you want from life?" he had asked.

"I justh want to be happily married and have kidths," she lisped.

"That's it?"

"Dathsit!"

They had clung to each other for better or for worse, in sickness and in health, for richer and for poorer, and in good times and in bad throughout all these years. No one had said you were supposed to be happy every day. That wasn't in the vows. Go read them again. Nothing in there at all about forever happy. You just do what you can with what you've got, and hopefully, you get by. You hold on to each other. Dathsit.

Time had explained this to both of them, explained it *hard*, and again and again, and they did the best they could with what they had.

Patrick (Don't call me Pat.) had flown down from LaGuardia for just one day. He needed to talk to Charlie in private, so there they were, sitting at the bar.

"Do you still love her?" Charlie asks as The Clash asks that question from the bar's speakers. Stay or go?

"Yes, sometimes. I think so," Patrick says, "But I don't know for sure anymore, if you know what I mean. I mean I'm not sure. I might, but I just don't know. She wants nothing to do with my friends."

"She's not that way with us."

"You and Donna are different."

It's always tease tease tease.
You're happy when I'm on my knees.

"At the start, it was great. We went places. We did things together. It changed, though. I grew. My circle widened. She stayed the same, like you always say, and not just her looks. She's gorgeous, but she says that all she wants is me. Not these other people. She doesn't even do Facebook, for crissake."

"And that's a problem," Charlie says.

"Well, yeah. I need her to be more social, especially to my business friends, but she won't do that for me."

"That's important to you."

"It is. I'm social. She just goes off into her own world when we're with other people. She wants to lock me in there with her, like we're in a prison cell. That doesn't work for me anymore, Charlie. To tell you the truth, it never did. I just can't do it anymore. My friends matter to me, and so does my business. And so does Facebook. It matters."

"But do you still love her?"

Patrick swirled the ice in his drink. Looked in there for an answer.

Abby texted that Trista loved the photos of the shells he was sending each day and she wanted to touch them all.

Tap, tap, tap.

Tell her as soon as we get back. Promise. You good?

Chip!

I'm fine, Daddy. Take care of Mommy and don't worry.
Have fun.
And bring back stories!

Tap, tap, tap.

Okay. Love you.

Chirp!

Love you more!

Tap, tap, tap.

Not possible.

The seashells were everywhere now. He thought about the time he and Donna drove Skyline Drive through a part of Virginia. They were young and curious and had gotten off I-81, a blur of concrete. Suburban people driving into nature. *So* unnatural.

Within the first quarter-mile, they saw deer and they pulled over to watch them. There are deer on parts of Long Island, but none like these. Donna and Charlie oohed and aahed.

They drove on and saw even more deer, each time pulling over to watch. There were deer up the ass along that pretty road. Deer, deer, oh, dear.

After about two hours of this stop and go, Charlie wanted to run down the next deer they saw. And its mother. The magic was gone. Like the seashells, there were just too many of them, and the road was too slow with all these tourists and their cameras. They'd never get where they needed to be if they stuck with this damn road, so they looked at each other, and at the first chance, they laughed and dove down the mountain and back into the river of cars and trucks that is I-81. Done with that. *Good.*

If I stay there will be trouble.
If I go there will be double.

The seashells, like the sand, were everywhere and beautiful in death, but there were so many of them, each representing a full life, once lived. The beach was a timeless graveyard. The surf, a dirge. The seabirds, crustacean pallbearers. Death everywhere. A cold front had reached down from the North and poked its nasty fingertip into the state of Florida and worked it around roughly. Fifty degrees, cloudy and windy. The sun is just a small bleach spot on the fabric of grey clouds.

Sucks.

"Can you afford to do this?" Charlie asks Patrick. They order another round. (What a surprise.) "I mean just leave her like that? She gets half of everything, you know, including the business."

"I know. I'll have to see. I'd hate to have to give her all of that, especially the business, but we'll see."

"Is there another woman?"

"There could be."

"Is she in the picture now?" He waits. "You know what I mean." He waits. Waits.

"Yeah," Patrick finally sighs.

"You've been with her."

"She used to work for me, but not for a while. We had a small thing then. She got married and had kids, but she's on her own now, so yeah, I've been with her. Couple times. We got a little thing going now. A little thing. Just a couple times. It was real good. I think it could turn into something good."

"Kids?"

"Yeah, three, and they like me."

"What's not to like? You're a likable guy," Charlie says. Patrick shrugs. "But I always thought you never wanted kids."

"Well, I did, and if I had known from the start that Bertha didn't, I don't think I would have married her."

"Didn't you ever talk about that when you were starting out? Dating? When you first got married? You didn't talk about having kids?"

"It was too late by the time we got around to it. And then she springs it on me. I was okay with it because we were having good times back then. But now all she wants is me. No one else."

"But you've had a good life with her?"

"It's been okay."

"Do you love her?"

"I think I gotta do what's right for me, Charlie."

"So you'll leave her. That's what I'm hearing. Do you have a place?"

"Yeah, I'll be okay."

"When will you decide?"

"Within three weeks. I'm giving myself three weeks."

"Why three?"

"I don't know. It's better than two, I guess."

"Okay. We're here if you need us."

"I know that. Thanks."

Patrick doesn't bother to ask Charlie how *he's* doing.

If you say that you are mine,
I'll be there 'til the end of time.

They drove across the bridge and down the highway to
Palm Beach to watch a film called *Brooklyn*. It was about a
young Irish woman who emigrates to Brooklyn (go figure)
in 1952 and meets a young Italian plumber, falls dizzy
in love, and secretly marries the guy. It's another mixed
marriage.

She returns to Ireland for a while because her older
sister, who was stuck with their widowed mother, dies, and
she doesn't know where her loyalties lie now - with her
secret husband, or with the dear old Irish ma?

While in that lovely country, she meets and, at the
urging of friends who think she is single, innocently dates
a handsome, but unworldly, Irish bachelor, who is about to
inherit a large farm and a country house from his elderly
parents. He wants her to stay in Ireland, her rightful home,
and make a life with him. He, too, does not know that she is
married. Oh, boy.

Should she stay or should she go?

It was a very appropriate film to see that week.

He asks Donna about a good container for the seashells,
which are becoming an impressive pile. They are in a store
in the mall where the movie theater is. This store caters to
the beach crowd. They have lots of those *Life Is Good* tee

shirts and hats, the ones with the silly, stick-figure people having fun.

Donna has one of those hats. He bought it for her years ago. It has embroidered pink-and-white flip-flops on the front, and that forever-uplifting *Life Is Good* logo above the strap on the back. The hat is Easter green and he remembers how good it looks against her blonde hair, especially when a light breeze and the sun are playing with her. She liked it when he bought that hat for her, mainly because he had thought to buy it (You look adorable.), but he hadn't seen her wear that hat in years. She had other hats now.

He asks her if she still thinks Life Is Good. "Ah, it's okay," she says, wrapping her arm around his waist. He laughs.

She shows him a green wooden box with a hinged cover. It reads Seashells on its top. "Pretty, but that's real glass there," Charlie taps the cover. She puts it back.

Later that day, they're in a dollar store and they settle on a pink, heart-shaped plastic bucket that comes with a small shovel. It was just Trista's size, and it was cheap. "Abby used to have a pink bucket like this. Remember?" Donna says, looking it over. "Just right."

When he pours the bag of shells into the plastic bucket they make the sound of a slot machine paying off. Lots of rattling and clicking. Winner, winner, chicken dinner.

Soon.

They were morning-walking the Singer Island neighborhood called Palm Beach Shores, like so many others their age. They began with the path along the Intracoastal and then worked their way back and forth through the grid of streets, like they were lacing a sneaker, or mowing a lawn, this way and then that way. They laughed at the fun mailboxes, some shaped like manatees, others like pink flamingos, and still others covered with seashells. They walked the mornings to burn calories so they could drink wine in the afternoons. Life is good.

"What does this street remind you of?" Donna asked.

He reached back through the treasure of their common memory and said, "That street we were on down here somewhere when we walked to mass that Sunday morning. We didn't have a rental car. We took a taxi from the airport to the hotel to save money. I don't remember what year that was. It was winter, though. That's why we were there. The houses here are similar, and the mailboxes, too, although *that* one is really *beyond* wacky." He points to a pink mermaid. Her breasts open to accept the mail. "I don't think they do that for the grandkids. I mean the mailboxes. It could be that older people in Florida just get childlike. I don't know."

"Could also be the booze," Donna says.

She reaches for his hand. He thinks about how soft hers is.

"Remember that day when we were dating and we went to Jones Beach to walk on the sand?" he says.

Common memory. Who in their right mind would trade that for anything?

"It was early-spring," she answers.

They pass a few more houses with their silly mailboxes and he wonders what it would be like to just stay here forever.

"That was the day I knew for sure that I loved you," he says.

She squeezes his hand. "You've told me that many times, Charlie." No trace of the lisp anymore. No surfer-girl part down the center of her hair either. It doesn't matter. He still hears The Beach Boys singing when he looks at her.

"It was so foggy that day," he says. "We couldn't see the surf, but we could hear it. And we were the only ones there. It was like being under gauze. The light was milky and the air was so still. Even the birds were quiet. Remember? I knew for sure then. I knew it was you."

He looks down at her and she is smiling up at him. She has a Lauren Hutton gap between her top front teeth. Such beauty. "We couldn't get enough of each other back then," he says.

"It was a long time ago," she says.

They were eating fish in a reasonable restaurant when his iPhone chirped a text from Patrick.

I'm not sure what to do.
What would you do?

He shows Donna the text. "I know what you'd do," she says. "You'd stick."

He starts to text back and then erases it. He starts again.

"Be careful," she says. "Wait. He's fragile."

The food arrives and they eat for a while. He picks up the iPhone and texts Patrick without showing her.

I would think about who I would want to be with 30 years from now, so that I had someone to help me be old.

"What did you write?"

He shows her. She nods. They eat in silence.

Chirp!

Wrong answer, man.

He slides the iPhone, forever filled with stories, across the table. Donna picks it up. Reads it. "He's done," she says.

"I know."

Patrick tells Bertha the next day. He doesn't wait out the three weeks. The rest of it is all brief, concerned-friend texts over a handful of days. No voices on the iPhone. No face to face. Just texts. Easier that way.

Cold front lingers. Fifty degrees and still windy on Singer Island. The sky has gathered into a surly gang of dark, grey clouds leaning on each other.

Snowing on Long Island.

Sucks.

Tap, tap, tap.

How is she doing?

Chirp!

She took it surprisingly well.

Tap, tap, tap.

Did you move out?

Chirp!

Yeah, I'm staying with a friend in New Jersey. The commute is a bitch, though.

Tap, tap, tap.

We're here if you need us.

Chirp!

"That's so sad," Donna says. "I'm going to miss her."

"We'll lose her, won't we?"

"That's the way it usually works," Donna says. "You knew him first."

"I think he still loves her in his own way, but he wants things to be perfect. Like it was for us in the fog on Jones Beach. Remember? When we were young?"

"That's not possible," Donna says.

2

Charlie always thought the best bars were the ones where you wouldn't see the same people again for the rest of your life. The un-Cheers bars. The bars in the airports, especially the ones on his way home to Donna, were such places. These were the bars of the rising, unexpected thunderstorms that arrived with their delays and angry rumblings, and endless possibilities. The bars he didn't expect to be in. They kept him away from Donna, sure, but they also brought him the stories that he needed to keep himself going. Good stories. Bad stories. It didn't matter to Charlie. He could work any story into something better than it was.

He never belonged to an airline club. The company wouldn't pay for that, and he couldn't afford it on his own. Besides, the club people weren't his people; the bar people were. The bar was better than the gate area where the young men splayed their legs and the children ran wild. During a storm, the gates were like the last days of Saigon.

He accepted delays as a part of life, and he cherished the stories that arrived with those delays, both the good and the bad. He pitied the red-faced people who yelled at airline employees. Thunderstorms and blizzards are not a choice, and the people with the red faces will probably die sooner than calmer people because they don't understand the simple grace of acceptance. They don't understand that Nature doesn't care about any of us. And besides, even if you could, do you really want to be flying through a thunderstorm?

He liked to take the stool at the corner of the bar if he could get it because, from there, he could watch more people, and especially the bartenders. Bartenders did the best they could with what they had, which was often-horrible people, and they worked for tips that many times didn't arrive because of the miasma of anger that often hung over the terminals during the days of delays. Charlie tipped well, even when times were tough. He saw the tips as his tuition.

The pours were sometimes stingy at the airports because of the shot-counting machines attached to the bottle spouts. It was better to drink house wine, and red worked best for Charlie.

Oh, and some airport bars had a policy of asking for ID, no matter what, and this was ridiculously delightful to watch. In fact, there's a sign right up there on the mirror behind the booze. Check it out:

NOTHING PERSONAL.
WE CARD _EVERYONE_.

This is probably the law, but many of the older people object to this nevertheless. They rail on about common sense being a thing of the past, and how government regulation is ruining this country, and it's all the president's fault. The bartenders wait patiently for the IDs, or they go wait on others while The Angry Old grumble on about the injustice of it all. "Hey, can't you see I'm *old*? Open your frickin' eyes!"

He once watched an old man snarl at a bartender, "You want to see *my* ID, kid? Hey, I was drinking booze when you were still calling shit poo-poo!" The bartender just stood there like a pallbearer, waiting for the coot's ID to appear. The coot looked around the bar with an I-sure-told-him smirk on his wrinkled puss. Charlie raised his glass off the bar an inch to the guy, smiled and shrugged. What can you do?

"Ridiculous!" the coot spat, skimming his driver's license onto the bar. The bartender nailed it with a quick finger before it slid off the edge. He picked it up, glanced at it, said nothing, handed it back, and got the coot's drink.

"Ridiculous!"

No tip.

That grouchy old bastard is gone now, never to be seen again. But, ah, his *story*. That stuck around, and it got better with age.

Charlie has the corner stool in a bar at O'Hare Airport, and again, during a thunderstorm that would make Steven

Spielberg smile. It had reared up like a dark-gray, wild stallion and pummeled every flight schedule in America. He glanced across the crowded concourse at the rain hammering the plate glass, trying to get in. He was waiting it out, wanting and needing to get home to Donna, but he was patient, as always. What can you do?

Take a seat and watch for a while. We're not going anywhere. There's an empty stool to Charlie's left, but don't take that one. *She* needs that one.

Here she comes.

She's tall with raven's wing hair. She slides onto her stool like warm butter onto hot toast. She tugs the hem of her skirt once, but not too much. She smiles hello at Charlie, crosses long legs with a nylon shush, and aims sea-green eyes at the bartender, whose legs lock.

"Classic Manhattan, please," she rasps. Somewhere, Scarlett Johansson just smiled in appreciation.

The bartender stands frozen for a moment, a moment. And then.

And then he reaches for just the right glass. He gets a new white towel and carefully wipes that glass. Looks at her. He holds the glass up to the light, but keeps looking at her. She smiles pure sin at him. Thunder booms. Rain sheets off the windows.

The guy to Charlie's right is about the same age as the lady and corporate handsome. He has been quietly sipping for a while. The bartender delivers the lady's Manhattan like a chalice. She accepts it. Sips. The bartender watches. A nod. A smile. Grand.

The corporate guy leans forward around Charlie and says, "Can you tie?" This is the first time he has spoken to anyone, other than to order his Scotch with two crisp words: Glenfiddich neat.

She answers him wordlessly with a cool gaze that brims with amused, mild interest. She places the Manhattan glass on the bar and slides it a few inches toward him, as if moving a queen across a chessboard. She reaches for the Maraschino cherry with manicured nails just as red. She twists the stem between slender fingers so that it spins this way. And then that way. A drop of whiskey falls off. She lifts the cherry to those magnetic eyes, gazes at it for a moment, and then past it right at him.

Blood-red.

Sea-green.

She leans her head back like she's going to shampoo that onyx waterfall of hair, and then she opens her mouth, smiling with those eyes. She lowers the cherry past pure-white teeth. It disappears, stem and all. She smiles at the ceiling, and then, achingly slowly, brings down those eyes, working her jaw all the way, and blasts a 50-caliber stare at the guy that could have raised Lazarus twice.

She works her jaw languorously. Mortal-sin smirk. Leans forward and toward Charlie, left arm folded on the bar, right hand lightly stroking her stockinged thigh. She sticks out her pink tongue, tip upturned. On that tip is the cherry stem, tied in a perfect knot.

She leans closer across Charlie. He breathes her in. Shivers.

The bartender, of course, has been watching this. Everyone with a pulse has been watching this.

The bartender looks at corporate-handsome, who nods. The bartender reaches into the fridge, and comes out with a gallon jar of Maraschino cherries. He puts the jar on the bar, and reaches down for a spoon and a clean plate. He spoons out a small pile of cherries.

The guy reaches, pokes with his middle finger, chooses two, pops them into his mouth, and moments later, offers his tongue to her with two stems, well-tied.

So there.

The bar goes church-quiet. These two are starring hot holes into each other. They say not one word.

She reaches an ivory left arm into Charlie's space. She has chosen the two best remaining fruits: Miss Cherry Universe, and her first runner-up. She lifts them by their stems, smiles at them, and then does what the corporate guy just did, only 1,000 degrees hotter.

Pink tongue out. Tip up. Two perfect red knots. Back in. Chews. Stares. Swallows. Stares. Challenges. Smiles. Eyes wide. *What?*

So there, *cubed.*

She's done. She considers Charlie. Sea-green bayonets. One eyebrow goes up. He raises his half-glass of house red, and smiles. To the victor.

She leans back. Sips her classic Manhattan and smiles at the bartender. Red fingernails moving slowly on her thigh, like a scorpion.

Not a word is said. This is *life.*

Somewhere out there on the concourse, at some horribly crowded gate stuffed with people who are going nowhere, a young guy is splaying his legs wide across three seats, sneering and playing Candy Crush on his iPhone. *Focused.* Focused on a *phone.*

He missed this.

He missed *life.*

Idiot, Charlie thinks.

And all of this Maraschino business happens in the time it takes for a young woman to drink a single classic Manhattan with imperfect strangers. She leans in and looks past Charlie at corporate-handsome. Smiles. *What?*

They don't exchange business cards. They never touch. They never get closer to each other than the width of Charlie, plus a few inches each side. Time holds its breath, waiting to see what will happen next. God is probably leaning off a cloud and looking down, wondering the same thing. The bartender finally understands why he was born.

She breaks the spell; pays with cash; tips 100 percent, and descends silkily from the barstool and clicks out the door, her scent lingering behind her like a pink contrail. She never looks back. Everyone who has eyes that work watches her walk. She melts the crowd as she moves through it.

Can you tie?

Charlie prays: Thank you, God, for sending us thunderstorms. *Thank* you.

The guy stays. Raises his glass slightly for a refill. Speaks to no one. People leave; others arrive. The story begins to marinate in Charlie's memory, and it gets even better with time.

Life.

Years have passed and he still thinks of her. The sea-green stare. The tick-tock of her high heels on the appreciative terrazzo. Her pink, upturned tongue with the two perfect red knots.

Thunder's applause.

Another time, Detroit airport, and another storm because Nature doesn't care about any of us. The bartender is slender with eerily beautiful, blue eyes that shine like menace. Boy-cut, natural red hair. A splash of freckles. Crazy Irish.

He's drinking the house red. She's working like a sled dog because of how many people are delayed, and she doesn't even have a bar-back to help her. She's not checking anyone's ID. The TV is tuned to Fox News, no sound.

The young guy who just grabbed the stool next to Charlie ("You gotta move fast!") is annoyed with her because he doesn't like to wait. He's an entitled drinker in the wrong bar. She notices his annoyance and makes him wait even longer.

He realizes that the fidgeting, the rolled eyes, the huffing, and tap-tap-tapping of the edge of his Visa card on the bar aren't working, so he takes a shot at charm, but it's *his* version of charm, which sucks.

"Hey, I like your *tattoo*," he shouts. Five or six people turn to look at the guy. Why so loud?

Her tat, a line of Chinese characters, is blue and beautiful across the back of her long neck, tickled by wisps of her short red hair as she moves.

"What's it mean? It looks Chinese. Hey, you *Chinese?*" Loud.

Clearly, she isn't Asian. He barks a laugh.

She's running out of glasses and quickly rinses a few for beers, ignoring him. He leans over, trying to see the back of her neck, and her legs, of course, but she's focused on the glasses and moving too fast for him, and now she's getting pissed.

"It says something in *Chinese*, though, right? Hey, can I get a *drink* here? I'm *talking* to you."

She's down the bar now. He huffs, and swivels toward Charlie like a left hook. "Hey, what do *you* think it means? Huh? *Huh!*" He leans into Charlie's space. Charlie figures this guy has probably already been refused at more than one of the concourse bars.

"I think it's something personal and very meaningful to her," he says. "Tattoos are forever, and hers is beautiful. Be nice."

The bartender is to the rude guy's back now. She shoots Charlie a look. Great hearing. Blue eyes blaze.

"Yeah, but it's *Chineeeeese*, man." the guy whines, leaning in more. Stale beer on his breath. "At least I think so. All those languages look the same to me." Leans back. "Hey, how come they don't just write it in *American*? You know? This is *America*, man! You think it means egg roll or something like that?" He laughs, glancing around at her, amused with himself. "*Egg roll*, humph."

She brings Charlie another house red. Smiles. Nothing for the young guy. Walks away.

"Jeez. Hey, what about *me*, Egg Roll?"

"You need to stop yelling at her," Charlie says. "Show some respect."

"Hey, screw you, man. I've been *waiting* here. I need a fuckin' *beer*. Hey, *bitch!*"

"Hey, *kid*," Charlie says, leaning in on him. "That's *enough!*"

She pivots, fuck-you fast. Three hard steps. *"You got ID, kid?"* Her hand is out, palm up, like a blade.

"What?"

"ID. *License.* You're acting like a nasty *boy*. What are you, like twelve years old? You with the *mouth*. You're in *my* bar. Let's see it, kid. *ID! Now!*"

That does it. He pushes back on his stool, which tips over. He flips her off, spits a *Fuck You!* at her, and another for the rest of the bar. He yanks his beat-up carry-on. It flips off its wheels and onto its side, which is always comical. He curses it, lifts it, bangs it back onto its wheels. It flips again. Even his luggage doesn't want to be with him. He lurches, bumps into a woman. She calls him an asshole, and loud enough for everyone in the bar to hear. They all applaud, relieved. He gets smaller, and is gone for good.

"Bully," the bartender whisper-hisses as she watches him go. She rubs the back of her neck.

Charlie smiles quietly into his wine glass. "Yeah," he whispers. "Bully."

The hopelessly delayed settle back into their drinks, and into their smart phones, of course.

Charlie watches her as she works. There's a bead of sweat on her forehead. She wipes it with the back of her hand, and keeps moving. He wonders what Donna is doing at home right now. He misses her terribly, but Donna also knows that storms don't care about any of us. There's another trip next week. He'll miss her then, too. He's thinking about being done. The young engineers are circling. Would Donna and he have enough to get by if he just quit? Would they be okay?

An older guy takes the stool the young guy had knocked over. The bartender alights for a moment, a red-and-blue, freckled butterfly. Takes his order.

She returns quickly with his Stella draught. Puts it on a cardboard coaster. Smiles at the guy. "Enjoy."

"Yep," he says.

She swivels toward Charlie. "How's your wine?"

"It's nice."

"More?"

"In a minute. Thanks."

"Want to know what my tattoo says?"

"If you want to tell me."

"Really?"

He nods. She leans in, cups a soft damp left hand around the back of his right ear, mouth close, breath like hot, minty wind tickling his ear. "It saaaays," she breathes into the center of his brain, "*Fuck . . . me . . . harder.*"

She straightens up, smoothing her fingertips across his cheek and lips on her way out, and gives him a lopsided, Katie Holmes grin, dimple and all.

"Surprised?" she asks.

The Stella guy says, "I missed that. What did she say? What does it mean?"

"It means courage," Charlie says, never taking his eyes off of hers. "*Courage.*"

"Oh," he says. "That's nice."

She smiles. Nails him to the wall with that smile. "Stay here," she says. Flies off.

He stares at the bottles on the shelves. Brown. Green. Clear. He's holding his glass and his hand shakes a bit on the stem. He places the glass on the coaster and tries to focus on Donna. She's probably watching The Weather Channel right now, or maybe checking his flight status online. He'll be home soon, but never soon enough.

Donna.

Donna

Deep breath. Let it out slowly.

Puff.

Blow.

Ten minutes later, she brings him another house red. "On me, hon. I hope your flight gets cancelled and you're stuck here overnight." Her hands are on her slim hips. Her head's bobbing yes, yes, yes to Marley's *Stir it Up* coming from invisible speakers. Blue-eyed menace. "I'd *like* that. *You?*"

Rain claws at the windows.

She moves like a dancer and keeps track of him with quick glances.

Stay here.

He sips.

Waits.

Stay.

Chirp!

DELTA AIRLINES

A change in our flight schedule impacts your upcoming trip.

Cancelled until tomorrow morning. Ten o'clock.

Tomorrow.

He stares at the bottles on the shelves. Glances at her down the bar.

Sips.

Waits.

Stay here.

Stay.

Another storm. Milwaukee. Charlie lowers himself onto the stool as if into a hot bath. He orders a Miller Lite. What the hell, it's summertime and it's Milwaukee.

"Hello, Irish. Do you want to up-size your beer for just a dollar more?" the bartender asks. She is pretty and probably nearly his age, and she has the look of someone who has touched life's ragged edges many times, but is still smiling at it all.

"Sure, why not?"

"Great answer. Do you want to add a top-shelf shot for just one more dollar?" She tosses a comical Vanna White gesture at the good booze. Just doing her job.

"I guess so. My flight's delayed."

"Yours and everyone else's, sweetheart. This place is gonna fill up fast. I'll watch your seat if you have to go shed a tear for Ireland. Miller Lite always does that to me."

"Thanks, young lady."

"My pleasure, young man. Would you like to enjoy the all-you-can-eat popcorn buffet for an additional dollar?" She fans her arm toward a popcorn machine that's the size of a small car and smells like the movies. Just doing her job. It's all about the add-ons.

"Sounds good," he says. "I've got the time."

"And we've got the beer," she says. "And let me guess. Jameson?"

Charlie smiles softly and nods. "You're good."

"That's what *all* the fellas say."

He sits and waits for the weather to behave, sips his up-sized beer and top-shelf shot and marvels at how well she did all of that to him, and in just 30 seconds. She sells better than he does. And he sells better than those scheming engineers with their social-network knives and razors ever will. None of them could do what she just did. She could sell you the coat you were already wearing. She'd kick their asses.

"Help yourself to the popcorn, Irish. It's fresh and it's delicious. I made it myself. Want another beer?"

He looks. It's half gone. "Sure. Why not?"

"My kinda guy." She smiles. Nice smile. *Real* nice smile. She reaches over and touches the back of his hand with warm fingertips. Lingers there. "You *with* somebody, Irish? Are ya?"

And then, just before he was done with the airports, he found himself at one that was all blue glass and chrome. Lots of hard surfaces and rounded edges. It was like drinking in a car dealership. This place had iPads cabled to the bar in front of each stool. This was something entirely new to Charlie. His flight was delayed, as usual, so he sat and fiddled with the iPad. It hooked him into *USA Today*. He skimmed news he already knew, and waited for someone to ask him what he wanted to drink, but no one did.

Charlie sat for about 15 minutes, watching the woman he thought was the bartender scurry in and out of what looked like a Dilbert cubicle. Each time she came out she rushed past Charlie and delivered drinks to scowling people waiting for the weather to get better.

The last time she rushed by, Charlie smiled and said hello. She didn't notice. She just kept the drink-delivery process going, scurrying between Dilbert and misery. Charlie tried three more times to catch her eye and she finally paused for a second to point at the iPad in front of Charlie. "Use that," she said, and was gone.

So he took another look. Turns out there was more on that iPad than the *USA Today* newspaper, stock-market reports, and what's up in the world of sports. There was also a menu. Charlie tapped his way through the menu and found the booze. They had red wine, five choices, but nothing called "house red." The least expensive red was $15 for a small glass, plus tax, and a mandatory 20% tip, with suggestions for a more-generous tip if you wanted to go there. Jeez.

Charlie looked around at the other people. Some were tapping. Others were sipping. No one was talking to anyone else at the bar. Those who were sipping were looking at their smart phones.

Charlie ordered the cheapest option, and in about five minutes, the runner appeared and placed the small wine glass on a paper napkin in front of him.

"Thank you," Charlie said.

"No problem," she said, and was gone.

Time passed and Charlie wanted another, so he tapped. There was no such thing as running a tab in this place. You entered what you wanted, one drink at a time, and the iPad would ask you to swipe your credit card again, but first, these words would appear on the screen:

Do You Have Enough Time?

"And isn't that a philosophical question?" Charlie says to the woman who is seated to his right as he points at the screen. She's about Abby's age and has just sat down. "Do I have enough time? What a question to ask an old guy like me," he laughs.

She quick-glances at Charlie's screen, and then back at her own screen. "It needs to know if your flight will be leaving before you get whatever you're ordering," she says, not looking up again from her screen.

"I'm ordering a glass of red wine. My flight's delayed," Charlie says.

"We're *all* delayed," she says, still staring at her screen, tapping through the pages.

"I thought it was asking me about life," Charlie says. "You know, do I have enough time. A deep, philosophical question. What would Socrates do?"

"Don't think. Just drink," she says without looking up. "It will be here soon."

"They have this Dyson Airblade hand dryer in the Men's Room," Charlie tries again with the woman to his right a few minutes later when he has his wine. He'd love to get The Chat going, just to pass the time. "It's right under an automatic paper towel machine. You know the kind you have to wave at to get three inches of paper towel? Those things are so stingy. Well anyway, the people have been using this Dyson as their garbage pail. It does look like a garbage pail, so I can see how that could happen. This one's stuffed to overflow with balled-up paper towels and going nuts in there. It never shuts off. It's just hanging there on the wall, screaming for help, a symbol of our times."

"You'll have to excuse me," she says, not looking up from her iPhone. "I need to catch up on my work. And I *have* a boyfriend."

Charlie glances. Facebook.

"Okay. Sorry to bother you," Charlie says.

"No problem." She doesn't look up.

He waits a few minutes. Turns to the 30-something guy on his left. "Have you seen the overstuffed Dyson Airblade in the Men's room over there?" he asks.

"I'm not gay," the guy says, not looking up, but leaning a few degrees away from Charlie.

"That's okay with me. Just looking to have a glass of wine and a chat. I'm not gay either. At least I don't think so. Never really gave it much thought, I've been married to Donna for so long. I'll have to ask her sometime, if I ever get home. I just thought the Dyson was funny. I've never seen anything like that before. It's going crazy in there."

"I've got work to do," the guy says. "Please excuse me." He's staring at his iPhone.

Charlie glances. Twitter.

Charlie looks around the bar at his fellow prisoners. No one is speaking to anyone else. Everyone is tapping a screen. He finishes his tiny, $15, plus tax and 20%-tip-to-someone-back-there red wine, and walks off, trying hard not to bump into anyone who is angry.

Donna.

Charlie and Donna were together on Singer Island, talking with strangers they had just met at this big happy rectangle of a bar that opens out onto the beach. The bartender, whose name tag introduces her as Paula - Edison, NJ, joins in their conversation. There was not an iPad in sight.

"Paula - Edison, NJ is a lovely name," Charlie says.

"I'm glad you like it," she says. "It's an unusual last name, but it works for me, at least in this joint."

"I have a buddy named Patrick. He's living in New Jersey these days. He doesn't want anyone to call him Pat."

"I know a lot of New Jersey Patricks, but they all go by Pat. They're tough guys."

"Patrick doesn't like sharing his name with the ladies," Charlie explains.

"Sounds like he may be lacking in confidence, if you know what I mean," Paula -Edison, NJ says, glancing crotchward.

"I'll mention that to him when I see him. I know it will cause him to carefully and prayerfully reflect upon his entire life thus far. Might even make him apply for the priesthood."

Paula - Edison, NJ. smiles at Donna. "Your fella's a bullshitter, right?"

"World-class," Donna says.

"It shows," Paula -Edison, NJ laughs.

"I think we need better nametags in this world," Charlie says a few minutes later. "I mean, it's nice to know a person's city and state of origin, but I think we'd be better off with nametags we could really sink our teeth into."

"Meaning?" Donna says.

"Well, how about if everyone wore a nametag with their first name, followed by their favorite food? What do you think of that idea, Donna Turkey Club? Wouldn't that get The Chat going?"

"I think that's a fine idea, Charlie Meatloaf."

The surrounding strangers all laugh because this is too good an overhead conversation to ignore. The skinny guy with the gray Hulk Hogan moustache and ponytail to Charlie's left reaches over and offers his hand. "Nice to meet you, Charlie Meatloaf. I'm Jimmy *Hot Dogs!*" He has a screechy, hee-haw voice that makes you wonder if life has been squeezing his balls.

"Pleased to meet you, Jimmy Hot Dogs. Do you know Nathan? He's famous in Coney Island, and major supermarkets."

"My oldest friend!" Jimmy Hot Dogs screeches. Laughs. Coughs. Marlboro.

Paula - Edison, NJ laughs with him, and then flies off to pour beers for other silly strangers who are drinking in the afternoon.

The TV plays a soundless homage to Ken Stabler, the Oakland Raiders quarterback who was dead. The news crawl reports that an autopsy showed he had CTE, a degenerative brain condition caused by getting knocked in the head a lot. The wages of American football.

"Did Ken Stabler *die*?" Jimmy Hot Dogs asks.

"Yeah," Frankie Meatballs and Spaghetti answers. "Colon cancer killed him, but he also had CTE. They can't prove that until they do the autopsy, though. That's why no one knew about it when he was alive. They have to wait until you're dead to figure out what's wrong with you. I blame Obamacare."

"If she could, my wife would get me tested for CTE this afternoon," Jimmy Hot Dogs says. "Cut my head right open like a melon and have a look inside. Whoops! Dead? Oh. Sorry!"

Paula - Edison, NJ hears this on her way back. "I'd probably ask for the same test if I were unlucky enough to be married to you, hot-dog boy." She gives him a good-natured poke and a fresh Jack Daniels.

He holds the whiskey to his ear and tinkles the ice like wedding bells. "Ah, married to *you*, Paula. A man can dream," he says. "A man can . . . *dream*." Dirty sigh, wiggled eyebrows.

"Dream on," Paula - Edison, NJ laughs.

"Yeah, well, you take out my brains and who's gonna notice? How long we know each other, Paula?"

"Too damn long," she laughs.

Townies.

Charlie notices the number 4 tattooed on the inside of Paula - Edison, NJ's left wrist. It's surrounded by flames, like you see on hot rods. He asks her what it means.

"You don't want to know," she snuffs.

Donna looks at Paula's arm, as do the others, except for Jimmy Hot Dogs, who knows all about it already. He dips his Hulk Hogan into his drink.

Paula flies away.

"Do you know why bartenders get busy all of a sudden like that, and then have time to stop and chat later?" Charlie asks Donna.

"I've never given that much thought, Charlie Meatloaf," Donna says.

"It happens because of Happy Hour," Charlie explains. "Everyone arrives and starts drinking at the same time because they don't want to miss out on the good prices."

"Okay. And the good chat, too. Don't forget that," Donna says.

"That goes without saying, but the drinking is like traffic. Ever notice how the drivers of cars stay together on the road and leave big spaces between bunches?"

"Yeah, car clump," Donna says.

"Right, car clump. I like that. Thanks. Well it happens because of the traffic lights. Clumps that start together, stay together. The drinking equivalent to that is what we're seeing here right now. It's why bartenders get busy and then suddenly have time to chat. People drink in bunches, and at about the same pace. I've made a study of this in many cities across this fine land of ours. I pay attention, young lady."

"And I'll bet you have a name for this phenomenon, don't you, young man?" Donna says.

"Most certainly," Charlie says.

"And that name is?" Donna asks.

"*Drink Sync,*" Charlie says, raising his glass.

"Of course," Donna says.

"But no syncing if you're planning on clumping," Charlie adds.

"Of course not."

Paula - Edison, NJ is back a few minutes later, gets them all more drinks and lingers.

"See?" Charlie says to Donna. "The Drink Sync linger. Time for The Chat."

"Okay, you really want to know?" Paula - Edison, NJ asks, offering Charlie the inside of her wrist.

"Yes, it's beautiful." He touches it with two fingers, like he's taking her pulse.

"It's for my father. He died six years ago. He was a coach in every sport you can imagine. He changed the lives of so many people. At his wake, some very famous men showed up to pay respects. They did! They said they owed their professional athletic careers to my daddy. He had them all under his wing when they were little kids. He changed people's lives for the better. *Lots* of lives."

Her wrist is still in front of Charlie. He folds his hand over the number and says, "Number Four, thank you for raising such a *fine* daughter, sir."

"Aww, you're sweet," Paula - Edison, NJ says. "All that, and a bullshitter, too." She laughs, turns to Donna. "You're a lucky lady."

Donna raises her glass. "I sure am."

"You're obviously an athlete," Charlie says.

"I *was*."

"What sport?"

"I was soccer, track, and gymnastics at different times." She's wearing beach-bar shorts, designed to inspire tips.

Her legs are whippet-thin, all taut muscle and smooth bronze skin. Rock-N-Roll legs.

"He raised you tough, didn't he?" Charlie says.

"He *did*," Paula agrees. "And he loved me like a daughter needs to be loved." A tiny diamond of a tear peeks from the corner of her eye. She touches the number on her wrist. "And I miss him so much." She kisses it.

She looks over her shoulder at raised empty glasses and flies off again to take care of business.

Drink Sync.

On Singer Island, the first overheard wisecrack can pull afternoon drinkers together like a fistful of wet beach sand, and just as impermanent. If they ever see each other again, it will be but for a brief time, a shared hour or two more with The Chat. It is sweet and quickly gone, like cotton candy, or summer, and then they'll move on to meet the rest of the strangers in their lives. If they do their jobs well, the townies will someday speak of them, saying, "Hey, remember that guy? Remember that gal? Remember that day? Man that was *fun!*"

The townies are the bookmarks of the good times on Singer Island. They get to stay forever.

John Chicken Parmesan and his redheaded second wife, Eileen Bacon Cheeseburger, who has Buick-bumper breasts and chunky, Lego-block legs, like Mary Lou Retton's, are three stools removed from Donna. They want in on the tattoo conversation.

John Chicken Parmesan mentions that he has wanted to get a tattoo, but he has been putting it off. He might do it on this vacation trip, though. Not sure yet. Gotta decide. Gotta pray on it.

"What will you get, and where will it be?" Donna asks.

"I'll get Psalm 116. It's a long one. It meant a lot to me during my divorce. He flexes his chicken bicep. I may have to work out for a while first, though. The psalm is a long one. My arm's too skinny to quote David right now."

"That's nice," Jimmy Hot Dogs says. "You need a workout shirt that says, Pumping for Jesus."

"I like that!" Eileen Bacon Cheeseburger howls. "Woo! Pumpin' for *Jesus!*"

"Or David," John Chicken Parmesan says.

"Jesus looks better on tee shirts," Jimmy Hot Dogs says.

There's a contemplative pause in the conversation for Jimmy Hot Dogs here.

Jesus? David? New Testament? Old Testament? This guy a Jew?

Born-again?

Not a Muslim, though, right?

Hmm.

Okay, so . . .

"How did you two meet?" Charlie asks, putting the Lionel back onto its track.

"Match.com," she says.

"I should have married Eileen first instead of the other one," John Chicken Parmesan says, forgetting about tee shirts. "But who knew?"

"Yeah," Eileen Bacon Cheeseburger giggles. "Who knew? I feel the same way about him and my ex. Yeah. My ex was like a pimple on my fat ass. The *worst*."

Jimmy Hot Dogs wipes drops of Jack Daniels from his Hulk Hogan. "I think I found *my* wife on Match dot DOOM!" he sputters, felling better about these two now.

"Where is she today?" Paula - Edison, NJ asks.

"She went to Target to buy a new broom," Jimmy Hot Dogs screeches. "The old one doesn't *fly* like it used to." Huge Marlboro hack.

Paula chuckles, shakes her head, turns to Charlie and Donna. "Want to know about this one?" She tugs the shoulder strap of the tight, wife-beater tee-shirt with the bar's logo aside. Five red hearts huddle like roses twined in thorns behind her right shoulder on smooth, tanned skin you just want to touch.

"That is so beautiful," Donna says.

"I wish I could have this part removed." She turns her neck like a bird, reaches back and pokes a red nail into the second heart. The largest one. "That's my ex. The others are my kids. I love my kids."

"What went wrong?" Donna asks.

"He cheated on me with my best friend and left us."

"Who could possibly leave *you*? Seriously. You are so fine, so nice." Donna says and watches another jewel of a tear appear.

"Well, *he* could. But then the bitch left *him*. So that's the way it goes, right? He's alone now, the bastard." She claps her Edison, New Jersey hands together, like she's knocking off road dirt. "He's alone now and I hope he's miserable." Catch in her voice. "Fuckin' *miserable*."

Someone raises an empty glass. She spots it and flies off on those slim, bronzed legs that everyone at the bar, men and women alike, can't help but watch.

Sweet Jesus.

He always thought the best bars were the ones where you wouldn't see the same people again for the rest of your life, and for good reasons. But they have all stayed with him, even after all these years. Some even haunt him.

And then came Clare.

3

Donna aligned herself with the sun, as the seabirds did with the wind. She thought seabirds were a pain in the ass. "They're thieves with wings," she says to Charlie. "I was sitting on my chair when a gull the size of a turkey swooped down and took a sandwich right out of this little girl's hand. Not here. Back home at Tobay. The kid was sitting right next to me. I can't stand the way the people push their blankets right up to where you're sitting. They're like an invading army. They think they own the whole beach. You shoulda heard her mother when the bird hit that sandwich. She was screaming, not so much about the bird, but about the sandwich. It was the only one she had brought. She was cursing the bird, and then she starts screaming at the kid for letting it happen. I don't know which was worst. As if the kid could have seen it coming. Damn birds."

"She'll see it coming the next time," Charlie says.

"I hope so."

They look at the gulls hanging in the air like laundry on a line.

"You like it here?" Charlie asks.

"Yes, this is a good beach. Fewer people here and the birds aren't as nasty. Well, not yet anyway. You gonna read?"

"For a while."

"What are you reading?"

"Thomas Hardy."

Donna likes books filled with murder. She goes through dozens of them each year, mostly on her Kindle.

"What are you reading?" Charlie asks.

"It's about a murder. It's a good one."

"What's the title?"

Her green eyes turn upward. She thinks. "I don't know," she says.

"Who wrote it?"

"I don't know!" she laughs, shaking the Kindle. "That's the trouble with this thing. There's no cover to open and close. The title and the author both get lost. I think it's a conspiracy against authors."

"Well, you could hit the button that looks like a house. That will tell you what you're reading," Charlie says.

"I suppose, but who wants to leave a good story?"

"It's good, though?"

"Yes." She returns to the unknown murder book by the unknown author.

"I'm going to take a walk," Charlie says, pushing himself carefully out of the beach chair.

"You okay? Watch your back."

"I'm okay. Just can't sit still. I need to move."

"Okay. I'll be here. We'll leave when you get back. Got your phone?" He checks his pocket, nods.

"Thanks."

"For what?"

"For putting up with me?"

"I've put up with worse," Donna says, hand over her eyes. She's smirking.

"I'm a lucky guy," Charlie sighs.

"You are. Go walk." She goes back to the murder book.

But only for a paragraph. She looks up and watches him trudge across the sand. He looks tired. She watches him dip below the sharp edge of the beach, where it slopes quickly to the Atlantic. He turns and she watches just his head moving low along the sand, hair still light brown. No gray at all. How strange that looks, just his head, and then he's gone. She looks at the cargo ship heading off somewhere. Looks at the people around her. They're not too close. Good. The gulls laugh. She goes back to the murder book.

When they were young, they'd go to Jones Beach and walk as far as they could from where most of the people were. They'd set their blanket (no chairs in those days) close to the dunes and away from the people, and he'd put baby oil on her back. She'd do her front, and then she'd do his back. She thought baby oil gave you a better tan. No one talked about skin cancer in those days. Who knew?

She'd lie on her back with eyes closed and listen to the gulls and the surf. He'd lie next to her and touch her hand. So warm.

Later, he'd roll sideways and kiss her, but only if no one was nearby. She'd bend up a bit, look to be sure, and then kiss him back. The gulls shrieked. The sand got stuck in the baby oil and itched. They'd hop up and walk into the ocean, hand in hand. The water was always colder than expected. She'd take a few tentative steps at first; get her feet wet, shins, thighs. Charlie would hold her hand. And then, not being able to take this slow torture anymore, they'd both dive under the next wave and bounce right back up, shivering. She'd squeeze the sea from her hair and hold his hand to fight the undertow as they struggled back out. They'd lean into each other on their way back to the blanket, drunk on love. They'd lay there and she would close her eyes and feel the warm touch of the sun on her skin and think of him. He was there with her, with them. Always.

Never really alone.

And the scent of the baby oil lingered into the night.

She read a bit more of murder, stopped and looked at the empty chair. She was happy he was finally done, happy for him. They had talked about this for years. Work hard, raise Abby well, save what they could, try not to worry too much, and finally have that special time just for them. Was it possible? So many they knew had died, and all too young. But what was young, really? And what was old? It was only time, days strung together like the beads of a rosary, each one precious.

Charlie's retirement had arrived earlier than either of them thought it would, but it was what it was, and the thought of him starting somewhere else at this age didn't make sense. Charlie was confident that they would be okay, but what did he know of money? And those young engineers had hurt him badly. Them and that new kid-boss with his fucking Kaizen. She knew that, but they never spoke of this. It was done and gone and she protected him now as he tried to fix himself, still not sure if he could do that. She wished he could get furious, but that was never in his nature, and that was okay. She loved his gentleness and the way he lived his life, and the way he loved her. Maybe he could just accept things as they are; like he used to be able to do before all of this happened. Maybe he could?

Time will tell.

She read a bit more and thought about the money. Would it be enough? What if it wasn't? What then? They couldn't depend on Abby for money. They wouldn't. She wondered if anyone would hire him at this age, and then felt ashamed for thinking that. They'd be okay. She'd see to it. They had planned, hadn't they? She was mighty, wasn't she? So the timing wasn't perfect. So what? She was good with stretching money. They just had to stay healthy until he got better. *If* he got better.

But could he?

Stop it, she thought. We're not that old yet, and he *will* get better.

I hope he will.

She looked at the sand, which had been there forever, and would always be there.

The sand.

Daddy.

She went back to her murder book.

A fly landed on her foot. She swatted and it flew off. She looked at her little feet. Turned them this way and that. Admired them. Most women her age had ugly feet. Hers were still beautiful. So was she. She had always seemed far younger than she was. She was in her early-forties when bartenders finally stopped asking her for ID, and they weren't kidding.

Charlie also looked at least 10 years younger than he was, maybe more. His hair was still light brown. No gray at all. Trim. Tall. Handsome. And he was such a good talker, and an even better listener. She thought that the stories kept them both young. They laughed so much, and they really liked people. This worry was a new thing. Maybe it would pass, but either way, they'd deal with it. Always had. She would protect him. Always had.

Could she?

"We'll be okay," she said to the sand, but the sand didn't answer.

Her toenails were cherry red. Fingernails can be any color, but a woman's toes must *always* be red, she thought. She had never worn those extreme high heels that make a woman's legs look great but ruined feet. She had been sensible, opting for size-five flip-flops in summer and flats when she absolutely had to give up the flip-flops because of the cold. It had paid off. She wiggled red toes in the sand. She wore a gold toe ring on her left second toe. Charlie had given it to her out of the blue. He said it made her look sexy. "*Sexier*," she corrected him. He laughed and agreed. "Okay, yes, *sexier*."

She thought of Trista and how she was now big enough to have her car seat facing forward. Trista said that this meant she was a big girl now. No matter the weather, Trista would take off her shoes and socks whenever she was in her car seat. Abby gave up trying to stop her from doing this. The four of them were driving to Chili's in the minivan when Trista held up her bare right foot, pointed at it, and said to no one in particular, "This is my *foot*. She is *beautiful!* She wants to go to a wedding." She started to sing the ABC Song because that's what they sing at weddings.

Donna smiled at the memory. "And these are mine, Trista," she whispered, holding up her small feet and wiggling tan sand from between red toes. She rubbed them with coconut lotion that filled the air with summer scent. The gold ankle bracelet dangled and gleamed. "This is my foot," Donna whispered. "And she, too, is beautiful. And she has been to *many* weddings."

Theirs had been small, just 50 people because that's all they could afford back then. Charlie and Donna were on their own, both then and now.

The wedding reception had been in a small Knights of Columbus hall. Nothing fancy but they were still together after all these years. She had danced with him in flats, and he had worn his rented tux and he held her like he was trying to absorb her. The vows they repeated after the priest at the mass said nothing about being happy every day. She hadn't thought much about that then, but they were still together. Still.

She looked at the empty beach chair.

Charlie had a few friends, and lots of business acquaintances. The friends were all car guys, which was funny because he couldn't tell one car from another. When he'd rent a car in some city he'd always shrug when the agent asked him which car he wanted. "Up to you," he'd say. He didn't know the difference between a Honda and a Bentley. A car was just a means of getting from here to his customers. The following morning, he'd have to hit the red button on the key fob to find the car in the hotel parking lot. He hadn't even noticed what color the car was when he picked it up and drove it from the airport. His thoughts were forever elsewhere.

He was also mechanically disinclined, which made being friends with car guys even more curious. She had wondered about this during the early years of their marriage, but along the way she realized that he attracted car guys because he listened really well, and car guys love to talk. Their wives were usually sick to death of hearing about the damn car, so the car guys talked to Charlie instead. He asked good questions and he listened like a champ to their explanations, even though she knew he didn't care about the cars, but he did care about people who had passion, and it didn't matter for what. He'd come away with wonderful stories, which he'd share with her. He lived for the stories, and his retelling was always better than the reality. He'd add stuff. And when he told Donna about what the car guys talked about, he'd add plenty of details. He once described the way Dennis moved his hand along a fender as if he was stroking a woman's bare thigh. "He did it slowly and appreciatively," Charlie had said, "And with great wonder and anticipation. And *hope*, Donna. Hope. It was beautiful to see."

And that telling made Donna like car guys, too.

She had bought every car they ever owned. He was always the driver when they went on a trip, but she was just better with the money. He listened to people and talked. She saved. She thought about the money again, now that he was finally done. Would it be enough? Would they be okay?

"Stop it!" she said to herself.

She glances again at the empty chair. Looks off toward the ocean.

A tanned, very fit guy, maybe 20 years younger than she is walks by on his way to the water. He's watching her on his way in, like a pilot approaching a landing strip. He diverts a bit. Lands. Smiles. It's a smile that goes over her like a wave.

"Pretty feet," he says.

Donna looks over at him. "Nice pecs," she answers, surprising him. She goes back to her murder book.

He's curious. Smiles. Considers.

"Do I *know* you?" he asks.

"Not a bit." Looks up again.

"*Could* I know you?"

She smiles, crosses her ankles, and goes back to murder. Says nothing. The gold bracelet dangles and gleams as she wiggles her red toes and the ring. He waits.

"Are you alone?"

She looks up at him again. Considers. Waits.

And then she looks at the empty chair, and up at the sun without shading her eyes.

"No. Never *really* alone."

She smiles with her eyes and goes back to murder.

He stands there for a while. She reads. He waits. She reads.

"Too bad."

He turns, and walks to the water.

She does not look up, just smiles confidence into her murder book as the warmth of knowing caresses her like sunlight on bare skin.

Daddy.

If you say that you are mine,
I'll be there 'til the end of time.

Charlie's finally back. He walks up and stops, blocking the sun. His pocket is bulging with seashells. She puts the Kindle into the beach bag. It's five short blocks from the beach to their apartment.

"You know you are still as beautiful as you were on the day that I met you." Charlie says.

"Really?"

"Yes, you never change. You sure you want to hang out with an old retired guy like me?"

"I'll keep you around for a while," she says, snaking a tanned arm around his waist.

"I am so lucky," Charlie says.

"Me, too, young man," Donna pulls him closer. "Me, too."

4

They gave themselves three days to drive from Long Island to Singer Island, and on the first night they stopped at a Fairfield near Richmond, Virginia. The clerk told them that if they decided to have dinner in the restaurant that was just across the parking lot, they would get a ten-percent discount off their check.

"What kind of food do they have there?" Donna asks.

"It's American. It's good."

"Do we need a coupon from you?"

"No, just tell your waiter you're staying here."

"Let's do that," she says to Charlie.

"Okay. I don't want to drive anymore today. It will be good to walk a bit, even if it's just across the parking lot."

"We'll have some wine," Donna says.

"Okay."

Their gangly waiter has a bit of raw acne nagging at his face. He tells them that he will be their server and that his name is Tom. Can he start them with something to drink?

"Yes, please, Tom. I'd like a pinot grigio," Donna says.

"House red, please, Tom," Charlie says.

Tom walks away. Returns in a moment. "What was that drink you wanted, *ma'am?*"

"Pinot grigio." He goes away. Comes back.

"I'm sorry, *ma'am*. What's in that *drink*?"

"Grapes."

The manager comes over. "I'm so sorry. Tom's new. He told me what happened. We don't have pinot grigio. Would chardonnay be okay?"

"Yes, thanks."

"And cab sav is our house red, sir. That work?"

"Yes. Thanks."

"You're very welcome. Thanks for choosing us."

Tom returns with the drinks. Apologizes. He's new. It's his first week. He touches his face with the pen. Are they ready to order?

"Yes."

He writes it all down while biting his lower lip. Repeats it back to them. They agree that all is correct and he goes away.

"Remember that restaurant in Ohio?" Donna says. "The same thing happened there with the pinot grigio. Remember?"

"That was years ago," Charlie says.

"Poor pinot grigio," Donna says. "It has a tough time outside of New York."

"The unknown grape," Charlie says.

A young couple arrives. They slide into a booth across from Donna and Charlie. They're holding their iPhones like prayer books, tapping with their thumbs, saying nothing to each other. Twenty-first Century acolytes.

Tom appears at their table and lets them know that he'll be their server and that his name is Tom. They order without looking up from their iPhones. No menu required. Townies. This throws Tom off his stride because it's not the sequence he expects. He fumbles for his pad and writes it all down. He repeats it back to them. Touches the pen to his face. They nod without once looking up. Off he goes.

"They're not talking to each other," Charlie says.

"I noticed that. They're talking with their thumbs to people who aren't here."

"Then why go out to dinner?" Charlie asks.

"I don't know. I suppose they're hungry."

"It makes me sad," Charlie says. "Why be together if you're not going to pay attention to each other? They've yet to look up. Gosh."

"You can't fix them, Charlie."

"I know, but still."

Tom returns with Donna and Charlie's food, all as ordered. "Tom," Donna says, "we're staying at the Fairfield and they told us that we get 10 percent off our check if we eat here. Is that true?"

Tom looks around for his manager, like a bullied kid looking for his big brother. "Um, I'll have to *ask*?" He scurries.

"He's like a plush toy," Donna says.

"He is."

"They still haven't said a word to each other," Donna is glancing at the young couple. "Now they're making *me* sad."

"They're thumb-praying," Charlie says. "Let's think of it that way. Their generation needs a *lot* of prayer. Let's pretend it's a good thing."

Tom's back and quite excited. "You're good for the 10 percent *discount*? I'll take care of it when I bring your *check*? *Okay*?"

"Thanks, Tom."

"No *problem*?" He's gone.

"Ever notice how young people turn every statement into a question these days?" Donna says.

"What do you mean?"

"Well? They talk like *this*? Like they need approval for everything they *say*? The last word of every sentence contains a *spring*? The octave goes *up*? Listen closely when he comes *back*?"

"Oh, yeah. I know what you mean. It makes them sound uncertain and weak, like they need approval for each thought they have before they can move on to the next thought," Charlie says. "It's like the way Canadians say, *eh?* after each sentence. And by the way, I know *why* they do that. People think Canadians are weak, but they're not."

"So why do they do it?"

"It has nothing to do with uncertainty. It has to do with *certainty*. I asked a Canadian on one of my trips about it and he told me *eh?* is an abbreviation."

"What does it stand for?" Donna sips her wine.

"Asshole."

She nearly chokes to death. Catches her breath, laughs out loud and says, "You mean like, 'Have a nice day, *EH?*'"

"Yeah. Canadians are very cool that way and *very* certain about to whom they are speaking."

"Good one, *eh?* " Donna says.

The young couple continues their iPhone-praying to social gods who are not there. They never speak to each other. They don't want to miss anything of life, except the people with whom they are having dinner, that being each other. They finish, pay the check and proceed out, tapping all the way.

"How do you suppose we got to this point?" Donna asks.

"We stopped telling each other stories," Charlie says. "And we stopped listening. The young engineers were like that. I'd be talking to them and they'd take out their iPhones and tap away. Mr. Ho Kim did the same thing. He kept touching his pocket to make sure the iPhone was still there. It's like they can't focus on actual people. They worship gadgets and electrons and anyone who is not physically present at the moment. In the future, I think there will be marriages between people who will never touch each other. They'll be putting these electronic buckets over their heads. Virtual-reality, they call it. That's going to replace making out."

"Not for me," Donna says.

"Me either."

Tom arrives to announce that it's Free Pie Wednesday. He is gleeful. Donna and Charlie are full and they don't want pie, free or not. Tom, however, being a growing lad, can't understand this. "But it's *free?*" he says.

"Okay," Donna says, not wanting to disappoint him. "But may we take it home, Tom?"

"Uh, *sure?*"

"Okay," Donna says. "Then one slice of apple and one slice of blueberry. Thanks, Tom."

"No *problem?*" Tom says. He's gone.

"Have you noticed the way the kids all say 'No problem' instead of 'You're welcome' nowadays?" Donna asks.

Charlie thinks for a moment. "You're right."

"Those are two very negative words. No and Problem. I miss the beauty of 'You are welcome.' Those are three very positive words. You. Are. Welcome. Three *gorgeous* words.

The first is about The Other. Next comes Are, which springs from the verb To Be, designating life. And then we finish with the most inviting word in the world, the blueberry pie of words: *Welcome*. I miss that. Why should there be the inference of a problem after a grown-up says thanks?"

"Thank you for that very complex, but nevertheless lovely, thought."

"You're welcome!"

Tom returns, as sad as a lame greyhound. He tells them that the free pie is only for in-store dining. He didn't know that, but it's on the menu in the fine print. He's new. This is his first week. He's sorry he missed it. He touches his face with the pen.

"That's okay," Charlie says. "We really didn't want it anyway."

"But I can bring it to you on clean plates with fresh forks and then you can put it into *boxes*?" Tom says.

"Will you bring us the boxes at the same time?" Donna asks.

"Uh, *sure*? I think *so*? No *problem*?"

"But you can't skip the step with the clean plates and fresh forks, Tom? You can't just put the pie into the boxes back there in the kitchen?"

"No, *ma'am*? That's not *allowed*?"

"Okay, Tom," Donna says. "Do what's right."

"No *problem*?"

Tom returns with the two slices of pie on clean plates with fresh forks, and also with two Styrofoam boxes. Donna immediately uses the fresh forks to slide the slices of pie off the plates and into the two boxes, leaving Tom with two plates and two forks that someone now has to wash. Tom watches all of this. Donna closes the boxes and smiles at Tom. "Easy as pie," she says. Tom doesn't get it.

"Can I get you anything *else?*"

"Just the check, please, Tom," Donna says.

"No *problem?*"

Tom's back with the check. He hands it to Charlie, who hands it to Donna. Tom watches this, not registering that Donna, and not Charlie, was the person who had asked for the check.

"*I* had asked you for the check, Tom," Donna says.

"Huh?"

"*I'm* paying."

"Oh. No *problem?*" He's gone.

She goes over the bill carefully, as she does with everything that has to do with money. Tom forgot to take off the 10 percent. The check also has this printed near the bottom:

Free pie. $3.95
Free pie. $3.95

Tom is scurrying by. "Excuse me. Tom?"

"Yes, *ma'am*?"

"You didn't take off the 10 percent. And free pie should be free." She points at the place on the check with the double $3.95 charge.

He stares at the check as if it has just arrived from space. "Um, that's not *right*?"

"Right."

"Um, I'll have to ask my *manager*?"

"Thanks, Tom."

"No *problem*?"

"Plush toy," Donna says.

"Yep," Charlie agrees.

Tom returns with the corrected check, now reduced by 10 percent, and the two slices of pie have found their freedom.

Free pie. $0.00
Free pie. $0.00

"Thanks, Tom."

"No *problem*? But, um, I wasn't able to give you the 10 percent off the free *pie*?"

"Why not?" Charlie asks.

"Um, the computer wouldn't do *that*? Because it was, um, *free*? It just *wouldn't*?"

"I would think you'd give us at least 20 percent off the free pie," Donna says. "I mean why not?"

"Or fifty percent off the free pie," Charlie says.

"Or a hundred percent?" Donna suggests.

"Huh?"

"It's okay, Tom," Donna says. "You're a fine boy, and you know how to follow the rules. You'll do well in life. Thanks."

"Um, no problem?"

5

They made it to Florence, South Carolina on their second day of driving and checked into another Fairfield. Fairfields are nice because they give you free breakfast, which really isn't free, but like free pie, it seems to be. Donna asked at the front desk about restaurants and got a photocopy list. They chose a Chili's about a quarter-mile away and decided to walk to it. There was a sidewalk all the way. It felt good to stretch their legs.

There was also a wait, but the place had a nice big bar with available stools, so they sat there instead of at a table and ordered. A burger for Charlie. A turkey club for Donna. Mike (no favorite food on his nametag) brought them their wine and set them up with paper placemats, and forks and knives wrapped in paper napkins, held in place by those sticky-paper wraparounds that the chain restaurants use. Charlie liked those wraparounds. He'd roll his into a tight tube, and then roll that between his thumbs and forefingers while he talked. It was a nervous habit.

"How you feeling?" Donna asks.

"I'm okay. A little sad, but getting better I think. A little bit. It was a good drive today. Lots of time to think and to talk. Thanks for listening to me."

"It's easy to listen to you, and I love you. Now please put the little paper tube down. You're making me nervous."

Charlie tosses it onto the bar and chuckles. "Sorry. I don't even realize I'm doing that."

"I know. Relax, okay?"

"Okay."

"Tired from driving?" Donna asks.

"Yeah," Charlie says. "I'm looking forward to getting to the island tomorrow."

"One more day on the road and then we can *really* relax," Donna says. She reaches over and squeezes his hand.

The bar is filling up and Mike's busy. A thirty-something couple hustles in and takes the two remaining stools on Charlie's side. The woman sits next to Charlie. They're both wearing NY Mets gear. Same shirts and hats.

"Hey, Let's go Mets!" Charlie says.

They turn to him and smile. They're both blonde and good-looking. "For sure!" the woman says.

"You live here?" Charlie asks.

"Yeah," the woman says.

"How do North Carolina folks get to be Mets fans? I'd figured you'd be rooting for the Braves."

"Oh, gawd," she says, "Braves? Fuggedaboutit. We're New Yorkers. Our jobs moved us here. No complaints, though. The weather's better here than back home. A lot better. How about you?"

"We're on our way to Florida to do senior stuff," Charlie says. "We're retired. We live on Long Island. Just heading down for a month to get warm."

"Niiice," the guy says. "It's good to be the snowbird. You going to spring training?"

"No, we're going to be on the Atlantic side of the state."

"Too bad," he says. "You could drive over and see a few games."

"I think we're just going to stay put and relax," Charlie says. "We have an apartment for a month on Singer Island."

"Where's that?"

"It's by Palm Beach."

"Niiice."

"You two meet at a game?" Charlie asks.

"No, we met at work," the woman says. "He used to be my boss."

"Oh. Who picked up whom?" Charlie asks. Smiles. Trying to get The Chat *really* going.

"Oh, we're not a couple," she says. "Just good friends."

"That's nice," Charlie says. "Some people think men and women can't be good friends without it being sexual."

"Oh, we have sex," the guy says, looking at her.

"Absolutely!" she says, "We're just not a couple."

"Really!" Charlie says.

"Yeah," the guy says. "It works for us. It's like a twenty percent Yes and eighty percent No thing. It depends on what's going on that day."

"That sounds like Pareto's Principle," Donna says. "Eighty percent of the effect comes from twenty percent of the cause."

"Yeah, you could say that," the woman says.

"So what's the cause?" Charlie asks.

"The Mets," she says. "If they win, we do it. If they lose, we don't do it. And we don't do it at all during the off-season."

"You're serious," Donna says.

"Yep," she says. "Been at it for a couple of seasons now. It works for us. Keeps us out of trouble with people we don't know. Right about now I can't wait for the season to start." She puts her hand on the guy's thigh. Gives it a squeeze.

"Safe sex," the guy says, covering her hand with his.

"Safe at home!" the woman adds, gesturing like an umpire.

"What about Spring Training?" Charlie asks.

"Foreplay," the guy says. "Practice."

"Yeah, that's not bad," the woman says, but still, the *season . . ."*

"April will be here before we know it," the guy says, putting his arm around her.

"What about a double-header, regular season?" Charlie asks.

"In-season rules," she says. "Two times for two wins."

"Rained out?"

"Postponed sex."

"World Series?" Donna asks.

"That's special," she says. "We go twice for each win. Doesn't happen too often, though, as you well know."

"All-Star Game?" Charlie asks.

"If a Met is in the game and he gets a home run then we do it," she says.

"Hmm, Metsex," Donna says. "Interesting concept. I like it."

"Yep," the guy says. "Works for us."

"It removes the burden of having to decide things," the woman says. "I hate having to decide things. I can never decide."

"Should I stay or should I go?" Charlie says.

"Yeah, The Clash," the woman laughs. "We just leave things up to The New York Metropolitans. Let their play decide for us. It adds a whole 'nother dimension to the game. Ya never know until the fat lady sings, right?"

"Niiice," Donna says, nodding again and again. "You wear the hats?" She points at their heads.

"Only the person on top," he says. "We take turns."

"Switch hitters," Charlie laughs.

"Play ball!" the woman says. Dirty wink.

Mike brings their food. He likes the Braves.

Chirp!

I think Bertha is seeing someone else.

Charlie passes his iPhone to Donna. "Wait," she says. He does. They keep eating and chatting with the fans.

Chirp!

YT?

Tap, tap, tap.

Yes, I'm here, Patrick. Does that bother you that Bertha is seeing someone else? I thought you were moving on.

Chirp!

I am, but still. . .

Tap, tap, tap.

You're seeing someone else, right?

Chirp!

Yeah, I am moving on, but Bertha's thing was that she wanted only me. That was the problem. She wanted just me. And now there's this other guy. I don't even know who he is, or how she met him, or how long she's been seeing him, or what she's doing with him. WTF! She could have been seeing this bastard when we were still together. She's posting about him on fucking Facebook! She Facebooking for him! My friends are reading it!!!

Tap, tap, tap.

But you're done with her, Patrick. Life goes on, right?

Chirp!

I know, but I don't like that it's going on so fast. I thought she'd wait a while, or better yet, just be alone. This isn't right.

"Your burger's getting cold," Donna says.

Tap, tap, tap.

I have no answers for that, Patrick. Sorry.

6

"Hardy again?" Donna asks, leaving over from her beach chair.

"Yes." Charlie shows her the cover. *The Mayor of Casterbridge.*

"Why do you stay with that stuff? Isn't it depressing?"

"He's the most miserable writer who ever picked up a pen," Charlie says.

"And you like that?"

"I need this right now," Charlie says.

"Why?"

"I read his books when I was a teenager. They moved me to tears back then."

"A lot moved you to tears back then," Donna says. "You think that's a good thing for you to be doing right now, Charlie? Crying?"

"I feel like I have to find a sadness that's so deep that mine will feel minor by comparison."

"I don't know," Donna says.

He reaches over and offers his hand. She takes it.

"Remember how we covered the sadness in our history with happiness when Abby asked about the grandparents she never met? They were all too horrible to tell about. Well, except for your father."

"I remember."

"So we made up happy stories about them. The fairy tales. My father didn't beat my mother. He was a prince. And she didn't beat me. She was his princess. We all lived in a big shoe. Abby grew up with those fairy tales and we never told her the truth. Why would we?"

"I agree, but why are you doing this to yourself now? Why cover sad with sadder? Why not look for happy? You can find happy if you look for it. You find it in the bars."

"I find a lot in the bars. It's not all happy."

"Okay, but you know what I mean."

"I do, but I've been thinking about my old friend, Joey. You know that kid I told about? The one who took karate lessons when we were young."

"Yes."

"Well, Joey told me that he got kicked in the leg during a practice once and he fell to the floor, moaning. The sensei walked over and asked him where it hurt. Joey pointed at his shin and kept moaning."

"Was he hurt that bad?" Donna asks.

"Not really. Joey said he just needed a rest, but listen to what happened next. The sensei grabs Joey's foot, the one on the other leg, and he starts smacking it with his bare hand, which is as hard as a sidewalk."

"What!?"

"Yeah, and Joey starts screaming, of course."

"Was this guy a sadist?" Donna asks. "What does this have to do with you?"

"Give me a second. The guy stopped smacking after a few more whacks and then he asked Joey how his *other* leg felt. The one he had gotten kicked in."

"Uh, huh."

"Well, by this point, Joey's foot is hurting so much that he's forgotten about the kicked leg. He tells the sensei that the first leg feels okay."

"So everything's relative, right?" Donna says.

"Yes, and that's why I'm reading Thomas Hardy. He's as miserable as it gets. I'm too old for fairy tales, and I know that most stories don't have happy endings. All stories end in death."

"Unless you stop telling them in the middle," Donna says.

"Yeah. Dathsit. But right now, I need the Hardy's stories. There is no such thing as redemption for anyone in any of his books. Take this one, for instance." He holds up *The Mayor of Casterbridge*. "This guy is the mayor of a town and very successful, but when he was younger, he got drunk at a county fair and had a fight with his wife. He winds up auctioning off her and his daughter to a sailor. I know. Crazy, right? Anyway, he's sober the next day, but his family is gone. He can never make up for this, no matter what he does. There's no redemption and no forgiveness. It's misery from cover to cover."

"And he dies in the end."

"Of course."

"And this makes you happy?"

"Happy because he shows me that things could always be worse. I've had some rough times lately, but I've also had some laughs. That's why I'm focusing on what *could* be worse. I'm trying, Donna."

"Maybe you should put that shit down and read something fun for a change," Donna says.

"Like what?"

"A good murder book."

7

There's another beach bar on Singer Island. This one tucks itself back into the building, like a kid hiding under the bed. It's a lovely place to sit and that's what Charlie is doing right now. He has no other responsibilities today. He's been settling into the idea of finally being done, but he still has an aching sadness that clutches at his core.

He's by himself because Donna wanted to sit in the sun. Again. That was her responsibility today. Charlie had had enough sun for awhile. I mean, how much sun can a person take? Charlie knew that Donna's answer to that question would be, "All of it."

She did use sunblock, but she also thought that cancer wasn't interested in her. She had made it this far without a problem, and her skin was still smooth and clear, and she was beautiful, so there you go.

She was also fine with him going out to find new friends. She had said that more than once, and he believed her. So here he is, watching the bartender. He's wondering if Donna just wants to get the hell away from him for awhile. Or maybe forever?

Stop it.

The bartender is petite, like Donna. She comes over and smiles. "You look sad, young man. Got the blues?"

He smiles back. "A little bit," he says. "I'm Charlie." He reaches over. She takes his hand. Her's is very soft, small, and damp.

"I'm Clare," she says. "Sorry about the wet hand." She giggles. "Occupational hazard." Lovely giggle. "And I'm sorry that you're blue, Charlie. You lose your best friend?"

"Nah, just a job. I was there for a lifetime, such as it was, and doing my best, or so I thought. They decided I was too old to keep up with them, and that was that. They were all about computers and social networks, and other hocus pocus I don't understand, or want to understand. I'm a people person. I just want to listen hard and then chat. That's what I was doing for all those years until the whole world changed and dropped out from under me, like a trap door. I never saw it coming."

"They fire you, Charlie? Just like that?"

"No, they just decided I was irrelevant, and then they encouraged me to retire early. *Strongly* encouraged me to retire early. Made me an offer I couldn't refuse."

"You don't look old enough to retire, Charlie," Clare says.

"Well, thanks for that. I didn't think I was, but here I am."

"Here you are."

"I'm pretty old," Charlie says.

"Me, too," Clare says.

"Yeah, right."

"So where's home, Charlie?" Clare asks.

"Long Island, New York."

"What are you doing down here?"

"We're here for a month, Donna and me. She's my wife. She's out on the beach right now. Loves the sun. I can take just so much of that. And gosh, you so are easy to talk to. Listen to me; I'm going on and on here."

"Well, thanks, Charlie. You're easy to listen to, and you've come to the right place. Maybe I can cheer you up. This is a good bar with lots of good people who like to listen and chat. But first things first. It's Happy Hour! What can I get you?"

"Do you have house red, Clare?"

"Sure. Cab sav okay, Charlie?"

"*Very* okay. Thanks, Clare."

"No problem."

Clare is a brunette, hair in a ponytail, and wearing shorts and a tee shirt, the Singer Island bar uniform. Pale gray Irish eyes, like damp stars. Upturned nose. Delicate, seashell ears with a tiny pearl in each lobe. Watercolor skin. No tats that Charlie can see, and there's a lovely elfin mischief about her.

She has to go up on a one-leg tiptoe and stretch her right arm high to reach the wine glass in the rack above the bar. He watches her as her short tee rides up. Her belly is tanned and as taut as an opened beach umbrella. She just manages to get the tips of two childlike fingers inside the rim of the glass. She wiggles it toward the end of the rack, catches it, flips it over, unscrews the bottle cap, and pours. She sets the glass in front of him, like it's been his forever. An heirloom.

She offers him the bottle cap. "Would you like to sniff the twist cap, sir?" she asks.

"No, I'm sure this is a fine vintage," Charlie says, holding up his glass, and smiling.

"It's good to have a sommelier at the bar," Clare says.

"Yeah, I'm classy as hell."

"I can tell," Clare says. She stands there and smiles at him. Just smiles at him. Her warmth goes right through his tee shirt. Others are waiting for drinks. She senses this behind her. She holds up one finger for them without looking back. Just a moment. The other drinkers turn and go back to their conversations. She'll be with them soon. They get it. She watches him deeply. Eyes like damp stars. A delicate strawberry fragrance he just notices now.

Charlie raises his glass and toasts. "First drink in this glass today, my dear," he says.

"Don't be blue, Charlie," Clare says. "This is where you belong, okay?"

Charlie looks at her. *Really* looks at her, as if for the first time.

"*Okay?*" she whispers.

"Okay," he says.

"Good. Stay here." She knocks the bar twice with her knuckles. "I'll be right back. Don't leave me."

Two big, squarish guys and a smallish one with a bad mustache just showed up. The little guy sits between the two squarish ones. To Clare, they look like Lego. They're all wearing Polo shirts and creased shorts. She figures business guys cutting loose.

And they all order the same drink: margarita with salt. Hey, it's Florida and the weather is just fine.

Clare sets down their drinks and smiles. The little guy in the middle picks up his glass and flicks the salt off the rim with the tip of his tongue, all the while giving Clare a look that belongs in a '70s porn flick.

"You know, I can make your toes curl," he says, and tongue-flicks the salt some more. Real fast. Then he licks the side of the glass, stem to top. "Curl 'em up real tight for you."

The other two guys look from him toward Clare.

"You can do that for me, eh?" she asks.

"I sure can." Flick, flick, flick. Lick.

"Okay, give me your shoes, little guy. Let's see if they're as small as I think they are. I'll try them on for size right now. See if they curl my toes. I'll bet they can. You have tiny feet, right?" She reaches out a hand and gives the guy a smile you could pour on a waffle.

The other two guys explode with laughter and smack the little guy on his back. "Man, she got you with that one," the guy on the right says. The guy on the left is trying to catch his breath.

"Better luck next time," Clare smiles. "Where you guys from?

"New York City," the guy on the left says.

"Here on business?"

"Yep. Convention."

"What's it like in New York?" Clare asks.

"Big City. Not like this tiny town," the little guy says. "You should visit someday. Maybe when you're on Spring Break. Where do you go to school?"

"Oh, here," Clare says.

"What are you studying?"

"Right now I'm studying New Yorkers." She looks around. "Enjoy, guys. I'll be back for more studying in a bit."

"She got you good, man," the guy on the left laughs. "Guys with small feet. You know what they say. Too funny!"

"Hey, I have no problem in that area. No complaints at all," the little guy says.

"Well, you'll never get a chance to prove it with this one."

"Can't win 'em all," the little guy says. Sips. Licks. Laughs.

"Let me get you a fresh glass," she says.

"This one is okay," Charlie says.

"No, a new glass will change your mood," Clare says. "You'll see. That one has served its purpose." She stretches up for the new one.

"They should lower that rack for you," Charlie says.

"Nah, the guys who work nights here are twice my size. And the reaching is good for my spine. This place is my gym. I get to scoot and stretch." She folds forward without bending her slim knees and puts her palms flat on the floor. Holds it like that. Charlie watches her vertebrae strain against her tanned skin, and then she straightens up and stretches high. Her tee shirt follows. She brings her arms out and down slowly to her hips and smiles with Christmas-morning eyes.

"See? Bar yoga."

"I do," Charlie says.

"You're nice," Clare says.

"As are you."

"Don't be blue," Clare says. "You now have a fresh glass, and a fresh start. Right here in this place."

"Okay, I'll snap out of it." He gives himself a light slap on his right cheek. Clare laughs and smiles wide. Lovely. One of her teeth, the right cuspid, is out of alignment, which makes her face even more interesting. He's noticing this for the first time, too. She doesn't put her hand up to cover it when she smiles. Charlie likes that.

A drinker down the bar raises an empty glass. "Don't leave me," she says.

"I won't."

She's back after a while, with a small bowl of chips. "My treat," she says and points at his glass. "More, Charlie?"

"Sure. Same glass is good. This is my lucky glass now."

"That's what I like to hear." (Gosh, that smile.)

"Clare, did you know you have a famous name?"

"Really?"

"Yep, Saint Clare followed Saint Francis of Assisi around. They were from the same town. I think they fed deer together. I might have seen them on Skyline Drive once years ago."

"Really?" She chuckles, like cool water on smooth rocks.

"Well, not about Skyline Drive. I made that part up, but the rest is true."

"That's nice. *You're* nice."

"Thanks. Clare also founded an order of nuns called the Poor Clares."

"Well, I get the poor part, but I'll pass on the nun thing," Clare giggles. Wind chimes now.

"She's also the patron saint of television." Charlie looks for a TV but there are none he can see. He's noticing this for the first time. How unusual for a beach bar not to have a TV.

"Patron saint of *TV*?" Clare says.

"Yep, and also of goldsmiths," Charlie continues.

"Ooo, I like *that*!"

"And laundry."

"You making that up?"

"Nope."

"How do you know all of this stuff?"

"I'm a good Catholic lad." Charlie makes the sign of the cross, and prays irreverently, "Spectacles, testicles, wallet and watch." Clare giggles. "Be right back." She scoots off to draw a Bud Heavy. Drink Sync.

Charlie looks again for televisions.

None anywhere.

Gosh.

A couple comes in and sits a stool away from Charlie to his left. They look like they're in their early-40s. The woman, also a slim, ponytail brunette, wearing a blue bathing suit and white cover-up, takes the stool one away from Charlie. He knew she would do this because she's with a guy. Guys in bars won't sit next to guys they don't know. It's like the urinal thing. A guy will *never* choose the urinal next to another guy if there are other urinals available, even if he knows the other guy, *especially* if he knows the other guy. It has to be a real emergency for a guy to do otherwise.

Charlie sips his wine and turns to the woman. She smells like the beach.

"May I ask you a question?"

"Sure." Nice smile.

"Did you have breakfast this morning?" Charlie also has a nice smile.

"What do you mean?"

"Breakfast. First meal of the day. I had some oatmeal. Donna, she's my wife, bought these packets that we put into the microwave. We're renting an apartment here for a month. It's not bad. I mean the oatmeal, not the apartment. Especially if you add some fruit to it."

"To the apartment?" she asks.

"No, to the oatmeal."

"Gotcha." *Real* nice smile. Works its way up into her crinkly brown eyes. Gorgeous now.

"Anyway, Donna's on the beach, and I've had enough sun for awhile. Figured I'd come here and make some new friends. I'm Charlie, and I'm shy." He reaches out a hand. She laughs and takes it.

"Shy, my ass," she says. "Jenny." A firm, challenging handshake, a black belt's handshake. He likes it. "This is my husband, Cliff. Cliff, this is Charlie. He eats microwave oatmeal for breakfast."

Cliff reaches over and shakes Charlie's hand. Smiles. "Hey."

"With a banana if I can get one," Charlie says to Jenny, continuing to shake Cliff's hand. "Bananas keep me regular. That's important at my age. I'm retired and I like a good push in the morning." He smiles, let's go.

Cliff looks at his hand, grimaces. They all laugh. Jenny's handshake is tougher than Cliff's. Charlie likes that.

"Why did you ask me about breakfast, Charlie?" she asks.

"It's the most important meal of the day, Jenny. Besides, on Singer Island, we all begin as strangers, but look where we are now."

And just like that, they're off and running.

8

The killer is in the car with the tinted windows. He's waiting for her to pull into her driveway. He's been tracking her car since she left her office with the bug he planted in the car's wheel well.

It wouldn't occur to Charlie to plant the bug in the car's wheel well, Donna thinks. If he was writing this story he'd ask Fred, or Dennis, or Bob about the best place to plant a bug in a car. Those guys would have dozens of ideas. Somewhere in their garages, one or more of them probably has an installation manual for planting bugs in cars, along with all the rest of their car-related shit.

Car guys.

There's a soft breeze. Donna puts down her Kindle, lifts the arms of her beach chair, leans back and closes her eyes. The surf is hypnotic today, steady and lovely. She's sitting right up against it. The tide is going out so she's okay. Now and then, a wave sneaks up close enough to tickle her tanned feet, but she's okay. She checked the lifeguard's notes on the whiteboard by his stand before she set up:

High-tide: 8:04 AM

Low-tide: 1:45 PM

Have a nice day!

The timeshare management rents lounges, umbrellas, and canvas cabanas in front of the big timeshare hotel over there. She needs nothing from these people because she brings her own chair and never sits under an umbrella.

She and Charlie had walked down here a few mornings when the tide was in and they watched the beach boy set up the long row of seating and shade for the timeshare people, who were probably still asleep, or having breakfast.

The beach boy drops a blue canvas lounge. Opens it. Wraps it in plush white towels. Works an umbrella pole into the sand with wide, back-and-forth strokes. Donna watches the boy's sinewy arms and legs and the taut, tanned skin of his back go through these rhythmic motions. Back and forth. Again and again. One after another. A long line of yellow umbrellas, like party hats, each pole buried deeply in the timeless sand.

Little surfer, little one
Made my heart come all undone
Do you love me, do you surfer girl?

She closes her eyes, smiles at the memory, hopes the beach boy grows up to be a good man.

A whiff of coconut. A gull laughs. She thinks of her father, gone these many years, and much too soon. The warm sun strokes her still-smooth, tanned skin.

She reaches toward the sun. Chokes back a sob.

Never *really* alone.

Daddy.

9

Clare appears.

"Jenny, Cliff, this is Clare and she is a precious elf."

"Hi, gang!" Clare says. "Charlie, I'm glad you found company. These two look like fun people."

"Did you have breakfast this morning, Clare?" Jenny asks.

"I did."

"And what did you have, young lady?"

"I had Pop-Tarts," Clare says. "Blueberry. My favorite."

"Really?"

"Absolutely. I'm a kid at heart."

"You old enough to work here, kid?"

"Shhhh."

"Okay," Jenny says. "Mum's the word."

"So what are we drinking?" Clare asks.

Cliff has a beautifully shaped, bald and shining head. He's wearing a red bathing suit and a light-blue **Mustang 50 Years** tee shirt. Black flip-flops. He orders a Corona, no lime. Jenny asks for a frosted strawberry margarita.

"Yum!" Clare says. "Salt?"

"What is margarita without salt?" Jenny asks. "Seriously?"

"I'm with you," Clare says. "Can't wait to get off."

"Need help reaching the glass?" Cliff asks as Clare does her stretch. He watches her.

Everyone watches her.

"Nope, I got this."

"You sure?" Watches her all over.

"Yep!" She flashes that white, slightly flawed/perfect smile.

Gosh.

"I have an idea for a bar," Charlie says.

"Tell us," Jenny says.

"It would have a car theme. All the stools would have seatbelts to keep us safe, and in front of each person at the bar, right here on the rail, we'll have painted dividing lines, and between each pair of lines, the letters SRS." Charlie touches the top of the bar with the sides of both hands. "You know, Supplemental Restraint System? Make-believe airbags. Wadda ya think?"

"I *love* it!" Cliff says. "And how about a gas pedal and brake instead of a foot rail?"

"That'll work," Charlie says. "If you need a refill, you just step on the gas and here comes the bartender."

"And if a lady doesn't like some guy who's coming on to her," Jenny adds, "she can just stomp on her brake and the creep's airbag will go off and knock him on his kiester."

"Bam!" Cliff says, pantomiming a punch to his nose.

"So what do you think?" Charlie asks. "Total safety in afternoon drinking?"

"Well, not for the guy who gets punched by the airbag," Jenny says.

"True," Charlie says, "But for the rest of us?"

"I like it," Cliff says. "They got TV in this bar?"

"I thought about that," Charlie says. "I considered twenty-four-seven NASCAR."

"Yeah, that would be good," Cliff says.

"But hang on," Charlie says. "Then I wondered what it would be like if there were no TVs at all in this place. What would people do without TV? Stop for a minute and look around."

Cliff and Jenny look.

"What are we looking for?" Jenny asks.

"TV," Charlie says.

They turn their heads this way and that. Look again. "Holy crap! There aren't any," Cliff says.

"Jeez," Jenny says. "I never noticed that. We've been yakking since we sat down."

"We don't need TV to have fun, do we?" Charlie's says. "Back in the day, there were no TVs in the bars, just The Chat and lots of laughs."

"Yeah," Cliff says. "Yeah! Hey, I like this even more now." He hoists his Corona. "*Fuck* TV."

Clare shakes her head and smiles. Ponytail sways. "Oh, Cliff."

"I'd drink in that place like it was nobody's business," Jenny says.

"Just like here, right?" Charlie says.

"Yeah, and I'd never shut up," Jenny says. "What's wrong with that?"

"Not a damn thing," Charlie says, clinking glasses with her.

"What shall we call this great bar?" Jenny asks.

"How about Crash?" Charlie says.

"I love it!" Jenny crosses her slim legs. One white flip-flop dangles off her candy-apple toes. "You a car guy, Charlie?"

Cliff leans over, waiting for his answer.

"I could be. Tell me about your old Mustang, Cliff."

10

Donna wakes up, lifts the beach chair's arms, sits up, and looks around. She's not alone. Four gulls are five feet away, staring at her. They could be in her murder book. They're separating like gang members now. Harder to kill them all that way. Black gull eyes staring at her beach bag.

Sandwich in there, lady? Give it up!

She glares at them. "Get outta here, ya bastards," she hisses. Throws a flip-flop at the biggest one. They rise about three feet and jump onto the wind like it's the running board of a getaway car. They screech a gull word that means *Bitch!*

She watches them go. They swirl over her, all pissed off. "Never *really* alone," she says to herself.

She looks to where his chair should be. Nothing.

She also looks around for the fit, tanned guy who liked her feet. Holds her palm over her eyes and scans the beach. Turns this way. And that way. Smiles quietly.

Too bad?

She wonders at possibilities and looks again at the empty space where his chair should be.

She can't fix him.

Only he can do that. She knows that for sure.

Can he? *Will* he?

All she can do is love him.

Is that enough?

She scans the beach again.

Too bad.

11

"Hello! Who are your new friends?" Donna asks.

Charlie turns and beams at her. "What a nice surprise! Pull up a stool. Clare? A pinot grigio for my daughter, please."

"Coming up!" Clare goes for the pinot.

Donna sits between Charlie and Jenny. "I'm not really his daughter," she explains.

"Really?" Jenny says.

"No, I'm his granddaughter. I've had a difficult week at the Junior High and I really need a nice glass of pinot."

"He doesn't look old enough to have a granddaughter," Cliff says.

"You a car guy?" Donna asks, smiling and looking at his shirt.

"I am."

"Been telling Grandpa Charlie about your ride?"

"Yep."

"He listening to you? Believing everything you say?"

"Yep."

"Asking great questions?"

"The *best*."

"That's my Grandpa!" Donna says. "Best listener in the world. He's pretty good with The Chat, too. Hi, I'm Donna."

"Cliff." Smile. Shake.

"Hi! I'm Jenny."

"Love your hair, Jenny," Donna says. "And your *eyes*. Wow! Van Morrison know about those brown eyes?"

Jenny laughs. "Thanks. I'm Cliff's brown-eyed girl. And my hair's a mess," She pushes it around. "But thanks."

"*I'm* a mess. You're lovely, and you should put those eyes away before the cops show up. Gosh." They all laugh. "I need wine," Donna says.

"May I see your library card and bus pass, young lady?" Clare asks, holding back the pinot grigio.

"Gimme that!" Donna lunges. Clare gives it up with a giggle.

"Donna," Charlie says. "This is Clare, who has left the order of the Poor Clares to minister to this needy congregation."

"Thanks for the daycare, Clare," Donna says, raising her glass.

"Somebody has to do it," Clare laughs.

"You let brown eyes like that into this joint?" Donna asks, pointing a thumb at Jenny. "That's dangerous."

"Yes, and so are your *greens*," Clare says, pointing at Donna's eyes. "I might not let you *out* of here. You're liable to knock down a plane with those."

Donna giggles. Sips. Flashes her eyes. Clare smiles back with that perfectly crooked cuspid. Doesn't lift her hand to cover it. Leans in. Smiles. Warmth flows back and forth between them. A Singer Island embrace without touching.

And so begins a beautiful friendship.

"How was the beach?" Charlie asks.

"Peaceful. I've had enough for now." She leans into him from her stool.

"Clare, would you please mark this day on the bar's calendar. This sun sponge has had enough for one day."

"Noted," Clare says.

"So what's the topic?" Donna asks.

"We've been talking cars and food," Jenny says.

"Do they have free pie here?" Donna asks.

"They do," Charlie says, "But it costs five bucks today."

"Oh well, then I'll stick to wine," Donna says. "Clare, thank you for knowing what pinot grigio is."

"No problem!"

She looks at Charlie. Small smirk. Common memory.

"You're adorable, Clare," Donna says.

"Thanks!"

"No problem," Donna answers.

"I have a food question for you, Jenny," Charlie says.

"Shoot."

"If you were being executed, what would you want for your last meal?"

"Executed?"

"Yes, this is Florida. They have the death penalty here. You don't stand a chance. Donna can tell you all about that. She reads murder books for fun. What would you choose for an appetizer?"

"Nachos."

"Good choice. Chili or chicken?"

"I'll go with chicken. I have to watch my weight."

"You're being executed," Cliff says. "Live a little."

"Okay, chili."

"Sour cream and guacamole?" Charlie asks.

"Why not?" Jenny says.

"I can bring you that right now," Clare says.

"She's under the warden's supervision, Clare," Charlie says. "Good as you are, you can't help this woman."

"Okay."

"You want some soup, Jenny? You're allowed to have some soup on Death Row," Charlie says.

"Sure, make it clam chowder."

"Great. We get the clams off the beach. They're beautiful, all very small. New England or Manhattan?"

"Manhattan. I had the chili nachos. Calories."

"Fair enough. And now for your main course. You may have anything at all. This is your very last meal. What do you choose?"

Jenny doesn't hesitate. "New York City pizza."

"Plain?"

"Are you kidding? Pepperoni and sausage."

"Coming right up. Now what about dessert?"

"They're going to kill me, right?"

"Yep. And soon."

"Okay, Italian cheesecake."

"Very good choices. We now know a lot more about you and what makes you happy."

"You're making me hungry."

"Here's another question," Charlie says.

"*How* would you like to be executed?"

"It's Florida. Don't I just get the lethal injection?"

"You actually have a choice here," Donna says. "You can pick the electric chair if you'd like, but I'd go with the needle. The electric chair really messes up your hair."

"But wait," Charlie says. "Since none of this is real, you have other options as well."

"Meaning?" Jenny says.

"Oh, hanging, beheading, stoning, crucifixion, gas chamber, firing squad, drowning, tossed off a cliff onto rocks. No offense, Cliff."

"None taken."

"You may also be drawn and quartered," Charlie continues. "You know, the whole buffet, and any other grisly thing you can think of. Ladies choice."

"I think I'll go with the needle," Jenny says. "Even though I hate needles."

Everyone nods. Best choice.

"And you get to pick a song," Charlie claps his hands. "What do you want to be listening to when you take your very last breath?" He drums his palms on the bar.

"Does she get to hear the whole song?" Cliff asks.

"Sure, why not. We have all the time in the world," Charlie says.

"Go with Jethro Tull's *Thick as a Brick*. It goes on for nearly 44 minutes," Cliff says.

"But I can't stand that damn flute," Jenny says. "I'm going to pick *The End* by The Doors. It's appropriate, and Morrison was hot. Jim, not Van."

"Well, that will give you about 12 minutes," Cliff says.

"How do you know all these song times?" Donna asks.

"I used to make cassettes," Cliff says. "You know, for the car."

"Oh, yeah. Car guy."

"More drinks?" Clare asks. They look at glasses and at each other. Why not?

"This is fun," Jenny says.

"It's about to get funner," Charlie says. "Since you're going to die, and very soon, you get to enjoy a final booty call. You may choose anyone throughout all of history. Make it a good one."

Jenny holds her chin, looks up at the top-shelf. "Okay, this is going to sound really weird, and I want you to know I am *definitely* not a lesbian, but if it's going to be the very last time, I gotta go with Jennifer Lawrence. Not

The Hunger Games Jennifer. The *Silver Lining Playbook* Jennifer."

"Yeah," Cliff says. "That works."

"Who would you pick, Charlie?" Jenny asks.

"Why, I'd pick Donna, of course." (Charlie is a wise man.)

"And how about you, Donna?" Jenny asks, "Would you go with Charlie for the final roll in the hay?"

"Nah, I gotta go with George Clooney. Sorry, Charlie." They all laugh.

"Perfectly understandable!" Charlie says.

"How about you, Cliff?" Donna asks. "Danica Patrick?"

"Hell, no. I'll stick with Jenny." He winks. "She's more dangerous."

"It's your last chance, Cliff," Jenny laughs. "It's not like I'll be yelling at you anymore. You'll be dead."

"I choose you."

"Aww, you're sweet."

"Glasses up!" Clare says. She's poured herself a shot of vodka. "Good choices all around, doomed souls." They clink glasses. Clare shoots the vodka like she was raised in a bar.

"How about you, Clare?" says Charlie. "Last booty call forevermore. Who's it gonna be?"

"Hmm, How about if I pick *you*, Charlie? You can tell me a bedtime story afterwards. Do I get a bedtime story before I die?" She tilts her head to the side. Smiles with that crooked cuspid. Twirls an index finger in her ponytail.

"Well, I'll have to get permission for that, Clare. What do you think, Donna? That be okay with you?" They laugh. Clare pouts.

Donna shakes her head. Smiles. "Poor Clare."

"Poor me," Clare giggles, and flies off to fill pints.

"Clare," Jenny says, "I gotta ask you something. Let me see your hands." Clare holds them out, palms up. "They're so small." Clare smiles. "How do you keep them so soft, working in a bar and all? I mean you're washing glasses all day long."

"Want to know my secret?"

"I do."

Clare turns, goes up on tiptoes and reaches for a bottle of Hangar One vodka, which causes her legs to go taut and her tee shirt to ride up again.

Pause.

Watch.

Deep breath. Let it out.

Okay, go.

"I use this," she says, showing them the label. "Just a little bit." She pours a few drops onto her left palm, and massages it into her skin. "Smell," she holds her hand out to Jenny. It's a soft smell, like vodka, which you would expect, but something else is in there as well. It's gone in a moment. All that's left is the softness, and the memory of what she just did.

"That's amazing," Jenny says. She holds Clare's hand like a small bird. Smells it again.

"It's better than lotion." Clare says.

"Doesn't it dry your skin?"

"Nope. I don't know why, but it doesn't."

"How did you learn this?" Charlie asks.

"Well, one day I was pouring for a customer and some of it spilled onto my hand. I didn't have a towel nearby so I just rubbed it in. I noticed the softness right away."

"Expensive lotion," Cliff says.

"Yeah, let's keep it our secret." She looks around.

A middle-aged drinker wearing a Notre Dame Fighting Irish tee shirt catches her eye and she's gone.

Jenny tells Cliff that she's going to order a double shot of Hangar One to rub on his bald head. "Maybe it will grow some hair," she jokes.

"My head's soft enough as it is, Jenny." He raps it softly twice with his middle knuckle.

"Well, yeah, that's true," she laughs.

Clapton's *Key to the Highway* comes on the juke.

Oh, give me one more kiss, darlin'
Just before I go.

'Cos when I leave this time, little girl
I won't be back no more.

Not a bad choice for the last song ever heard, Clare thinks as she draws the Fighting Irish guy's fourth pint of Guinness.

12

"I'm going to hop in the shower," Donna says.

"Go ahead. I'm checking something." Charlie is at the black lacquered table with his iPhone, trying to figure out which singer the island was named for. Maybe the birds?

"Hey, Donna," he shouts from the small table toward the tiny bathroom, which isn't far away.

"Yeah?" She left the door open to let out the steam.

"This place is named for the guy who built Palm Beach. His name was Paris Eugene Singer. His daddy was Isaac Merritt Singer, the sewing machine magnate."

"That's interesting."

"Yeah, my iPhone tells good stories."

Charlie clicks on more links. He knows Singer sewing machines. They were every young woman's perfect present when he was a teenager. The girls would go to stores like J.J. Newberry and S.S. Kresge to buy patterns, and then they'd make their own clothes, but he knew nothing about Singer himself, so he clicked away.

He's still at it when Donna comes out of the shower, green robe open, rubbing her blonde hair with a white towel. Gosh.

"You ready to go to the prom?" Charlie asks.

"Give me like ten minutes," Donna says. "My glass slippers are still in the dishwasher." She walks over; looks at his iPhone. "What's with the Statue of Liberty? You homesick?"

"No, this is great stuff. Turns out this guy, Isaac Merritt Singer, was quite the ladies man. He just couldn't keep it in his pants. He was a bigamist, too. He finally had to move to Europe to get away from the law in the States. He never came back."

"Some people just can't resist temptation," Donna says.

"For sure. Paris was his twenty-third kid. No one knows how many more kids there were, legitimate and illegitimate, or how many women, but this guy was *busy*. Here, look at this. Isabella Boyer Singer, the last wife, gave birth to Paris, the Singer who developed this island. She also had an affair with Frederic Bartholdi. She was his model for the Statue of Liberty." Charlie hands her the iPhone. Donna sees a not-very-pretty Victorian woman holding a boy's hand. They're standing next to Lady Liberty's copper face when it was still in parts in France. It has the same face. "Isn't that amazing? I'll bet that kid is Paris."

"I'm going to get dressed. Let me know when you come up with a real singer."

Charlie keeps clicking links and reading. He leans in, reads more. "Hey, Donna?"

"Yeah?"

"Singer's partner in the sewing machine business was Edward Clark. Together, they built The Dakota on Central Park West and Seventy-Second Street."

"That's where John Lennon lived and died," she said from the bedroom.

"So there's your singer," Charlie said. "Imagine."

"Any other singers live in The Dakota?" She's in her bra and panties now.

Charlie pauses. Looks at her. Sighs and taps some more. "Well, Yoko, of course, if you want to call her a singer."

"I don't." She puts on khaki shorts. Zips up.

"And Roberta Flack. You know, *Killing Me Softly*?"

"That appeals to me," She slips on a green tee shirt.

"I figured it might, murder girl. Oh, and Rosemary Clooney also lived there, as did Leonard Bernstein. He didn't sing. He conducted."

"I know that." She steps into white flip-flops. "What did Rosemary sing?"

Charlie taps. "*Come On-a My House* and *Mambo Italiano* were her two big hits."

Charlie taps. "And you know what else? She was George Clooney's aunt!"

"Hey, my last booty call. Yea!"

"Yes, poor me. Lucky George."

"Hey, speaking of last booty calls, that was nice of you to pick me. If I still knew how to blush, I would have blushed."

"Well, you're my best girl."

She moves in with a hug. "You keep talking like that I'm going to have to call George and tell him it's off."

"He'll be heartbroken."

"Think so?"

"Absolutely. You are the cutest woman in the world."

"Clare's also cute."

"Adorable, and better yet, she knows how to pour, but she's got nothing on you, kid."

"Aww, thanks. Wasn't that crazy with the Hanger One vodka?"

"Yeah, I wonder if the vodka company knows about that. Or her boss."

"She makes me miss Abby," Clare says.

"Me, too. It's nice to be with young people who still know how to talk to grownups."

"How old do you think Clare is?" Donna asks.

"I don't know. Twenty-two?"

"She's thirty-five. I asked her when you were off shedding a tear for Ireland."

"Wow. I know I should be amazed, but I'm married to you, and you've been pulling that same trick for as long as I've known you. May I see your ID, young lady?"

"I have it here in my bra, sir. Would you like to look?" Donna kisses him. "You're such a bullshitter. I love you. I don't even mind that she picked you as her last booty call forevermore. Shows she has good taste, and that she's very smart. She'll have to fight me, though."

"Do you know what she had for breakfast? Blueberry Pop Tarts."

"She told you that?"

"She told Jenny,"

"And Jenny asked Clare about breakfast because?"

"Well, you know. The Chat," Charlie says. Smiles.

Donna shakes her head, laughs. "You still got it, Charlie. Let's go get something to eat, and then maybe later I'll let you tell *me* a bedtime story. *After*."

"I'll do my best," Charlie says.

"You'd *better*."

> *If you say that you are mine,*
> *I'll be there 'til the end of time.*

13

In Charlie's dream, Donna is sitting and reading on her beach chair. He gets up and finds the pink, heart-shaped bucket filled with seashells. The sand is easy to walk on today. He drops one shell at a time back onto the beach, in a pure circle around Donna.

"Should you stay or should you go?" Donna asks, looking up from her murder book on the Kindle.

"I will stay," he says. "Forever."

"There is so much beauty in that pink bucket," Donna says.

He drops more shells around her.

"Thank you for finding them," she says.

"Do we have enough time, Donna?"

"For what?"

"For us."

"We have all of it, Charlie," Donna says. "All the time in the world."

He drops more shells.

"What will Trista say?

"She'll understand," Charlie says.

"And Abby?"

"Abby is going to be fine. She's strong, and she has us now, and she has Trista, and a daughter is precious, the most precious thing in the world."

"I know," Donna says. "I know."

He circles his wife of all these many years with a protective ring of seashells, each one perfect, she at its center, always. He leaves just two seashells in the pink bucket. One is communion-dress white, the other colored the lightest bronze and rainbowed three times with ivory, like a beautiful painted toenail.

"These two are for Trista," he says, showing her.

"They're just right. White first, the other for later, when she's older. And then you'll find her a red one when she's older still. What will you tell her in your dream, Charlie?"

"I'll tell her that the other shells asked to stay on their beach because it is so beautiful here, and it is their home. You and Abby and I will take her to visit them here some day when she is older. Together, we'll find them all again. But meanwhile, these two seashells, the most beautiful ones of all, will live with her, and they will use their ocean magic to bring sweet dreams to her each night, and they will love her forever, and never ever leave her alone."

"And what little girl wouldn't want that?" Donna asks.

Sunlight and a soft breeze play in Donna's hair. She's wearing the Easter-green hat he gave her years ago. She's laughing with her green eyes. She reaches up for him.

"Forever, Charlie. Forever."

Life Is Good.

14

Although they weren't formally introduced, Abby and Hank were together on the day they were born, which is not a very unusual thing to have happen. Babies are born every day in hospitals all over the world. In Abby and Hank's case, a pediatric nurse set them side by side in their little glass baking dishes in the Maternity Ward nursery of Plainview Hospital. A pink name card for Abby, a blue one for Hank. They arrived three hours apart (Abby is older), and screaming like they couldn't wait to get at life. The same obstetrician delivered them both. Again, not at all unusual. Happens every day. Doctors have many patients.

They went home with their parents and life moved along normally for both suburban babies. They lived in the Town of Oyster Bay on Long Island, but not in the same village within that large town. They both walked at about the same age (again, Abby was first by a week). They entered kindergarten in different schools on the same day. There's nothing unusual about any of this.

During the spring of their junior year at two different high schools, Abby and Hank both thought about where they might work for the summer, and this is where fate stepped in.

It arrived by way of friends of both of their parents, who knew someone in the Town office who could get the kids good summer jobs that paid more than they would have made at McDonald's. That's the way things work on Long Island. It's always good to know someone who knows someone. What helped a lot was that Abby was probably the smartest kid in her school (she would be valedictorian of her graduating class), and Hank was his school's star athlete (both football and baseball). Everyone loved these two popular kids.

Summer jobs for kids of friends in the Town of Oyster Bay ran the gamut from painting fire hydrants, to collecting garbage on the beaches, to mowing lawns in the parks, and various other things that a very large Long Island town does for its residents. One of the top jobs was to work at Tobay Beach, which nuzzles up to the Atlantic Ocean and is just about perfect.

Tobay Beach takes up a nice stretch of the 120-mile-long barrier beach that reaches from Coney Island to Montauk Point and protects the South Shore of Long Island from the anger of the Atlantic Ocean. Tobay lies just east of Jones Beach, which is a state park, and always very crowded on sunny summer days. Tobay, however, allows only town residents, so life there is slower. If you live in the town, you just have to buy the sticker and you're good for the whole summer season.

So, fate.

In their first summer working for the town, Abby and Hank got hired to stand in a small booth at the entrance to the parking lot. If they saw the sticker, they'd wave the driver through. If they didn't see the sticker, they'd ask for the car's registration, collect the fee, and put the sticker on the passenger-side window.. Easy as pie.

As summer wore on, most residents had their stickers in place, so the job of checking them got easier and easier. By late-June, the kids working the booth weren't really looking at the cars; they were looking at each other, and that was certainly the case with Abby and Hank.

And naturally, the subject of birthdays came up, and when they learned that they shared a common one, the next question, of course, was *where* were you born, and then the other questions that led to their joint, "Oh my god!"

Abby went home and told Donna and Charlie, and they dug through old photos taken of the baking dishes in the hospital's nursery, and there they were, side by side. Abby and Hank. And Abby, raised on fairytales, now had her very own.

Also in the nursery that day, but not in any of the photographs, and in a baking dish three babies away from Abby, was another just-born infant. His blue card read,

Cyrus. A different obstetrician delivered Cyrus and she went quiet as his little head emerged from his mother. He had a very large, round, screaming-red hemangioma on his forehead, just above his little nose. It extended horizontally to the center of each of his little eyes. This unfortunate birthmark caused all of the people who visited the nursery to gasp, and then go silent. Poor kid.

Years later, Cyrus' and Hank's paths would collide, but no one knew that on the birthday that they shared with Abby and the other infants in the nursery. The collision would happen for the same reason that strangers become graveyard neighbors.

Murphy is born. Roselli is born. They do not know that they will spend eternity buried next to each other in Saint Charles Cemetery on Long Island, where the stones of identical dimensions look like rows of black and grey postage stamps, licked by death, and mailed to God.

Murphy and Roselli will never meet in life, but the connection in death has always been there for both men. They were on a journey that would end with them side by side, six feet under, but it is only in death that we can see this.

And what, you may wonder, are the chances that this particular seashell over here, this pure white one, should lay atop this other seashell that looks like a pretty painted toenail, rainbowed three times with ivory, and this on a beach with trillions of seashells hugging a sea with countless more. Why *these* two together in death? And why should Charlie Molloy, recently retired, stoop to pick them up and place them in his pocket? Why these two? How many events had to take place for this to happen? Does life work us the way the ocean works a shell? No shell comes out the same; some have more scars than others. Is this pure chance or something deeper?

How many events does it take to set Hank and Cyrus on their collision course? Millions? Trillions? No one knows. We don't think of such things when we're busy making plans, when we're wondering whether we should stay or go, over and over and over again, each day of our lives. Why this way? Why not that way?

A man and a woman, unknown to each other and living in different parts of the world, work hard and save money so that they may travel to France to tour and eat beautiful food and drink gorgeous wine, and perhaps, one blessed Friday, walk the labyrinth in the nave of Chartres Cathedral. This has been their dream for years.

These two, though, unknown to each other, and through some wonderful mingling of millions of tiny decisions made individually, are about to meet. Is this random? Or have they always been on a collision course within their separate lives?

She steps onto the labyrinth's narrow path and winds her way back and forth toward the sacred center. She stops to pray there, and then works her way out of the labyrinth by the same path, turning and turning and turning within this beautiful, ancient symbol of life's journey. All the while, she is considering her past, her present, and her future. It takes her an hour to complete this rhythmic walking meditation and prayer.

She meets the man as he is going in the opposite direction because the labyrinth is not a maze; it is a continuous, twisting, holy path, like life, and it is both long and narrow. They meet, a bit awkwardly. Smile. He moves left, as does she at the same moment. A dance. Then they move together right. Dance again. They stop moving and laugh, each a bit embarrassed. They are the same age. They each find the other attractive.

And then something perfect happens. They share a brief, light embrace. It seems so natural to touch this other person, this other life, whose journey is now joined with yours in this single moment. Touch, and move on into a future no one will understand until death arrives. Or stay? Stay and change everything else.

The moment asks, *"How?"* and *"What if?"* and *"What now?"*

Decide:

> *Darlin' you got to let me know.*
> *Should I stay or should I go?*

Who will sit next to you in the bar on that next airport concourse, Charlie? And the time after that, Charlie? Who then? And will she change your life forever, Charlie?

Will you stay?

And will she haunt your dreams?

And how did you come to these shared moments on your way home to Donna, and to Abby, and to Trista?

How many events had to come together to make it all happen the way it did, Charlie?

And isn't it all just so perfect, even when it seems impossibly flawed? Isn't it, Charlie?

Even when it hurts you terribly?

Stay or go.

There are unseen threads that connect all of us throughout all of time. The connections are apparent only in death, and none who go there get to tell the living.

But there will always be Murphy and Roselli, side by side, reminding us that all of this is true. Some call it religion. Others call it fate, or karma, or juju. Most just ignore it.

Nature doesn't care what we call it, or not call it. Nature doesn't care about any of us. Not one bit. Only *we* care about us. And only if we want to. Love is a choice.

And fairytales often have monsters.

15

"Mom, can you believe this?" Abby said. They were in the kitchen, putting together a salad for dinner. Abby was washing each leaf of lettuce like it was the face of a baby. "It's like Hank and I were married in another life. We grew old together and then died on the very same day because we couldn't live without each other. And when we got to heaven we laughed and said, 'Let's go back and do it all over again!' So we held hands and jumped off the cloud and into that nursery. We were born side by side, Mom! Like in a fairy tale."

"I know," Donna said. "I was there. Remember?"

"But you didn't know then, Mom. No one knew. Hank and I had to discover that for ourselves. And we did. Things like this don't just happen. This was meant to be, Mom. I just know it; and I love him *so* much."

Donna, tough as the years had made her, got a bit teary with this, but also a bit uneasy, which she couldn't understand. She thought of that long-ago springtime walk in the fog with Charlie on Jones Beach. Love on the beach. It happens. It's always possible. And here it was again. Or so it seemed. It could be. Who knows? And they *were* born together. So why this uneasy feeling?

She thinks of her father. The sand castles. The brilliant sunlight.

The sand.

"Help me, Daddy," she whispers.

That first high-school summer, Abby and Hank got off work and walked through the pedestrian tunnel that goes under Ocean Parkway and onto the beach. Many of the people, and all of the lifeguards, had left the beach by then. Some people lingered, though, because this was a beautiful time of day. The sky was hummingbird blue and the light breeze stroked them like a lover.

"Which way do you want to walk?" Hank asked. He was still in his Town uniform and getting the attention of the remaining young ladies on the sand. Hey, baseball and football.

"Let's walk down to the nudie beach," Abby said. "That's always funny."

It was a half-mile or so west of the pedestrian tunnel. Nudity isn't legal on the beach, but nobody bothers the people who *really* like the sun. They're down there by themselves. Now and then, one of the men, and it was mostly men, would stand when curious people wearing clothes strolled by. The random man, almost always a coot, would look out to sea, hands on hips. The walkers, usually young people like Abby and Hank, would keep their eyes straight ahead and giggle, straining their peripheral vision like pulled rubber bands as they passed by.

On this particular late-afternoon, a coot with skinny legs, a flabby ass, a pencil eraser of a penis, and a saddlebag scrotum, came strolling down from his blanket. He wore Ray Ban sunglasses and nothing else. He was smoking a cigarette held in a six-inch-long plastic holder that would have looked just right between F.D.R.'s yellowed teeth. He timed his approach to coincide with the kids passing by. Did it on purpose. When they passed, he was six feet away from them, posing with gnarled hands on knobby hips, cigarette holder up in his teeth, like a plastic erection. Smoke wafting in the gentle breeze. Big smile on his sun-broiled, wrinkled puss.

"Hey, mister," Abby says. "Where do you keep your matches?"

The naked coot says nothing. He turns on sandy soles and trudges back to his blanket, saddlebag scrotum keeping cadence like a petulant pendulum, dignity, such as it was, intact.

And Hank thought that was hilarious. She could be so funny. He, not so much. Well, actually, not at all. He was mostly serious, and he knew that. He went at life like it was a playbook, and Abby said that this quality made him seem very grown-up to her. Together they seemed just right. She thought they filled in each other's gaps, but Hank had more gaps than she knew about that first summer, more than she could ever have imagined.

"I mean, if he used one of those plastic lighters I wouldn't have had to ask where he kept it," Abby said. "But matches?"

Hank chuckled. Just a little, but he did. It made Abby happy to hear him chuckle.

16

Cyrus was having a lousy childhood. The hemangioma did not fade, as the doctors in the hospital said it would by the time he was 10 years old.

Lois, Cyrus's mother, was a single mom, who still lived with her parents. She didn't know for sure who Cyrus' father was. She thought of that angry hemangioma as the mark of her sin, and it turned her to constant prayer.

Oh, and to alcohol. It was hard for her to hold the child, or even to look at him. Her parents tried to help, but they were also troubled by the horror of the boy's face. Cyrus grew up neglected and alone with his turbulent thoughts.

And children can be cruel. In the fourth grade, a fifth-grade boy on the playground called him Cyclops instead of Cyrus and that horrible nickname stuck to him like a brand. He fought the larger boy for saying that. Knocked him down and kicked at his face until a teacher pulled him off. He tried to do more but the teacher held him. He kicked the teacher.

They sent him home and told Lois he needed professional help, which she could not afford.

His grandparents put a TV in his room and left him there most days with the door closed. He ate in there as well.

When he returned to school, he spent a lot of time in the nurse's office, curled up and still on the couch, hands over his head. He mumbled it was a headache. He had one every day. No teacher was ever unhappy to see him leave a class. He had an ominous kind of stillness, like a slingshot being pulled back too far.

He never really had a chance.

17

Abby was the valedictorian of her high school and she made a wonderful speech. Everyone said so. She and Hank had applied to the same Division-Two school. Abby got a partial academic scholarship, and Hank got the same for athletics. They took loans to cover the rest.

Charlie and Donna drove Abby to the campus and got her moved in. They hugged and kissed her, and hoped for the best as they drove home, each deep in their own thoughts.

"Are you with him now?" Charlie asks, hands gripping the steering wheel.

"I'm always with him," Donna says, looking at the road.

"I miss you when you're with him," Charlie says.

"I'm with both of you," Donna says, turning toward him.

"It's not easy sharing you with someone who is dead," Charlie says, looking ahead.

"I can't help that," Donna says.

"I know."

Quiet.

"He died, but he never quit on me," Donna says.

"I know."

"Never quit. He's still with me. I may be small but I am *mighty*."

"I know," Charlie says.

Quiet.

Quiet.

Like a grave.

Read the vows again.

Read them!

Abby and Hank both majored in Business because if you're good at business you can make money, and money meant freedom to these two. They had watched their parents struggle, and Abby and Hank wanted life to be different. They got serious and they made plans. Abby wasn't as funny now as she used to be. She needed to focus. Hank told her that all the time. Focus for *them*. Life was like a football game, a very competitive sport. You planned your work, and you worked your plan. That's how you win, and winning is important. Second place is for losers.

They'd be okay if they just stuck to their plan. They needed to get serious and they needed to work hard.

Hank wanted a life that was as organized as a water molecule.

Four years passed quickly. Abby graduated with honors. Hank with a larger-than-expected student loan because he had to drop sports halfway through. He just wasn't able to handle the practices and the heavy academic load at the same time. The work was so hard. He knew he would never play professionally, so he focused on Business instead.

He missed the cheering crowds, though. Missed them a lot, and he resented Abby a bit for making the academic work look so easy. It was easy for her, sure, but what about *him*? Why should *he* have to be the one to give up something *he* loved? He never spoke to her about these feelings, though, so they grew inside of him like cancer.

"You need to ask him, Hank." Abby said.

"Why do I have to ask him? Why can't I just ask *you*, like I just did?"

"It's traditional," Abby said. "And it's important to him. I'm his only daughter. You have to do it. Do it for me. Please."

"I just don't see why I should have to."

"Please."

"Hello, sir."

"Sit down, Hank. And please call me Charlie. We've talked about that before. You're dating my daughter. It's okay for us to use first names. Okay?"

"Um, okay." Hank sits on the couch and starts working his hands between his knees. He's wearing jeans, running shoes and a Jets jersey: Joe Namath.

"So you texted that you wanted to get together and chat for a bit. And here we are. So what's up?"

"Well, um, sir. *Charlie*. Abby and I have been seeing each other since high school, and I know you know that." Hands wringing. "And we're done with college now, and, um, we both have good jobs, and a great, workable plan, and I'd like to ask your permission to ask Abby to marry me."

Charlie smiles. Leans in. Puts his hand on Hank's knee. "Please look at me, Hank." Hank looks up from his hands. "Abby is our only child, Hank, and a daughter is precious to a man, the most precious thing in the world. I need you to understand that."

"I do, sir." He looks back at his hands.

"That's good. I also need to know that you will take care of our girl and be true to her always. Please look at me."

Hank does, and with a start. He's not used to people telling him what to do. He was the quarterback. Not anymore, but still. He's supposed to be the one doing the telling. "I *will*, sir." Strain in his voice.

Charlie gets up, holds out his hand. "That's what I needed to hear, Hank. She's my world."

"I understand, sir." Hank takes his hand limply. Doesn't stand up.

"Good." Charlie says. "You have my blessing. I hope she says yes. When will you ask her?"

"I want to keep that private, sir."

"Uh, uh. No more of this *sir* stuff. Call me Charlie. We're going to be family." He puts his hand on Hank's shoulder. "Let's have a drink and celebrate!"

Charlie has several glasses of cab sav. Hank has one can of Mountain Dew.

18

"That wasn't so bad, was it?" Abby says.

"I still don't understand why I had to do that. Was it really *necessary*? I felt like I had to kowtow to him."

"It's tradition, Hank. It's important to him. I'm his only child."

"Well, I'm glad it's over."

"Are you glad I said yes?"

"Of *course* I am!"

Donna explained to Abby that they'd be able to give a gift, but they wouldn't be able to pay for the wedding. They had to watch their money at this point because of what was going on with Charlie's job. The future was so uncertain.

Abby said she and Hank didn't expect them to pay for it, and that they would keep it small, as Charlie and Donna had kept their wedding small. They'd be able to swing it on their salaries. They both had gotten good jobs, and their financial future looked bright. They were working their plan.

"Are you disappointed that they can't pay for the wedding?" Abby asked Hank later that day.

"No, I'm okay," he said. "I know your parents don't have much money. It does move away from tradition, though."

"What do you mean?"

"Well, it's traditional for the bride's parents to pay for the whole wedding. My mother was sort of expecting that. She read about it in an etiquette book she got from the library. Who does what? You know. Tradition. Like me having to ask your father for his permission to marry you. You insisted on that because it's tradition, right? Well, my mother doesn't understand why the expense of the whole thing should fall on us. She likes tradition, too, and I gotta tell you, she's a bit disappointed in your parents."

"Your mother can't afford to pay either," Abby said.

"I know that, Abby. But she shouldn't have to pay for anything. She's the mother of the groom, not the bride. It's tradition. I know you believe in that. I thought your folks would step up more. So did she. You know. Tradition."

"They're doing what they can, Hank."

"That's what they say, but still."

The wedding was small and lovely, and everyone got along. They had a buffet dinner and a cash bar. Abby and Hank bought a small house on Long Island to start, and they set out to work their plan.

Six years passed and then, just before Saint Patrick's Day, on a bright Sunday afternoon, Abby called Donna to tell her she was pregnant.

"That's wonderful!" Donna said. "I'm so happy for both of you. Happy for us! When is the baby due?"

"The doctor said on September 15. I'm finally going to be a mommy!"

"It's so wonderful, Abby. Here, let me put your father on. He's chomping at the bit." She handed the iPhone to Charlie and he gushed over his only child's good news.

"Is Hank there? Good. Put him on," Charlie said.

"Hi, Charlie."

"Way to go, Hank! I'm so happy for both of you. For all of us."

"Thanks, Charlie."

"Got a preference? Boy or girl?"

"Well, I just hope it's a healthy baby, Charlie."

"That's what I like to hear! We're so happy for both of you."

"Thanks, Charlie. Here's Abby."

"Oh, Daddy, I'm so happy!"

"So are we, sweetheart. I love you so much."

"I love you, too, Daddy."

"Here. Here's your mother. I love you."

"Love you, Daddy."

Charlie wipes at a happy tear. Pours himself a nice glass of cab sav.

"They're so happy," Abby says.

"I hope they'll be good grandparents to him," Hank says.

"They will be. And you're sure it's a *him*?" Abby says.

"Hey, I hope so. I want a little guy I can play ball with."

"You can play ball with a girl, too, you know," Abby says, laughing. "My father played ball with me all the time."

"It's not the same, Abby. A man needs a son. It's traditional. My father always said that, I mean before he died. A son carries on the family name. It was important to him. I was his only son, his only child. You know he died before I made the varsity. He never got to see me quarterback or pitch. I need a little man to take to the ballgame. I need it for him, for my father. I want to watch my son quarterback his high-school team. I want to watch him pitch a no-hitter. I want to take pictures of him to the cemetery and show my father. I want to hear the crowds cheer for my son like they cheered for me, like my father never got to hear. That's important to me, Abby. You need to *understand* that. I need to do this for *him*."

"Wouldn't he have liked you if you had been a girl, Hank?" Abby asks. "I mean, I wouldn't have liked it, but would *he* have liked it?"

"I don't know. Girls are different," Hank says.

"And why are we different?"

"They just are. A boy looks at his father and says, *'Dad! Dad!'* Girls just play with dolls."

"That's not true," Abby says.

"That's been my experience," Hank says, face stern. "I'm not going to fight with you about it. *Enough* talk about this."

"And what if we have a girl?"

"I suppose we could sell her," Hank says. "Good-looking girls go for big bucks these days. We'll sell her to the Saudi Arabians. We'll be set for life."

She gives him a playful punch.

He's not laughing, but Hank hardly ever laughs. He was just kidding, though, right?

Right?

Hank goes to the obstetrician with Abby to get the results of the tests. The baby is healthy and growing and all looks right with the world. Nice strong heartbeat. Great news all around.

"Do you want to know the baby's sex?" the doctor asks.

"Absolutely!" says Hank. Abby nods excitedly.

"It's a girl,' the doctor says. "Congratulations."

Wonderful!" Abby says. She hugs Hank. He's looking at his hands.

"You seem disappointed," she says as they drive home.

"No, it's great," Hank says. "Really. Just great."

"You wanted a boy. I know that."

"No, a girl's fine for now. We can try again for a boy. I think they should be close in age, though. Not more than a year apart. That would be just right. You okay with that?"

"One at a time, okay, Hank? It took us so long to get pregnant this time. We'll see."

"It's *important* to me, Abby. I *explained* that to you. It's *important!*" He snaps a bullwhip glare at her. Strangles the steering wheel.

Neither of them speaks again during the rest of the ride, which is not very long, but it feels like days to Abby.

19

Cyrus didn't go to college. Didn't even consider it. He had left high school midway through his senior year and took a job in a supermarket. He asked to work in Frozen Foods, which meant that, regardless of the season, he had to show up for work dressed for winter. This was a job that few wanted, so they hired him on the spot.

They kept the storage freezer at zero degrees Fahrenheit, and that's where Cyrus spent much of his time. He'd unload the refrigerated delivery trucks, and move the heavy cartons of frozen meats, fruits, vegetables and ice cream into the freezer, stacking them carefully. He'd quickly prowl the store's freezer cases, still wearing his heavy clothes, head always down. He kept everything properly stocked. His boss was pleased with his work. No one bothered Cyrus while he worked and he didn't bother with anyone else, and that was just fine with him. He was very used to being alone. He preferred being alone. No one stared at him when he was alone.

He wore those layers and a heavy black overcoat every day. He kept his collar up. He also wore a black woolen cap, pulled way down over his forehead, whether or not he was at work. Some people thought that this was cool because The Edge, the guitarist for U2, also wore a cap like that. The Edge did it because he had lost his hair; but for Cyrus, the goal was to cover his birthmark, which had actually grown over the years. It bulged out of his forehead, red and angry, like it was looking for a fight.

An operation to remove it was beyond his means. A doctor at a walk-in clinic that his mother had taken him to when he was a boy said there would be a large, horrible scar if they tried to remove the hemangioma. "Don't worry; it will go away on its own."

It didn't. It just kept getting bigger, or at least it seemed that way to Cyrus.

Some people still called him Cyclops from time to time, but no one ever did that more than once. Cyrus had grown large, and he was very strong from lifting cases of frozen foods. And his rage simmered constantly, just one or two degrees below the boiling point.

His mother still prayed ferociously, and since her parents' passing, she had really let herself go. She drank even more of the Gordon's vodka, starting just after she woke up each mid-morning. Her parents had left her the house and their savings, which allowed her to get by. Cyrus lived in the basement and paid her a small rent out of his supermarket paycheck. It was enough to keep her senseless most days. They rarely spoke to each other. If they passed in a hallway, his mother blessed herself quickly and repeatedly, and muttered prayers, and roached away from him.

Cyrus drove a used Saturn Ion that had been recalled for faulty airbags, but he had not gotten the word about that. Even if he had known, it's questionable whether he would have brought it to the dealer. He needed the car to get to work in the freezer, and he hated sitting in waiting rooms, no matter where they were. People stared at you in waiting rooms.

Can't have that.

20

Hank's watching ESPN. There's a Low-T commercial on with some sorry old guy who reminds him of Charlie. "You know what, Abby?" Hank says. "I think your father's an asshole."

Abby looks up from the laundry she's folding and putting into a blue plastic basket.

"This guy reminds me of him," Hank says, pointing at the TV. "Maybe your father needs some testosterone. He's always bitching about the young people at his job. He thinks they're all out to get him. From what he tells me, those people are just working their plan, just trying to get ahead." Hank sips his Mountain Dew.

"That's not very nice," Abby said.

"What?" He points the green-and-red can at her. "That he's an asshole?"

"Please don't talk about him like that, Hank. He's my father."

"Don't I know it? He's been telling me that since the day I met him. You're his *life*, his only *child*. You're *precious*. Blah, blah, blah. And it gets worse the more he drinks."

"Why are you doing this, Hank?"

Hank throws the empty can at the wall. Abby jumps back.

"*Why?* Because your asshole father thinks he's the only one under a lot of stress. He should try working where *I* work. I'm trying to move up, work my plan and move up, but these old bastards are in my way. They make more money than I do, and I work harder than they do. You know why they make more money? Because they're older than dirt. Your father would fit right in with those old assholes. They could sit around and complain to each other all day long."

"Please don't say that, Hank."

"You know what? If he's not happy, he should just quit and go do something else." He stands up. Pantomimes a baseball bat swing, and smiles at his imaginary ball clearing the fence in center field. "Yeah, something else. Something new. Oh, wait. He doesn't *like* new, does he? He just likes old. He doesn't want anything to ever change. Boo hoo."

"There aren't many jobs for guys his age, Hank. And yes, he is old-school. And yes, the world is changing and he's having a tough time adjusting to it."

Hank swings for the fences again. "Let him show some initiative, Abby. Like I do. I'm sick to death of his moaning about his job whenever we all get together. Let him grow a pair of balls."

Abby leaves the laundry and walks toward their bedroom. "I'm pregnant, Hank, and you're being mean to us," she holds her belly.

"Yeah? So go piss and moan. Both of you. Just like your father does."

She leaves, says nothing. She can't find funny anymore. Hank goes back to his ESPN. Sports are important.

Abby sits on her bed. Holds her belly. Rocks. They can't find out. They can't. I can't share this with them. This would be too upsetting to them. This isn't the way it was supposed to be. We were born together. They can't know about this. It would hurt them. Can't. I can't do that to them. Just can't. Must keep it a secret. Must.

Our secret. She hugs her unborn daughter. *Ours.* Okay, baby? Okay? No one else. Just us.

Shhhh. Shhhh. Shhhh.

Abby's obstetrician gave her some early screening for, among other things, Down syndrome. The test came back negative for that, but positive for the potential for preeclampsia.

"What's that?" Abby asked.

"It's a condition where your placenta doesn't work as it should," her doctor explained. "Your body is showing signs that you may get it as you move closer toward term."

"Is it serious?"

"It can be serious, but we're going to monitor the rest of your pregnancy very closely and we're going to take good care of both you and your daughter. There's a good chance she'll come early. I want you to rest as much as you can in the coming weeks, Abby, and not get upset. It's important that you stay calm."

At 33 weeks, Abby noticed that she was suddenly gaining more weight than she should be gaining. Her hands and her face were swelling. Hank told her to stop eating so much. He didn't want a fat wife. What would his friends say? But she wasn't eating any more than she had been eating before, and she *was* eating for two now.

She called the doctor and he saw her that day. Her blood pressure was very high, and a further test showed protein in her urine. They admitted her to the hospital immediately.

Charlie, Donna, and Hank (three plastic chairs away from them) waited outside the delivery room for hours. The TV on the wall was locked into a *Growing Pains* marathon from the '80s. Charlie wished he could kick in the screen. Hank was smiling along with the laugh track.

"Shouldn't you be in here with them?" Charlie asked Hank.

"I don't like blood," Hank said, still watching the TV.

Charlie and Donna looked at each other.

"Does this get ESPN?"

The baby was arriving three weeks premature. It was Monday afternoon in late August. Charlie and Donna sat and watched doctors and nurses rush in and out of the room. No one would tell them anything. It was like watching the end of the world from front-row seats. Hank, glued to his show, smiled at something Kirk Cameron said.

Charlie, of course, had used his iPhone to research all he could about his daughter's condition. He knew that the only cure for preeclampsia was to deliver the baby. He also knew that the pitocin the doctor gave Abby would rush her labor, but it could also put the baby in danger as her premature heart raced in response to that drug. But if the baby were allowed to stay too long in Abby's womb, Abby's blood pressure would continue to skyrocket, and that could cause her to stroke, or even die. Her kidneys could also fail from the super-high blood pressure. A C-section was not a good choice because of Abby's blood pressure. The doctors were orchestrating this crazy medical balancing act between mother and child, and between life and death.

Darlin' you got to let me know.
Should I stay or should I go?

Abby told Charlie afterwards that the high dose of magnesium the doctor administered to lower her blood pressure had caused her to lose her sight for a time.

"It was horrible, Daddy," she said. "It was total blackness. I thought I would never see again, and the shaking was uncontrollable. It was like being in a freezer, but I wasn't cold. I just couldn't stop shaking. I felt as if the baby and I were trying to murder each other. It was horrible. I'm so glad to finally be done, and I'm so glad that she's okay."

"Thank God," Charlie said, squeezing her hand.

Charlie had hated this infant. Hated her like mortal sin until she stopped assaulting his only daughter. But once he saw her tiny innocence - she lying still with all those tubes - he began to love her desperately. Abby was safe, and this child, this precious granddaughter, was here now.

"Yes, thank God," Charlie said again.

"Do you want to hold her?" Abby asked.

"No, she's too small," Hank said. "You hold her."

"Will we be able to have more children?" Abby asked the doctor a few months later.

"I would *strongly* advise against it, Abby," the doctor said. "Your preeclampsia is so severe that another pregnancy could cost you your life."

"Would my son survive?" Hank wanted to know.

The doctor looked at him, not sure he had heard correctly. Hank just waited for his answer.

"No one can say for sure," the doctor finally said. "I do believe it could kill Abby, though. Perhaps you two should talk more in private."

"Is that a hundred percent certain?" Hank asked. "That she would die?"

"Nothing in life is a hundred percent certain," the doctor said.

"Other than death," Abby added.

"Yes," the doctor said. "Other than death. I really advise you against it, Abby."

Hank was looking at the diplomas on the doctor's wall. "I think we should get a second opinion," he said.

"That's your right," the doctor said, never taking his eyes off Abby, who had never taken her eyes off Hank.

"Hank? Abby said. Nothing. *Hank?*"

"It's okay, Abby. We'll get to the bottom of this. There are other doctors. Don't worry. We'll work our plan." He was wringing his hands, not looking at her, or at the doctor. "We'll get it figured out. I owe that to my father."

They can't know. This would kill them. *Kill them.* Must keep it a secret. Must. *Must.*

Shhhh.

Abby looked at the blue tattoo on the inside of her left wrist. Their daughter's name, Trista, in a swirly, girly font. It was in the exact place where a doctor would take Abby's pulse.

Trista means sorrow.

Hank had insisted on that name for his daughter. "It's a pretty name," he said. "It speaks to me. It's symbolic and *traditional*. I hope you're okay with it."

"If that's what you want, Hank," Abby whispered.

"*Yes*, that's what I want."

Hank also insisted on the tattoo. He chose the tattoo parlor and the design. From now on, *he'll* be the quarterback in this family. *He'll* call the play.

Trista. It *spoke* to him.

Trista.

Sorrow.

Yes indeedy.

21

It was a warm Sunday morning and the walk from the hotel was lovely. They had never been to this little church. It was old and in need of repair. There weren't many people there, 40 at most, and they all seemed to be older than Donna and Charlie.

They arrived 20 minutes before the start of the mass and sat on the right-hand side, as they did at home each Sunday. The pews were of old wood, no cushions. Charlie went in first. She always insisted on that. It put her closer to the collection basket.

They sat in the quiet and held hands, and this was Charlie's silent prayer that day:

Thank you, Lord, for life, and for love, and for this precious day.

Thank you for my wife, and our daughter, and our granddaughter, and our children in heaven.

Thank you for all that you've given me by your grace and generosity.

Thank you for all that you've taken away from me through your wisdom, for you know what's best for me. Always.

And thank you for all that remains, for it is far more than enough.

I love you, Lord, and I ask only that you continue to guide me in your way, for I am a weak man, and I cannot possibly do this on my own.

Amen.

He crosses himself with his right hand, still holding Donna's soft hand with his left. He squeezes. She squeezes back. He does not say Spectacles, Testicles, Wallet and Watch. What happens at the bar should stay at the bar.

The priest, an elderly man in green vestments, the color of hope, comes down the aisle, preceded by an African-American deacon in white, and a female altar server at that awkward age. She's carrying the crucifix. Everyone stands.

The mass begins and both Charlie and Donna smile at the old priest's Southern drawl. It's like syrup on Sunday pancakes. It makes them feel warm and welcome. He explains that he is visiting from Virginia because their pastor is on a retreat. He tells a bit about his home parish and how well he's been eating since he arrived here in beautiful Florida. He mentions the good weather, and what a fine man the deacon is, and how the deacon is a retired police officer who served this community well for many years, may God bless him. He tells them that the coltish altar server's name is Kristen, and that he's so happy to have her with him at this mass. She smiles, head down, and blushes.

The poetry of the Roman Catholic mass proceeds and all is as expected. Everyone stands up and sits down at the proper times, or as Donna says, "We did our Catholicsthenics." The old priest ambles to the lectern, opens the Bible to the bookmarked page, and reads the Gospel slowly and thoughtfully.

When he is done, it is time for his homily. He speaks without notes. He mentions this and that and the deacon answers with Amens! Charlie and Donna think about how un-Long Island this is, and they love the revival nature of what the deacon brings to this service.

"Hallelujah!" Charlie whispers in Donna's ear. She gives him a shut-up poke.

"I'd like you to consider," the old priest says, "how some people spend money they don't have, to buy things they don't need, to impress people they don't like, and how very sad that is."

"Amen!" says the deacon.

"Amen!" two people in the congregation answer. Charlie and Donna look at each other. Smile.

"And not only is it sad, but isn't it also *silly*, my brothers and sisters? Isn't it about as *silly* as a dog chasing its tail?"

And he goes on from there for 10 minutes or so, talking about the folly of people and how they often work so hard for things they don't need, and how simple life could be if people would just slow down a bit, and look around, and do something selfless. And he's saying all of this in that smooth drawl that makes everyone within earshot want to go take time and walk the beach and be peaceful. Just go *love* somebody.

"And worry about nothing, my friends, because our Lord is sitting right there next to you. He promised us that whenever two or more of us are gathered in his name he would be there with us. Yes, he said that, and I feel him now. Don't you? Scooch over a bit and give Him a hug. Go ahead and do that. He's waiting on you. Just *waiting* on you. And say hello to your neighbor while you're at it. Go on now. Say hello."

People smile and turn a bit awkwardly toward their neighbors. They say hello, and feel better for it.

"There, wasn't that pleasant?" the old priest drawls. "Not so hard to say hello to a brother and to a sister. To get outside of your worries and think of them for a moment. Not so hard at all. And doesn't that feel so good? *Sooo* good."

"Amen!" the deacon says, huge white smile on his dark face. "Amen!"

"So don't worry, my brothers and sisters. Don't worry at all. We are here for but a short time and we are here to love one another, as Jesus commanded. And don't you go making too many plans because while you're planning, God is laughing. Yes, he is. He *is*. So just *live* life. Just *love*. Just *be there* for each other. He'll see that. He'll see that and he'll be there for *you* when you need Him most. Truly, He will."

A chorus of Amens!

He leaves the lectern, crosses the altar, pauses to bow and then goes to his chair to sit for a bit. Gives everyone a few moments to digest those delicious words, to marinate in the love he just made in this holy place.

He stands. The small congregation stands with him. He moves on into the most sacred part of the Roman Catholic mass. There is such peace here.

A half-hour later, Donna and Charlie are walking back to their hotel. They hadn't rented a car on this trip. They needed to save money. Didn't matter. The day was lovely and a slow walk did them good.

"Man plans," Charlie says.

"God laughs," Donna says.

They hold hands and walk on. So true.

"And look at that silly mailbox," Charlie says.

22

Trista was a year old and walking. Abby had pulled Trista's short hair up into a small ponytail that stuck straight up from the top of her head a few inches. Abby called this a hair geyser. She had invited Donna and Charlie over for some cake, and some wine, of course. Chocolate cake goes very well with wine.

They stayed a few hours. Trista was wonderfully covered with her first birthday cake and having a messy, grand time.

"She could pitch for the Mets," Charlie said, as she flung another handful of cake on the floor. "I'm thinking knuckleballer. You never know where it's going next."

They left when it was time for Trista's bath.

Hank sat watching ESPN. A can of Mountain Dew on the end table.

Abby brought Trista, all clean-and-squeaky, over to Hank for her good-night kiss. Hank kissed the air and leaned around her. Sports are important.

"Do you want Daddy to read to you?"

"*Mama*," she said.

Hank harrumphed. Didn't look up from the ESPN. "I can't friggin' believe you *missed* that catch," Hank said, leaning in on the TV. Sports are important.

Abby read and sang as Trista curled up with her lovey blanket. She smelled like clean soap and baby shampoo.

"Goodnight, my love."

"Ni."

"I love you."

Snuggle. "Lup."

She sits near him on the couch. He keeps watching the ESPN. "Did you have a nice time?" she asks.

"Your father's an asshole." he says, not looking away from the TV.

"Please don't say that."

A commercial comes on. He gets up, goes to the fridge, pops another Mountain Dew.

"It's true," he says from the kitchen. You listen to him complain about the young guys at work? Again?" He strolls back, flops onto the couch. "How many times do we have to hear the same story? Why doesn't he just leave if he's so fucking miserable?"

"We've been over this, Hank. He has no place to go. He's trapped. He doesn't handle change well. And I think he's scared, but too proud to say so. It scares *me.*"

"Yeah, well there's a reason for that. I mean, having nowhere to go. He's an asshole. No one else would have him. They probably don't even want him anymore on his current job. He's just an old fool."

"Please, Hank."

"I'll tell you what, next time you invite either of them over, let me know so I can be somewhere else." He stabs the remote with his thumb. Switches over to ESPN2.

"What changed you, Hank? Why do you act this way?"

"What *changed* me? You want to know what *changed* me." He throws the remote at the wall. The batteries fall out, skid across the floor. Abby sucks in a breath. Sinks deeper into the couch. He scrambles up, leans in on her. She holds up her hands, preparing to be hit.

"What *changed* me? I got all these *women* that are sucking the life out of me." His hands are flailing, forming fists. Abby turns her head, squeezes her eyes closed. "I got the women at work. I got your mother. I got Trista to support, useless as she is." Leans in harder. "*Look at me!*" *She does.* "I got you, who won't support me, or *obey* me. And then there's your asshole father, who *acts* like a woman. Oh, he is soooo *sensitive!*"

"How am I not supporting you, Hank?" Abby sobs. "How am I not obeying you?"

"You gotta *ask*?" He moves in closer, bends over her, eyes crazy-wide. Abby cowers.

"Okay, how about *this*? I need a *son*, okay?" He's inches away from her face now. Spittle leaves his mouth and lands on Abby's right cheek. She doesn't dare touch it. "That's what *I* need. *I* need a little man to play ball with, to watch the TV with, to carry my father's name, to be my *son*. To show to my father at his grave. He's *dead*, Abby. Do you realize that? He's dead. He needs a grandson! He needs to see his name carried on. You gonna give me my son, Miss Precious Daughter of a Total *Asshole*?"

She says nothing.

"No, *right*? *RIGHT!*" He straightens up. Glares at her.

"Hank, you know what the doctors said. All four of them that you took me to see. They all said that having another child could kill me."

"But none of them said for *sure* that my *son* would die," he shouts.

"Oh, Hank, you don't mean any of this."

"I *don't?*" He spits a laugh. "I'm finally being *honest* with you and you're telling me I don't *mean* any of it."

"How can you know for sure that it would be a boy?"

"If it's not, we'd have options," he says. Big confident smile. Working his plan.

"You're serious, aren't you?"

"I am."

"You'd force me to have an abortion? You'd kill your unborn daughter?"

"How can you kill something that's never been born?" Hank asks.

"But she would be your *daughter*. Just like Trista."

"You mean Sorrow? I need a *son*, Abby. With you or with somebody else. It really doesn't matter to me anymore who it is. It's just what *I* need. It's what my *father* needs."

"Your father is *dead*, Hank!"

"Don't you *dare* say that!"

"I think we need counseling."

"No, you know what *I* need? *I* need to get the fuck out of here." He grabs the car keys from the hook and yanks open the front door.

"Please don't go!"

"*Don't?* You're telling *me* what to do? Okay, how about *this*? I'll tell *you* what I'm gonna do. I'm gonna go for a long drive. We started too soon, Abby, and we never finished what we started. You're damaged goods, and I miss the big crowds and the cheers that I had in school until I had to give it all up for *you* and that useless kid, and I'm sick of it. I feel like I'm in prison here. We're *done*. You keep Sorrow. I don't want anything to do with her. I never did."

"Please don't, Hank. Please don't go off like this. Please don't leave us again. We need you!"

"I'm done with both of you. DONE!"

"Please don't shout," Abby pleads through tears. "The baby is sleeping."

"Fuck you both. I'm out of here."

She follows him. He shoves her back. She falls on the concrete. He gets into the car, stabs the key, twists, bangs the gearshift and knocks over the garbage cans backing up. *Fuck!*

He's gone.

Shhhh. Shhhh. Shhhh. Can't tell. Can't.
Daddy.

Cyrus had been forced to work late, because of the damned Customer Appreciation sales. *Fucking* customers! He is simmering with rage. He needs to get to his dark basement where no one can see him.

Four-way stop signs ahead.

"Fuck it!" He nails the gas.

The other car flashes into his peripheral vision. *"Fuck him!"*

He T-bones Hank's Chevy. Nearly drives right through it. No seatbelt on Hank tonight.

Cyrus, who never got the word from Saturn about the Ion's airbag flaw, is also not wearing his seatbelt. He never does. What's the point? Nobody cares about him anyway. He goes through the tinted windshield, which he thinks has been staring at him for the past two years.

The hemangioma is no longer an issue.

Nothing is.

The woman who lives on the Northeast corner, in the blue house with the white shutters, stares out her window in horror and then calls 911.

A big crowd gathers.

No one cheers.

Abby sits quietly at home. ESPN is still on, but she's not watching it, or hearing it. She wonders if he'll come back this time. How could she have caused all of this pain? Has she ruined her marriage because she could not die for him?

She gets up and goes into Trista's bedroom, stands by the crib. Looks at her one-year-old daughter, sleeping softly. She touches her short blonde hair, and she looks at the tattoo that moves with her pulse:

Trista.

Sorrow.

Trista.

Sorrow.

Abby places her hand on her baby daughter's back. Feels the warmth of the life she made with her fairytale husband. "Mommy's here. Mommy's here. Mommy's here. Mommy's here. It's our secret. Our secret. Our secret. Shhhh."

Abby's prayer.

23

"When is your birthday, Clare?" Charlie asks.

"Oh boy, here we go," Donna says.

"Are you going to get me a present, Charlie?"

"Sure, and I'm going to tell you about your Conception Day."

They're at Clare's bar because there's a gentle rain on Singer Island today, and being tucked back inside the big, rectangular bar is wonderfully cozy.

"Conception Day?" Clare says.

"Yes, the day your parents decided that you were a mighty fine idea."

"Okay, I was born on January 27," Clare says. "You just missed it. And I'm not telling you how old I am." She winks at Donna.

"Your secret's safe with me, child," Donna says.

"I figure you're about twenty-two," Charlie says.

Clare smiles. "I'll take that."

"So would I," Donna says.

"Okay, January twenty-seventh, a winter baby, but a springtime conception," Charlie says. "Your parents decided you were a fine idea on or about April 27."

"Unless I was a surprise."

"Nope," Charlie says. "You were definitely planned, Clare."

"How could you possibly know that?" Clare laughs.

"I have special powers," Charlie says. "And besides, the whole world needed you. Your parents knew that. You know that, too."

"I like that."

"April twenty-seventh." Charlie says. "That was a beautiful spring day. No rain."

"How do you *know* that?" Clare asks, laughing and shaking her head.

"I look at you and I can tell, Clare."

"Where does he come up with this stuff?" Clare asks Donna.

"He's a world-class bullshitter. You know that."

"Hold that thought," Clare says, and she's off to refill a margarita. Drink Sync.

"She's a Lime Day baby," Donna says.

"Yep."

A round couple is drinking across the bar from Charlie and Donna. Their barstools groaned when they arrived and clambered onto them. They're looking at lunch menus, and actually talking to each other about what they should get, rather than texting someone who is not there.

"Do you want a big meal, or just a sandwich, or should we just share an appetizer?" the round girl asks the round guy.

"Share?" He's incredulous. Share generally doesn't work for this lad. "How big are the appetizers?" the round guy asks. "I don't think splitting just one is a good idea. We need more than just one. How big are they?"

"I don't know how big they are," the round girl says. "I'm here for the first time, just like you. We're on vacation together, right? How the hell should I know how big they are? I've never eaten here. You're asking idiot questions."

"Okay, right. Take it easy. I'm just asking. Don't get your shorts in a knot."

"Well ask *her*," she points at Clare.

He waves. Clare scoots. "Hey, big guy. What's up?"

"How large are the appetizers?" he asks. "How many should we order?"

Clare looks at him. Considers. She goes up on tiptoes to check out his belly. "Show me that bad boy," she says. He pushes up from the stool, and not easily. The stool says, "Ooof." Clare scrunches her face. Holds her chin with her right hand. She figures XXXL. "Better get three," she says. "*Minimum.*"

"Yeah?"

"Definitely," Clare says.

They order monster chili nachos, a dozen deep-fried mozzarella sticks, and two dozen hot wings.

"That should keep you smiling for a while," Clare says. "And there's plenty more food back there when you need it." She points toward the kitchen.

"How do you stay so trim," the round guy asks Clare.

"Why, by serving *you!*" She reaches over and pokes her little index finger deep into the round guy's bushel-basket belly. She gets away with this because, well, she's Clare.

"Yeah," the round guy laughs. He grabs his belly with both hands and gives it a good shake. It bounces twice and settles down, hanging over his belt like a trash bag filled with sludge.

"More drinks?" Clare asks Charlie and Donna.

"Is the Pope a Jesuit?" Charlie asks.

Clare laughs. Wags a finger. "Careful there, good Catholic lad. That's the Holy Father we're talking about now."

"Yeah, but he's a cool guy," Donna says. "If he was here, I think he'd be drinking with us."

"No doubt," Charlie says. "I like this guy. He lives in a small house. He's a man of the people."

"You think the Pope's a good tipper?" Clare asks.

"I don't know, Saint Clare," Charlie says. "Vows of poverty and all that, but I'll bet he has some great stories. All those years in the confessional. Mmmm."

"You think you could pry those out of the Holy Father?" Clare says.

"No chance," Donna says.

"I'd love to give it a shot," Charlie says.

"What do you think would be his choice of booze?" Clare says.

"House red," Charlie says. "Good and cheap. Box wine. A man of the people."

"What music would he want to hear if he was being executed?" Clare asks.

"Hmm, I'm thinking *Stairway to Heaven*." Donna says.

"That works," Charlie says.

Clare laughs, shakes her head. "We're all going to hell."

"There's still time to change the road you're on," Charlie sings.

To which, Donna adds, in her best Robert Plant, howl, *"Oooooo, and it makes me wonder."*

"Stop it!" Clare laughs.

Somewhere in the world, Jimmy Page is shaking his head.

"So, Clare," Charlie says when she returns with their drinks. "Have you ever noticed how many babies are born just before Christmas?"

"Now that you mention it, Charlie, yeah, I have. I've been working this bar for a while. Those pre-Christmas kids arrive every year, at least they do for the townies. I can't speak for the tourists, but it's probably the same. People are people, no matter where you go."

"Do you know why that is? The timing, I mean."

"People want to have special Christmases? I don't know. I never gave it much thought, Charlie."

"Count back nine months from Jesus' birthday. Or better yet, just count ahead three months from Christmas. Either way will give you the same answer. What holiday do you get?"

Clare face-scrunches. Her gray eyes go wide. "Saint *Patrick's* Day!" she says.

"Exactly," Charlie says. "It's those *Kiss Me; I'm Irish* tee shirts the ladies wear. They actually work."

"Wow."

"Ah, but *you*, Clare, you are *very* special. Your parents made you on or about Lime Day."

"Lime Day?"

"Yes, it arrives every spring."

She looks at Donna. "I've never heard of it."

"It's a national holiday," Donna says. Sips her pinot.

"Really?"

"Absolutely. Charlie will tell you all about it. There's no stopping him now." She raises her glass.

"I've never heard of Lime Day."

"That's a shame, child," Charlie says, "Do you know that one special day in the spring of every year when the buds on the trees are just about to burst open and they're that perfect shade of lime green?"

"Uh, huh."

"That's Lime Day."

"What's the date?"

"This is the best part, Saint Clare. It varies. And everyone gets to call it. It's usually late-April, at least it is in New York, but you have to watch the leaves very closely from day to day wherever you are. When you think they can't possibly get any more limey then they are right now, you call it and that's it. Lime Day!"

"But what if the next day turns out to be even more limey."

"Well, then you're a loser, Clare," Charlie says. He goes sad and sips his wine. Shakes his head slowly, as does Donna. "And you must then bear the burden of being a loser for an entire year. Poor Clare."

"Poor Clare," Donna confirms.

"Poor me," Clare laments.

"Indeed," Charlie says.

"And this is national holiday?" Clare asks. "Really?"

"Absolutely," Donna says.

"How long has it been around?" Clare asks. "I've never heard of it."

Charlie looks at his watch. "About five minutes," he says. "Give or take. Longer in other versions, but this version, about five minutes, maybe six. Tops."

Clare looks at Donna, who smiles and shrugs. "What did you expect?"

"You're right," Clare says. *"World-class."*

"None better," Donna says.

Clare goes to get the round couple's nachos, and fried cheese, and hot wings. And lots of napkins. The nachos look like a very large pile of violated autumn leaves. The round guy goes wide-eyed. He licks his lips. So does the round girl. He positions the pile in front of himself and takes a selfie with his iPhone. He looks at it, shows it to the girl. "Let me take one," she says. He slides the plate over to her and she takes a selfie with her own iPhone. Looks at the pic. Moves the nachos a bit. Takes another selfie. Looks at it. Does the same with the other two plates. It's difficult to get her whole self into the picture.

"I'm wondering why some people can't eat anything without first taking a photo of it," Donna says.

"And why they have to be in the photo with the food," Charlie adds.

"Facebook?"

"Yeah, probably."

The round girl takes another selfie, this one from about a foot away, and without the food. She makes a pursed-lip, Zoolander face. Vogue. She looks at the pic. Considers it. Moves her hair around a bit. Takes another. More pout. Checks it. Takes another from a bit further away. About 18 inches this time. Checks it. Looks around. Digs into her purse.

"Did you bring the selfie stick?" she asks the round guy.

"Forgof fit," he says though a mouth filled with chicken wings.

"Shit. What am I supposed to do *now*?" she asks. She puts the iPhone down, folds her arms under her breasts, like she's carrying two large bags of groceries.

"I could take one for you," the round guy says. "Or we could get the girl to do it." He points a chicken wing at Clare down the bar. She's drawing an IPA. The girl.

"Not the *same*," the round girl says. "I need to be in charge of the photo shoot." She puts the iPhone down on the bar. Eats a chip. Grumps. Looks at the iPhone. Picks it up. Takes another selfie. Full-arm's length this time. Tries to get her grocery-bag breasts into the shot. Checks it out. No good. Needs a wider angle. Much wider.

"*Shit*. I hate this! We need the selfie stick." She stuffs a fried cheese stick into her mouth and burns her tongue. "*Shith! SHITH! DATH HOT!*" Spits the cheese onto the plate. Takes a sip of her cold Bud Heavy. Takes a selfie of her tongue. Checks it. Blows on the cheese. Puts it back into her mouth. Still too hot. Spits it out again. "AAARRRGGG!"

"Sorry," the guy says through a mouthful of hot wings. He waggles his empty pint glass at Clare. The girl.

The round girl looks at him. "You eat like a pig," she says, and puts the twice-spit cheese back into her mouth. Not too hot now.

"Sorry. Urp!"

"Shith? Dath hot? She sounds like a young me," Donna says.

"Yeah," Charlie says, "but *your* lisp never needed hot cheese."

"It was hot enough as is, right?" Dirty wink.

"Dathsit," Charlie says.

The round girl is scratching cheese off the plate with her fingernail and stuffing it into her damaged mouth. Scratch, stuff. Scratch, stuff. Scratch, stuff. The round guy is reaching in to do the same, but she plays good defense. She picks up the plate and licks it. Glares at him. He backs off, leans back on his stool. Let's out a long sigh. Looks at the plate longingly.

"Now *that's* sexy," Clare says to Donna.

"Yeah, in its own peculiar way, I suppose it is," Donna agrees.

24

The police arrived at the house. Abby answered the door and knew something bad had happened. She figured they had arrested Hank for speeding, remembering the way he had knocked down the garbage can. Maybe he had gone to the bar and had some drinks, although that would have been really unusual. He hardly ever took a drink. Maybe he was in jail. But if that was the case, wouldn't Hank have called her? She could get him a lawyer. *Would* he have called her?

But wait. Cops don't show up at the wife's house when the husband gets arrested, right? At least they don't on TV. So what's going on here?

And these two guys look so uncomfortable. She steps back and thinks of Trista in her crib.

"Mrs. Kruger?"

"Yes."

"Is your husband Henry Kruger?"

"Yes. Hank. We call him Hank. What's wrong?" Another step backwards.

The older cop tells her. She reaches around to grab at something solid, but there's nothing there. The younger cop is good. Fast reflexes. He catches her before she hits the floor.

Charlie and Donna are at the house within 20 minutes. The cops explain what happened, and what Charlie and Donna need to do next. Hank's body is at the morgue. His car is totaled and impounded for a safety inspection. There will be paperwork.

Donna is staring holes through the wall, wandering inside of herself, deep in her recent memories. Thinking. Processing. Remembering.

Protecting.

They can never know. *Never* know. I must keep our secret. It would kill them to know. We were born together. It wasn't supposed to be like this. They *can't* know. Not ever.

Shhhh.

Charlie is holding Abby, big as she is, but a daughter is never too big that a father can't hold her. He's rocking her back and forth, as he did when she was a child.

"Hank was going to the store to get milk for Trista," she sobs. "Everything was fine. He told me how much he enjoyed seeing you both at Trista's birthday party," she lies. "He gave Trista her bath and read her a story," she wishes. He tucked her in. Sang her a song. The one she likes. The Barney song. I love you. You love me. We're a happy family." Abby sucks in a breath. Racks a sob. Grabs at her fairytale, but it's like trying to hold smoke.

Not ever!

"I can't believe this is happening, Daddy. He loved us *all so* much. He loved Trista. He loved you and mom. He loved me most of all, Daddy, and I will never stop loving him. We were perfect. Born together. We were perfect. A fairytale. Like the ones you used to tell me, only better. You know that. He *can't* be gone. He *can't* leave us."

Charlie hugs his only daughter to himself. Tries to pull her inside himself, where she can be safe.

"Oh, Daddy, Hank *loved* you. He really *did*. He thought you were the greatest man in the *world*. He wanted to be just like you. How could this have happened?"

Charlie holds her and rocks her, strokes her hair. "Shhhh, honey. Shhhh." He looks over at Donna, who is as quiet as granite. She's looking at the wall, not at them. She's remembering things. Small things. A terse word snapped. A sideways look at Trista. Small demands, said with an edge to his voice. "*Pick* that up. *Turn* off that light. *See* what she wants. *Answer* the door." Abby's meek reaction to all it.

Donna *knows*.

Hank's work friends come to the wake. They look somber for a few minutes in front of the closed casket, and then they gather at the back of the room. They talk, and not so quietly, and then they laugh. They talk business, of course. What else is there?

Well, sports.

They laugh a bit louder. People look at them. They switch to whispers, but not really.

Who killed him?

Some loser who worked at the supermarket.

The supermarket? No shit? How much could that *guy have made?*

Not much and he was driving a fucking Saturn, for Christ's sake. What a shit car that is.

Hit hard enough, though, right? Laughs. Too bad for Hank, but that's the way it goes, right? Shit happens.

Hey, wait a minute; this means his job is open! How much did he make? Any idea?

The family stares at them.

The work friends figure they'll go outside for a smoke. They can laugh as much as they want out there. No problem if they're outside, right? They'll stay maybe a half-hour? That good enough? Maybe twenty minutes. That acceptable? Fifteen? What's traditional? Anybody know? Jeez, I gotta take this call.

They all leave without saying goodbye to Abby, or to anyone else. He's not coming to work anymore anyway, so really, who gives a shit? And they'll never have to put up with *her* again. *Good riddance!*

None of them go to the funeral mass. It's on a workday. How could they possibly give up a workday? Hank would do the same thing, right? He'd understand.

How much did he make? Any idea?

Hank's insurance policy covers the funeral, and there's plenty left for Abby and Trista for a very long time. *Very* heavy term-life policy. It was part of the plan, and one of the few times that Hank gave in to Abby, who was always thinking of Trista.

He insisted that the insurance premiums come out of her paycheck, though, and not his. "If you ever decide to give me the *son* that I need, I'll split the cost of the policy with you," he said. "But *this one's* on you." He waved a dismissive hand at his only daughter.

25

"Sell the house and live with us."

"Okay, Mommy. We will."

26

Chirp!

"Who's that?" Donna asks.

Charlie looks at his iPhone.

She's all over Facebook with this guy. Facebook! And now she's hanging out with his friends. She's posting about how nice his friends are, and how much she's enjoying their company. Lots of pics. It's making me nuts!
She would never do that for me!

"It's Patrick."

"What's up?"

"Bertha likes the new guy's friends," Charlie says.

"She couldn't stand Patrick's friends. Except for us."

"I know. She has such fine taste."

"Yeah," Donna says. "We are just peachy."

"I don't know what to say to him. He tells me he's moving on but he can't stop watching what she's doing now that *she's* moving on. He's stalking her."

"Let it wait. You're allowed to have a vacation. Be with *me*, okay? Shut it off."

"You're right." Charlie holds the button until the screen goes black.

Waiting in the cloud for Charlie is:

Chirp!

YT?

Chirp!

YT?

Chirp!

Where the fuck are *you, man?! This is getting serious!!!*

27

"We're heading home tomorrow, Charlie," Jenny says. "I feel miserable. It's cold back there."

Cliff is wearing a black tee shirt that reads:

Leave me alone. I'm only talking to my Mustang today.

"Am I allowed to talk to him?" Charlie asks Jenny.

"I'd leave him be," Jenny says. "He's miserable. The cold and the job await. Real life. Ugh."

"Okay, then let's focus on you, young lady. This is International Jenny Day. Did you know that?"

"I did not, but I like it," Jenny says. "Here's to me!" She raises her salted, frozen strawberry margarita.

"To Jenny!" Donna says.

"To Jenny," Cliff mumbles.

"Aw, c'mon, Cliff," Donna says. "It's not so bad."

"Wait 'til you have to go back," Cliff says.

"Perhaps we never will," Donna says. "What do you think, Grandpa Charlie? Want to stay in Neverland forever?"

"Works for me."

"Could you really live here?" Donna asks.

"I think so," Charlie says. "Everything moves more slowly here. I like that. And we talk more here. It's nice."

Clare alights. "Ah, Saint Clare," Charlie says. "It's always a joy to see you. May I please have a refill? I request this only because my glass is empty." He points at it and sighs.

"Who could say no to you, Charlie?" Clare says. "I mean, seriously."

"This is why you are my shining star, child." Charlie says.

Clare twists the cap. Pours to the rim of the glass.

"And yet another reason why I love you, child." He carefully raises the glass to his lips.

"Don't spill the holy water," Clare says.

"Jenny, do you watch *The Bachelor* on TV?" Charlie asks.

"Of course," Jenny says. "I have girl parts; therefore, I am compelled to watch that show. It's in the Girl Rules."

"My darling Donna also watches that show, but more with aggravation than with anticipation each week as I sit lonely in another room and read Thomas Hardy. She fills me in on the happenings the next day. I listen with care because I love her, and because listening is less expensive than divorce."

"What in the show makes you aggravated, Donna?" Jenny asks.

"I'm aggravated that the bachelor is always a boy instead of a man," Donna says.

"What do you mean?"

"Well, look at what went on the other night. There he is, down to three girls, each one an emotional Cuisinart. The show lets the boy take each on a *special* date. You know. The *special* date." Donna puts quote marks in the air.

"You mean the date where he gets to sleep with them, right?" Jenny says.

"Yes, exactly. He's sampling the goods before making a choice, like he's choosing between three fancy cars and wants test drives. He's doing this in front of the rest of them. It's what everyone watching is waiting for. It's all gauzy lighting, rose petals and silky sheets. A bit of groping and then they cut to a commercial. When they come back from the commercial, he's done. Quick Draw McGraw."

"Well, they can't really show anything more than that," Jenny says. "It's family TV."

"Yeah, he loves them all alike and he just can't make up his mind," Donna says. "Family TV, my ass. He's an adolescent twit. I'd like to see one of those girls chase him with a claw hammer."

"I'd watch *that*," Cliff says.

"I mean these *girls*, and I say *girls* because these are *definitely* not women, they're drooling over this *boy* even though he's sleeping around for the whole world to see. And the *girls* are hanging out with the other *girls* who are sleeping with him. 'Oh, but I love him soooo much!' What *woman* in her right mind would put up with that shit?"

Charlie looks over at Cliff. They both shrug.

"What?" Donna says, looking from one to the other. "You think the guy's *right*?"

"No," Charlie says. "I think we're just wondering how the guy pulls it off."

"Yeah," Cliff says.

"He pulls it off because the show is *fixed*," Donna says. "They're all *acting*. None of this crap would ever happen in real life. There'd be murder."

Clare's back.

"Clare," Donna says. "Would you ever go on *The Bachelor* TV show? Let's say the producer walked in here right now and invited you to be on the show. All expenses paid. You'd have to compete with all those crying cupcakes that they find somewhere in America. Would you do it?"

Clare's hair is pulled back in a French braid today. She looks delicious.

"If I went on that show," Clare says, poking her right index finger onto the top of the bar. "It wouldn't be much of a show. The guy would want to run off with me before the first commercial in the very first episode, and that would be that." She snaps her fingers.

"And what would you tell him?"

"Well, before we went *anywhere*, I'd tell him that I'd consider him only if he could grow a pair of man balls, and right now. And he'd have to prove it to me."

"And how would he prove it?"

"I'd give him an Irish polygraph."

"What's that?" Donna asks.

"I ask tough questions. He gets to talk. I decide."

"I like that," Donna says.

"It's what real women do," Clare says.

"Okay, Clare. I'm with you," Jenny says, "But suppose you're dating this guy and he starts looking at other women. What do you do then?"

"Looking's okay. Can't help that. We're all human. He looks. I look. It's all good," Clare says. "So is flirting. Flirting keeps us all young, and it's fun. But *getting with* them is *not* okay. Not if you want to be with *me*."

"Good answer," Donna says.

"But what if he does get with them?" Jenny asks.

"What if he does?" Clare says. "Well then I would drop his balls into my frozen margarita machine over here." She pushes the button and the machine grinds and growls with promise. "And while he was still wearing them. How's *that*, ladies? Work for you?"

"Yep!" Jenny says.

"She's adorable," Donna says.

"And lethal," Jenny adds.

"Clare, one more," Donna asks. "What do you think about all those girls putting up with what they put up with on that show?"

"They're *girls*."

"Not women, right?" Donna says.

"Not at all," Clare says. "Pfff."

"How can you be so wise at such a young age?" Charlie asks.

"I work in a big bar on a small island, Charlie. And like you, I pay close attention." Sweet smile.

"Okay, Clare," Jenny says. "I'm with you. The guy's a boy. I'm so done with him, and with that dopey show. Thanks for the best International Jenny Day present ever."

"You're *welcome*." Clare says, showing, that beautiful, uncovered, misaligned cuspid.

28

Trista's second birthday arrives, a date that sticks up on the calendar like a rusty nail. Trista will always share her birthday with her father's death day. She knows him only by the photographs that hang in her room. Hank doing this. Hank doing that. By himself in all but two of the photos. He's with Trista in those two. He looks uncomfortable in both, barely touching her. Not smiling.

Abby baked a chocolate cake and Donna and Charlie gave Trista her birthday present, some Fisher Price Little People that Donna had gotten on sale at Target. Trista tears the pink wrapping paper and laughs at the toy. "Opit!" she says, and Charlie opens it.

"I wish her daddy could be here," Abby says.

Donna is quiet. "I miss him so much," Abby says.

Quiet. Breathing deeply.

"We had a fairytale marriage, Mom. Just like you and Daddy."

Quiet. Puff. Blow.

"We did, Mom."

"Not all fairytales are happy, Abby."

They sit at the kitchen table as afternoon light filters into the room through windows that no one has washed for a while. Abby looks at the streaks and listens to the tiny sounds of the neighborhood. Donna looks at Abby, breathes deeply, and waits. Waits. Waits.

Waits.

"Well, *your* marriage is happy. It's *always* happy." Abby says, still looking at the streaks.

"Not always, Abigail. We have had our moments. In good times and in bad. For better and for worse. In sickness and in health, for richer, for poorer. You know."

"It's better since my hearing isn't so good," Charlie says, trying to lighten up the conversation.

"Our life was *perfect*," Abby insists.

Donna looks hard at Charlie. He stands up.

"Let's go play with the Little People," Charlie says to Trista. "You can show me what Little People can do." He unhooks her from the booster seat and carries her into her bedroom.

Donna reaches over and places her hand over her daughter's hand, the one with the wrist tattoo.

"He loved me like Daddy loves you, Mom. And he loved Trista like Daddy loves me." She's crying.

"Is that what you remember, Abby?"

"What do you mean?"

"Not all fairytales are happy."

"What do you *mean*?"

"You were fighting, Abby. More him than you, but it wasn't perfect. I know."

"How do you *know* that? How can you *say* that?"

"I can say it because you are my daughter and I love you. And I *know it* because I have seen much of life, and have been married for a long time, and I know people, Abby. I pay attention. You were having tough times, and I know it had something to do with Trista. Things changed with your pregnancy."

"How can you *know* that?"

"Because I watched Hank with her, and with you. He was cold to her, and then he got even colder to you, and probably because of the preeclampsia. I think he wished Trista had been a boy. His manner said it all. The sports. The TV. Little tells. And I *know* what Trista's name means, Abby. The name *he* chose. I *know* what her name means. It means sorrow."

She knows. Oh my god, she knows. *How?* How! *She knows.*

Abby's tears turn to thunderstorms, dams breaking. Donna moves and holds her close. "Cry, my darling. *Cry.*"

"He was leaving us, Mommy," she sobs.

"I know."

"He was so *mean* to us, Mommy."

"I know."

"But *how* could you know?"

"Because you are my daughter and you are precious to me. He wasn't perfect, Abby. No one is."

"But you and Daddy."

"Not perfect. Not even close."

"But I wanted our life to be a fairytale, like yours. Hank and I were born side by side, Mommy."

"I know that, Abby. I was there. It's *not* a fairytale, though. It's just a life. But that's okay. That's all we get, daughter. Just a life. But what a precious gift that life is, and how many are denied that life, and today, on Trista's second birthday, we are going to start *celebrating* life, and we're going to *keep* celebrating life because that's our job while we are here. We are going to live as best we can, and love each other as much as we can, and hope for the best. That's all we can do, and that's *real*, Abby. That's real. Shhhh. No more fairytales for any of us, Abby. No more. Okay?"

"Trista *matters*, Mommy," Abby sobs, "Even if she isn't a boy. She *matters,* Mommy!"

"You bet your sweet ass she matters," Donna says. "And so do *you*, child. So do you." She holds her close. Holds her close. Holds her. Close.

"I love you, Mommy. I'll tell you some day what he said to us before he left us. He was so cruel."

"Shhhh. That can wait. Today we return to living, okay? It's our little girl's birthday."

Sobs. "Okay, Mommy. Okay."

Sobs.

"Why are these Little People so little?" Charlie asks Trista.

"*Little!*" Trista shouts.

"Yes, they are. You're a *giant*, Trista. A great...big...girl! With a *birthday*!" He lifts her, swings her up over his head. Runs her around the bedroom. "You can *fly*, Trista! You can fly like a big bird!"

Trista laughs until she can barely catch her breath. "Happy birthday, Trista!" Charlie says. He pulls her into a deep hug. Kisses her cheek. Kisses her hair. Closes his eyes because he's tearing up. She smells like chocolate cake and Johnson's Baby Shampoo. "Happy Birthday, my love. Happy, Happy Birthday."

"*Happy*, Trista!" she says. Tinkling laughter.

"Yes, big girl. Happy. That's what we'll try to be. We'll try hard. *Happy*. You and me."

Charlie also knows. He's known for almost as long as Donna has known. Charlie pays attention, especially to Donna. He knows people. And he's *nobody's* fool, old or otherwise.

Curtis Hayden was wrong. He was both cruel *and* wrong. Charlie knows that now. Maybe someday he'll be able to share with Donna what that cruel boy did to him on his last day at work.

Maybe someday.

29

Tap, tap, tap.

Sorry I didn't get back to you. What's up?

Chirp!

It's like I wrote. She's with this other guy. She's hanging with his friends. She likes them. It's all over Facebook. My friends are saying stuff about it. They're laughing at me. I feel like an idiot. I can't take much more of this.

Tap, tap, tap.

How goes it with the new lady and her kids?

Chirp!

That situation has shit the bed. She just wanted me to take her kids to their sports and whatnot. I asked her to be with my friends and she said that she didn't have time for that

*right now. She had to put her kids first. I wished her well. I
don't know what to do now. What would you do?*

Tap, tap, tap.

*I would think about who I would want to be with 30 years
from now,
so that I had someone to help me be old.*

Chirp!

Wrong answer again, man!

Tap, tap, tap.

Honest answer, pal. It's from the heart.

30

Abby takes another sip of her morning coffee. She's still in her workout clothes, sitting at the kitchen table, reading *Newsday*. The paper is thin with fewer ads these days because most of the stores advertise online.

But *Newsday* is one of her father's habits, and she likes starting her day with him. She could get her news online, of course, but it makes her feel good to continue their ritual while he's away.

He's awake before anyone else each morning, usually before dawn. He starts the coffee pot and then walks down to the end of their driveway in his robe and slippers. He carefully bends to pick up the paper. It's always in a clear, plastic bag. Two, end-to-end, if it's raining. When Abby was small he would blow up the bags and let her pop them. He called *Newsday* the *Daily Pop* in those days, and Abby believed him.

Charlie looked both ways down the dark street each day, but he never saw the person who delivered the paper. In the *Daily Pop* days, Charlie would tell Abby that a mermaid delivered the paper. "She rides a big seahorse," he said. Abby would try to wake up early to see the mermaid, but Charlie explained that the mermaid sees her when she's sleeping and knows when she's awake. Like Santa.

Or a fairytale.

She opened the paper to the weather page first. Another habit. "Let's see if the sun is going to rise tomorrow," Charlie would always say to her. Abby smiled as she noted that the sun would indeed rise, and at 6:48. The weather looked good for the next few days - cold, but no snow, which made Abby happy, but probably would have made Trista sad. What kid doesn't like snow?

Abby turned to the front pages and sipped coffee. The politicians were still at it. "We have the best politicians money can buy," Charlie liked to say. "And they're always on sale!" She turned the page and there was this brief story.

Husband Attacks Wife and Friend over Facebook

Nassau County Police say Patrick O'Toole, 45, attempted to enter the Westbury house where neighbors say he had lived with his estranged wife, Bertha O'Toole, 44. Mr. O'Toole allegedly banged on the front door while waving an Apple iPad and screaming that she had to "like his friends."

Michael Pechman, 46, a friend of Mrs. O'Toole, answered the door and Mr. O'Toole struck him numerous times with the iPad while screaming. "She can't like you on Facebook if she doesn't like my friends."

A police spokesman said that when they arrived, Mr. O'Toole repeatedly swung the iPad at them as well, while screaming that he didn't like them. The officers subdued him and brought him to Nassau University Medical Center for psychiatric evaluation.

Mr. O'Toole was unhurt by the iPad attack. "He hit me with the flat part," he told the police. "It really didn't hurt, but I hope he gets help."

Abby didn't know all of her parent's friends, and she had never met Patrick or Bertha, so the story didn't register as anything other than just more craziness. She flipped the page and read on. Macy's was having a sale. Trista called her to play and she set aside the *Newsday* for later.

The local paper on Singer Island didn't cover the story. It was a tiny Long Island story, a part of the craziness. Charlie never really cared for any of Patrick's friends. He had that in common with Bertha, but he never said anything about it to Patrick. They were the sort who, as the old priest had said, spent money they didn't have to buy things they didn't need to impress people they didn't like.

None of those people would think to call Charlie with the news. They didn't really know him, and they were thinking mostly of themselves.

"Did you ever hear back from Patrick after that last go-around with the texts you showed me?" Donna asks. They were walking the beach. Sixty-eight degrees on Singer Island. Twenty-five degrees on Long Island.

"Yeah, he sent three texts. Charlie opens his iPhone and reads them:

Tap.

"I can't take it anymore, Charlie. She's making me crazy."

Scroll.

"She won't like my friends."

"That's a little scary," Donna says.

"Yeah, he told me that living with her was like being locked up. She liked him too much. Now he says she won't like him. What the heck does that mean?"

"Facebook?" Donna says. "That's all about liking, isn't it?"

"Beats me," Charlie says

"Did you text him back?"

"I did, but he hasn't answered. I may have pissed him off with my text about growing old together. I answered him truthfully, though. I really feel that way."

"Angels could do no more than that, Charlie."

"Yeah, I know, but still."

"Life's complicated," Donna says.

"So is marriage."

"Got that right," Donna laughs.

"He said he had to do what was right for him. I guess he figures this is the right thing at this point, whatever it is. He needs to work it out. I can only do so much for him, Donna. I can't fix him. I'm still not sure I can fix myself. But I told him I was here if he needs me. What more can I do?"

"I guess you'll hear from him when you hear from him," Donna says. "You're a good friend."

"I'm trying."

One day is fine and next is black
So if you want me off your back
Well come on and let me know
Should I stay or should I go?

31

"I'm going to sit on the beach."

"What a surprise!" Charlie says.

"We need some stuff from the food store for dinner. Would you mind going alone?"

"I'd be happy to go, but I will miss you terribly."

"Such a bullshitter," Donna says.

"I *will* miss you, but I do like going to Southern supermarkets. They have clean bathrooms and they offer to help carry groceries out to your car. They also bag for you and tell you to have a nice day. That could make all the difference in the world. Suppose you wake up wanting to have a shitty day. Someone in the Bakery Department smiles and tells you to have a *nice* day, and there you go. All fixed."

"But only if you're willing to listen," Donna says.

"Of course. There is always choice. Hey, if I'm hell-bent on having a shitty day, I'm going to have a shitty day. I'm a New Yorker. Don't tell *me* what to do."

"Yes, it's all very adult," Donna says.

"And so very civilized. I like it. Got a list?" Donna hands it to him.

He glances down the list. One of the items is Saucy Susan, an old-school duck sauce that has been around longer than Charlie has been on the planet.

"Saucy Susan. Looks like you're making something special," Charlie says.

"It's a recipe I saw in a magazine. I think you'll like it. Goes together real fast, and it's both sweet and sour, just like you lately."

"Ooooo kay. We need wine?"

She just stares at him. "Okay, I'll get wine."

He gets to the store and pulls the handle of a shopping cart. It sticks to the one in front. He yanks harder. Bounces it. No good. He tries the one in the next row. Same thing. Next row. The cart comes loose. It has a wobbly front wheel. He rattles down the aisle, looking for Saucy Susan."

But Susan's not in that aisle. Or that one either.

Nope, not in Spices, or in International Foods.

Not over here either. He looks at the empty cart. No answer there.

Charlie continues his search, picking up the other items on Donna's list as he goes. Now he's by the long meat case. The butcher, a huge man with arms like tree limbs, is loading chicken parts into the case. Give him a chainsaw and he could be in a horror movie. "Excuse me. Do you know where I might find Saucy Susan?" he asks.

"Who she?"

"It's a sauce," Charlie says. "Like duck sauce, only different. I'm not sure how it's different, but it is. It's old-school."

"I don't know, man," he says. "Let's go look."

"But you're busy. I can keep looking."

"No problem. Let's go."

He leaves the chickens in the aisle and quick-walks Charlie back to all the places Charlie had just been.

"I looked here already," Charlie says.

"You sure you got the right name?" the butcher asks. "Saucy Suzzie?"

"No, it's Susan, not Suzzie."

"Yeah," the butcher says. "C'mon." Charlie follows him to the deli counter. "Hey you know where Saucy Susan's at?" the butcher says to the deli guy.

"No," the deli guy says. " I ain't been with her since high school."

"No, fool! It's like *duck* sauce," the butcher says, laughing. Charlie's also laughing; so are the deli customers.

The deli guy comes out from behind the counter to join the search. "Be right back," he says to the customers who are standing there holding small pieces of paper with numbers printed on them. He leaves these people, along with the ham, the cheese and the rest of the cold cuts to fend for themselves.

They go back to the same places they had been before.

"Think we should ask the manager?" Charlie says. "I can go do that."

"Let's all go do that," the butcher says.

They find him at the Courtesy Desk. "Hey, boss, where the Saucy Susan at?" the deli guy says.

"What that?" the manager asks.

"It's like duck sauce," Charlie says, taking a step forward and showing him the photo on his iPhone. Amazon sells the stuff by the case.

"We ain't got that," the store manager says, looking away. He shakes his head. He glances back at Charlie. Looks away again.

"You should check the computer," the butcher says. "We didn't know what it was either. Go ahead; look at the computer."

"We ain't *got* it," the manager says.

"You sure?" the deli guy asks.

The manager freezes them all with a look.

"Okay guys," Charlie says. "I'll go with what the manager says. He's the boss. But let me explain what's at stake here. I'm going back over the bridge to the lady of the house, and without Saucy Susan, who is on her list." He shows them the list. They all take a look. "She's going to tell me that we didn't look in the right place for Susan, and that's trouble, right?"

"*Damn* right," the butcher says. The deli guy nods. So does the store manager.

"So may I please have your word as foodstuff professionals that we all looked far and wide for Saucy Susan and she absolutely does not live in this store?"

"You got it," the deli guy says. The store manager nods and goes back to his business. The butcher slaps Charlie five.

"Thanks, guys." Charlie goes and gets a bottle of ordinary duck sauce to replace Susan (as if anyone could) and heads for the register. On his way there, he thinks again about the wonderful hospitality of a Southern supermarket. Those guys dropped everything to help someone on a hopeless quest, desperately seeking Susan. Even at the expense of other shoppers. So what if those other customers never return to the store. These guys showed that they cared. True Southern hospitality at its best.

The cashier is young and Donna's diminutive height, but probably weighs as much as three Donnas. But that's okay with Charlie. After all, this is America and this young lady works in a food store. It's all good.

He loads the vegetables onto the conveyer belt first. The cashier picks up a cucumber and stares at it. Above the register is a picture book with photos of dozens of fruits and vegetables. Trista has a similar book. Beneath each photo is a name and a code. She flips through all the pages and stares again at the cuke. Finally, she turns to Charlie, holds it out and says, "What dis?"

"Cucumber," Charlie says. "It's on page two." He points to the picture book.

She looks again. "Oh," she says. "Dis one *bigger*." She looks again at the big cuke and punches in the code from the book, and then moves on to the three avocados in the plastic bag. She pokes at them and tries to read the tiny labels through the plastic.

"Avocado," Charlie says. She looks up at him. "Page one." He points.

She nods. "Thanks."

"You're welcome."

Next comes the cantaloupe. She's palming it like a basketball and flipping through the book. She looks at Charlie and says, "Dis a coconut, right?"

"Nope, cantaloupe," Charlie says. "Same page, though. Three. You really should get to know fruits and vegetables. They're good for you."

"Huh?" she says.

Charlie hands her cash and she hands him his change.

"Thanks," he says.

"No problem," she answers, and then, under her breath, "*motherfucker.*"

Charlie loads the groceries into the trunk of his car and walks the cart back to the front of the store. When he gets back to the car he buckles up and shifts into reverse. He moves back a few inches as he glances into the rearview for the first time. There's a young guy walking by back there. Big guy. *Real* big guy. He practically fills the rearview mirror. How did Charlie miss this guy? Why didn't he look in the rearview before lifting his foot off the brake?

The guy smacks the trunk with both hands. "Hey!" he booms. "You looking? You fucking *looking*?"

He's around the car in an instant and knocking a thick knuckle on Charlie's window. "Roll it!" he says. Charlie does. The guy reaches in and backhands the left side of Charlie's face. Charlie tries to blink off the pain. His eyes are tearing.

"What the *fuck* you think you're doing, old man?" the guy says, leaning in.

"I'm sorry," Charlie says.

"You *ought* to be sorry," the guy snarls. "You ought to be out of this car, too."

Charlie's sphincter tightens. "I have to get home," he whispers.

"Oh, yeah? How many more people you gonna run down on your way there, old man?"

Huge fist. A set of key, each peeking from between thick fingers.

"Maybe next time it will be a kid, huh? You got no business driving, old man. Now you just back up slow and I'm gonna stand right here and watch. Do it *now*. You go fast I'm gonna punch a hole in your windshield and pull you out through it. You got it?"

"Yes, sir."

"Good. GO!"

Charlie puts the car in reverse and backs out slowly. The big guy is a man of his word. He stays put, but he also holds the tips of his keys against the side of Charlie's car and presses as the car creeps backward. Charlie hears the grinding sound and stops.

"I tell you to stop, old fool? *Keep going.*"

Charlie does and the gouge grows long across his car's door, and onto the front left fender, and then up across the hood. Just for good measure.

"There, that'll do. Now go home and die, motherfucker," the guy says, banging the hood with a thick fist.

Charlie heads home.

Wishes he *could* die.

Donna walks in, just back from the beach. "What happened to your face?!"

"I turned to look for the Saucy Susan and I banged into a display. It was stupid of me. I'm okay. Don't worry."

"Did anyone help you?" She comes close. Touches his face with her fingertips.

"It's nothing. They didn't have the Saucy Susan. I got everything else." He takes her hand gently away from his face. Steps back. Turns toward the grocery bags to avoid her eyes. " And I got duck sauce. It's not the same, I know, but I hope it will do. Sorry."

"Did you see the car? My god, what happened to the car? It's all scratched up."

She steps closer. Tries to touch his face.

"Some kid must have done that when I was in the store." Holds up his hands. "I'm okay. It's okay. I already called the insurance company. I sent pictures. We're covered. They'll take care of it when we get home. Don't worry."

"Gosh, what an afternoon," Donna sighs. Shakes her head in frustration. "I should have gone with you."

"No, it's better that you went to the beach. Really. It's better."

Must keep it secret.
Must.
She can't know.
Can't.

32

Trista's third birthday arrived, no longer a rusty nail on the family's calendar. Chocolate cake and wine, and more Little People from Target to play with. They celebrated together at home.

As the months went by, Abby and Donna had sat often in their now-shared living room. It all came out, painfully at first, and then easier with the salve of time. Abby told her mother what Hank had done to her, and said to her, since Trista's birth, and before. The fairytale never really was what it seemed to be to those looking in. Abby had woven a story born of the fairytales of her youth, told many times by parents hiding their own secrets.

But the time she spent with her mother, this strangely powerful woman, changed her. Donna had given her birth, and now she was guiding her back into life. Donna listened with a ferocious intensity, and the force of her listening brought out a rage in Abby as she recounted all that had happened, now seen through clearer eyes.

"Let it *loose*. Get *angry*," Donna demanded. "It's okay to be pissed off. Push it further than that, Abby. Get *furious*.

Rage, daughter. Get nuts *now*, and I promise you this will *never* happen to you again. Trust me, my child. Trust me and get *furious*. Not everyone can do this, but I know you can."

"Can *you*?"

"I can," Donna said.

"When did you?"

Quiet.

Quiet.

"When *did* you?"

"This is not about me," Donna whispered. "This is about *you* right now. It's *your* turn."

"When did you?"

"No, I won't tell you. Not now."

"Why?"

"It's not time."

And so Abby did, and did, and did. She raged like a madwoman, and the pain pulsed out of her like poison purged.

But there was one more question that needed an answer.

"Mom, did Daddy want a boy instead of me?" Straight-up, brutal question, like a right cross. Hard, wary eyes behind it. *"Truth*, please, Mom. Truth. Did he?"

Donna moved closer, and the gentleness of this woman, sheltered behind her acquired toughness, bloomed like

May. "Let me tell you a story. It's one I've never shared with you."

"What?"

"I had three miscarriages after you were born. None of the pregnancies lasted more than two months. They happened one right after the other. It was a terribly sad time for us, but we had you, and you were perfect, and we got on our knees and thanked God for you every single day. We still do, Abby."

Abby began to cry. Donna reached out and held her.

"It's okay. It's okay."

"What happened?" Abby sobbed. "I feel so bad for you. All those babies, lost."

"We finally stopped trying," Donna whispered into Abby's hair. "Your father was worried that I would be hurt if we tried again. He had a vasectomy. It was *his* choice. He did it to protect me."

"Oh, my god, Mom. I never knew," she sobbed.

"You were a child, Abby. All of this happened before you were three years old." Donna rocked her. "We told you about the first pregnancy, that you were going to be a big sister. Mostly to share, because you are the flesh-and-blood proof of our love, but you were too young to understand what that meant, and we were also young, and we were so excited. It was just words, cooing between joyful parents and their beloved child.

"You never knew I lost the first baby, Abby. You were a baby, too. We never mentioned the other pregnancies to you. I had a feeling that none of them would come to term. I can sense things sometimes. I just knew. I don't know how I knew, but I did. You were going to be the only one for us."

"That is so sad, Mommy."

"It is, Abby, but we have *you*, and you are all that we have ever needed."

"But it's so sad."

"*Life* is sad, Abby, but it's also joyous, and often hilarious. You take the bad with the good. And your siblings are in heaven and safe from harm forever."

"I love them, Mommy."

"And they love you, and your father, and me. Believe me; they do."

"So did Daddy want a boy? Is that why you were trying?"

"No, Abby. He wanted another girl. He was so in love with you. He wanted another just like you."

"Really?"

"Really."

"But what about sports and all that, the stuff Hank needed. Carrying on the family name. Men want sons."

"Men want *life*, Abby, and they want *love*. That's the big difference between men and boys. Men know this. Girls are every bit as alive as boys, and I think even more capable of love. You've heard your father say, a son is a son 'til he takes a wife, but a daughter's a daughter for the rest of her life?"

"Yes, and it's true," Abby says. "I remember when he told Hank that he wasn't giving me away at our wedding. He was willing to share, but he would *never* give me away. I was just too precious. I never told Daddy, but that really pissed off Hank."

"He didn't see the same magic in Trista."

"No, he didn't. He cared about carrying on the family name. Did Daddy worry about that?"

"Throw a stick in this town and you'll hit a Molloy," Donna says, "No worries about that."

Abby laughs. "Yeah, that's true. But what about sports?"

"Well, Abigail, you had plenty of them, didn't you?"

"I did."

"And your father was there for you at every game, even when you were riding the pine pony?"

"Yes."

"Girls rock, my love," Donna says.

"Even when we're on the bench?"

"Even when we're on the bench." Donna says, and hugs her daughter.

"Daddy is a special man."

"He is. And you know what I think makes him special?"

"What?"

"He loves people, no matter how old or young. He tries to understand everyone, and to learn from everyone. It was tragic to watch those young engineers on his job go after him the way they did. And that new boss was so cruel to him. That's your father's weakness, Abby. He finds it very difficult to change with the times, and especially with the technology. He's okay with his iPhone because it tells him stories. But he's not good with the *culture* that the iPhone brings. He lives much of his life in the past, and through the lives of others by way of their stories. Both of these qualities slow him down, and the world is not slowing down; it's speeding up. He got stuck somewhere back there. Those young people caught him when he was at his most vulnerable, as did his boss. I understood why they did this. They were all boys, not men. They were childishly selfish, and they hurt themselves by missing out on what he had to teach them. They could have learned much from him about life, but they chose to hurt him. To break him. They were boys."

"Boys can be cruel," Abby says.

"No one knows that better than you."

Abby bites her lip, nods.

"There's another thing about your father that's very special."

"What?" Abby asks.

"He loves women. Absolutely *adores* them. It was what first attracted me to him. You can see it in the way he treats us. He is always there for us, and when he was traveling, he couldn't wait to get back to us. The man positively *adores* women."

"Do you think he ever cheated on you, Mom?"

Quiet.

"Did he?"

Quiet. Tiny tear. Sniff.

"No. Never."

"How can you be sure?"

"Because if he had, I think he would have told me."

"You do?"

"Yes."

"Why?"

"Because it's his nature. He can't keep secrets. I have to believe that."

"Do you think he's been tempted? He's a handsome guy, and he looks so much younger than he actually is. Just like you. And he was traveling all the time."

"He did tell me a story once about a trip he made to Detroit. There was this young bartender and this drunk who was giving her a hard time about her tattoo."

"Her tattoo?"

"Yes, it was here." Donna touches the back of Abby's neck. Lingers there a moment. "It was Chinese characters. Right here." Donna tickles the spot. Abby smiles. "The drunk made fun of it. Your dad said she had red hair and freckles, but the guy called her Eggroll. He wouldn't stop."

"What a jerk," Abby says.

"Yes, and your father stepped up to defend her."

"So what happened?"

"The guy left in a huff. Later, the bartender brings your father another wine. She asks him if he wants to know what the tattoo means. He says, 'Sure, if you want to tell me.' She whispers this into his ear." Donna leans in and puts the redhead's words into the center of Abby's brain.

Abby's eyes go wide. She laughs. "She actually *said* that? To *Dad*?"

"Yep. Said even more afterwards. He got stuck in Detroit that night."

"And what happened?"

"He came home to me the next day."

"And he *told* you about all of this?"

"Yes. We were in bed."

"Were you upset?"

"Why would I be upset? He told me."

"You are so tolerant."

"No, I'm not, Abby. All that happened was that she saw in your father what I see in him. She gave it a shot. He came home to me, though. Always has. That's life. Women come on to him because he adores them, and appreciates them, and is forever drawn into their spell."

"I've never thought of him that way."

"You're his daughter."

"I am."

"I was in a restaurant in New York City with him a few years ago. We were having a nice lunch. He calls over our waitress and tells her he wants to pick up the tab for this single woman that was sitting a few tables behind me. I glanced around. She was by herself and maybe eighty years old, maybe more. She was well dressed, but in an old-style way, like she had gotten to the restaurant in 1947 and had been waiting for someone to arrive ever since. She was small in a worn-down way, and your father told me later that she would dab at her mouth with the corner of her napkin after each bite, like she was taught to do it that way by her mother when she was a little girl, back during a time when manners really mattered. Your father tells our waitress to tell the woman that a secret admirer paid her tab because she is beautiful."

"That is so sweet," Abby says.

"It was more than sweet; it was caring, Abby, and so human."

"So what happened?"

"The woman finished her meal and took another sip of her coffee. She dabbed with her napkin one last time and looked off into space, like she was trying to remember something. Then she gestured for the check. The waitress went over to her and leaned down to tell her the news.

"The woman's eyes went wide and she looked all around the restaurant. This is going on behind me. I can't see it. Your father keeps his full attention on me, but he's watching her, too, and he's filling me in. The woman looked and looked. Her eyes were so bright. And then she smiled and took out this delicate white hankie and dabbed at her eyes. She continued to look around. She looked at

your father. He looked at me, keeping the mystery alive. I
know that she must have felt loved at that moment, and I'm
sure she felt beautiful. She touched her hair and she smiled,
and for a few moments she was young again, desired
again, and that's what mattered to your father. He wasn't
looking for anything other than her check. That's who he is,
Abby. That's how much he loves women. So are you still
wondering if he wanted a boy?"

"Nope," Abby says.

"Good."

"Mom, can I ask you a personal question?"

"Anything, within reason."

"I've seen the way men look at you. I've watched
that since I became aware of men. How do you feel about
them?"

Donna laughs and her green eyes get even brighter.
"Oh, daughter of mine!"

"No, tell me."

"Okay, I'll say this. I do love *men*, but to me, being a
man involves more than just owning a penis. There are a lot
of boys out there in the world and they can be adorable, and
they usually are, but they're not *men*. Do you understand
what I mean? Not all boys grow to be men, and I have no
time for boys, other than to giggle at them."

"But what about *men*?"

"What about men?"

"Have you ever?"

"Let me ask you a question, Abby. Why did you hold all of this about Hank inside of yourself while it was going on? Why didn't you talk to us?"

"I wanted to protect you both, Mom."

"Protect us, Abby? From *life*?"

"Yes, I suppose."

"That's not possible. No one can protect any of us from life. It's beautiful and cruel, and all at the same time."

"I understand that now."

"I know you do."

"But have you ever?"

Quiet.

They sit. Hold each other and rock like two small boats tied together.

Shhhh.

After a while, Donna whispers. " Do you know what your name means? Have you ever looked it up?"

"No," Abby peeps.

"*Father's joy.* That's what your name means, my love. It's a name as old as the Bible. *He* chose that name for you. You are his joy. And mine."

33

"I got you both a present," Abby announces. They're having dinner, a nice meatloaf that Donna put together, along with garlic mashed potatoes, gravy, niblet corn and hot biscuits. Charlie's favorite. Trista is eating Kraft mac and cheese, her favorite.

"A present?" Charlie says. "What the occasion?"

"It's I Love You Day," Abby says.

"That's every day," Donna says.

"Exactly. So here's what I got you both." She hands them a page she printed off the Internet. It has a photo and description of a small apartment on Singer Island, Florida.

"What's this?" Donna asks.

"It's where you're going to spend February," Abby says. "It's all paid for. I want you to go down there and relax. Celebrate retirement. You deserve it."

Charlie and Donna look at each other. "Oh, this is too much, Abby," Charlie says.

"Yes, we couldn't possibly accept," Donna adds, forever thinking about the money, both theirs and Abby's.

Abby holds up her hand. "None of that from either of you. It's done. Trista and I wanted to do this for you. And don't worry; we'll be fine."

"But this must be so expensive," Donna says.

"Surprisingly affordable," Abby says. "Trust me. I have the insurance money, and the money from selling the house. The business is doing well, and we're all living in the same house now, right? You did that for us, so let us do this for you."

"Abby?" Donna starts, and stops. She's smiling. So is Charlie. "Thanks."

"Go buy yourself some new flip-flops, Mom. Sit on the beach and be beautiful. And, Dad, maybe get some new cargo shorts. You'll need a lot of pockets to hold all the stories. I also want to get you airline tickets and a rental car."

"Oh, please don't do that, Abby," Charlie says. "If we're going, I'd love to drive there. That will give us a lot of time to talk along the way, and you know I enjoy driving. And maybe we'll meet some interesting people along the way. Get some good stories for you."

"Okay, Daddy. Whatever makes you happy works for me."

And that's how Donna and Charlie came to be on Singer Island that February when it was cold and snowy and angry on Long Island.

But about Abby.

34

Donna held two-year-old Abby close as the child shivered with fear. She wrapped the blue towel tighter around her. "Bad," Abby cried, looking at the ocean. "Bad!"

"I know, baby. The wave knocked you down, didn't it?" Abby nodded furiously. "Bad!" A grey and white gull soared close overhead and screeched a laugh. Donna looked up at it, cursed it silently.

"But you told Daddy that you wanted him to let go of your hands, didn't you?"

"Yes," she sobbed.

"Did you turn around and look for me, so I could see what a big girl you are?"

"Yes!" Abby said.

"You don't have to do that, honey. I know what a big girl you are. You don't ever have to look for me to see that. I *always* know, and I always *will* know."

Abby quieted and snuggled.

"I'm going to tell you a secret that I want you to remember forever, okay?"

"Secret, Mommy?" Abby looked up from inside the blue towel. Smiled.

"Yep, a *big* secret, one that not many people know. And those that *don't* know will always be knocked down, like you just were."

"What's the secret, Mommy?"

"Promise not to tell?"

"Yes."

"Cross your heart?"

"Yes." Abby pulls her hand out from under the blue towel and makes a cross on her chest.

"Okay, here's the secret." Donna looks around to make sure no one else can hear. "The ocean is *sneaky*," she says. Abby looks confused. Donna nods her head, very seriously. Up and down three whole times. "Verrrry *sneaky*!" She hugs Abby and jiggles her back and forth. Abby giggles. "Verrry, verrry *SNEAKY*!" Donna says with a monster voice. Pokes Abby in both sides. Abby goes nuts.

"Sneaky!" Abby squeals.

"Yes, my love, and this is why you must never, ever, ever turn your back on the ocean. If you do, it will sneak up on you and knock you down. Just like it did before. So promise me you won't ever do that again."

"I won't, Mommy."

"Even if a big fishie is chasing you?" Donna says, and pokes Abby in the belly again.

"Fishie in the *water*," Abby says.

"That's right," Donna says. "That's why you have to watch the ocean. Don't let it send a big fishie after you." Poke in the belly. Squeal. "Or a big WAVE!" Another poke. Giggle fits. Hugs.

They sit quietly after that. Abby still wrapped in the blue towel, Donna looking over at Charlie, who has been watching. He should never have let go of her hands. It's his fault.

"And honey," Donna says. "One more secret."

Abby looks up?

"This one you can tell to *anybody*. It's a secret to share.'

"Secret to share."

"Yes, are you ready for it?"

"Yes." Giggles.

"Your daddy loves you. He loves you more than anything and he will always be there to protect you, just like he beat up the ocean today because it knocked you down. Did you see him kick it? I sure did. He kicked that ocean right in the balls."

Abby looks over at Charlie.

"And that's my secret," Charlie says. "I kicked the Atlantic Ocean in its balls for you, Abby. Did you hear it rumble? I sure did. No ocean likes to get kicked in the balls, but this one deserved it. Don't mess with *my* girl, Atlantic Ocean."

Abby pushes out of the blue towel and climbs onto Charlie's lap.

"I love you, big girl," he says.

"Love you, Daddy."

"Do you want to take a walk?" Charlie asks.

Abby looks at Donna.

"That will be fun, honey. Go walk with Daddy."

She watches them walk off, hand in hand. She is so small next to him. So small.

Her father made sand castles with her so many years ago before he got sick and lingered into weakness. She didn't understand how this could happen to him, or to her, or why.

"You are my magic girl," he would say as he upturned a bucket of wet sand, patted the sides of the bucket and then lifted it carefully. "You can build castles out of the beach. Look at how beautiful this is, and it is all yours."

"I love it, Daddy."

"And I love you, big girl."

"I'm not big, Daddy," Donna giggled. "I'm small."

"Maybe you are, my love, but you are mighty."

"What is mighty, Daddy."

"It means that you might do anything in the whole world that you want to do, Donna. You are *mighty*. That's what it means."

"I love you, Daddy."

"I will always love you, Donna. Even if I'm not here."

"Where will you be, Daddy?"

"I will be the sunlight on your skin, and the wind in your hair." He touched her warm back above her swimsuit.

"That tickles, Daddy!"

"I will be with your forever, Donna. I promise. I will always be there."

"Can we make the castle bigger, Daddy?"

"Yes, as big as you want it to be."

"Can it be mighty?"

"Yes, like you."

A gull glided over their heads and shrieked a laugh.

He died that Thanksgiving Day.

Donna's lisp appeared for the first time that Christmas Eve.

"I mith Daddy tho mush," she said.

"Don't talk like that," her mother scolded. "You sound like a *baby*."

They walk down the beach, never turning their backs on the ocean. Charlie points out the pretty seashells. He picks up a big clamshell and holds it to Abby's ear.

"Can you hear the ocean?" he asks. "It's whispering to you. It's saying, keep watching me. Keep watching me. Keeeeep Waaaaaaaaaching Meeeee."

Abby's eyes go wide. "I hear it!" They walk some more. Abby holds the shell like a telephone. "Can I take the shell home, Daddy?"

"You bet."

"Will the ocean talk to me at home, too?"

"It will always talk to you if you listen for it, but never turn your back on it again, okay?"

"Okay."

They went to the mall a week later and Abby asked for a shiny balloon she spotted at a kiosk. It was star-shaped and golden. When they got home, Abby was sitting on the floor with the balloon, holding it tightly to her right ear. Her eyes were looking at the ceiling.

"What are you doing, sweetheart?" Charlie asked.

"I'm listening to the sky, Daddy."

Charlie stood there in wonder. "Thank you, God," he whispered. "Thank you for letting me live long enough to hear those gorgeous words."

Twenty-one-year-old Charlie was nervous. He had never done this before, and he never planned to do it again. He thought it would have been easier had her father been there instead of her mother. Donna said he would have gotten along well with her father. They were alike in a so many ways. The biggest way being that they both loved her unconditionally.

"Do you want some?" Mrs. Doyle asked Charlie, offering him the dirty jelly glass filled with gin and a bit of tonic. Her robe opened up as she reached out. He saw a nipple.

"No, I'm fine, but thanks," Charlie said, looking down and picking at a thread on his jeans that wasn't there.

"What's that?" Mrs. Doyle said, leaning closer. Again, the nipple.

"What? This?" Charlie moved his hands toward the imaginary thread. "Just a thread or something."

"Let me see?" Mrs. Doyle said, reaching for the inside of his thigh. She squeezed him there.

"No, it's okay," Charlie said, shifting his legs to the side and sliding back on the couch. "I'm good."

"Don't be nervous, boy. Mama's not going to bite you."

Charlie stood up. "Actually, I need to ask you for your permission to marry Donna," he said quickly, trying to change the subject. "That's why I'm here."

"You should be asking my husband. That's man's work, giving away a daughter, not that she's much to give away. But he's not here, is he?" she said, looking around the room. She lifts a doily from the couch arm. "Anybody home? Nope." Takes a pull on the gin. "He left us long, long, long ago." Wave of the jelly glass. Back and forth. "Long, long, long ago." Like a child's song. "Loooong ago." Big, deep sip.

"I know."

"At least he left his cop's pension for me," she said. "It's not much but it got us this far. That and the insurance on the house. We did the best we could with what we got, boy."

"I know."

"So you want to take my baby away from me, eh? That's what you're here for, right? To take my baby away from me?"

"Yes, Mrs. Doyle. We're in love and we want to marry, but I want to ask your permission first."

"And what's to become of *me*?" she asked, lighting another unfiltered Camel.

"We'll always be there for you," Mrs. Doyle. "Donna and me."

"My baby and *you*? You're a boy." Dismissive wave of the Camel.

"We'll be there for you. I promise."

"Promise? Yeah, I've heard that before."

"I mean it."

"She talks like a *baby*. You know that, right?"

"I know she has a lisp. She can't help that. I think it's endearing."

"*Endearing*, what a nice word." Hack! Pulls the dirty tissue out of her sleeve. Spits. "Endearing. I never thought of her that way." Pulls on the gin. Puts the tissue back.

"I do. I think of her that way all the time. I love her."

"She doesn't listen, you know." She jabs with the Camel. "She doesn't. You'll see. She thinks she's in charge of everything. She's not, but she thinks she is. She thinks she's so fucking high and *mighty*." Hack. "All the time *mighty*. Makes me sick."

"I love her."

"Well, if that's the case, and if you want to marry a *baby* who doesn't listen then more power to you, boy. That's what I say. Take her off my hands. I've done enough for her. She's all yours, and good luck to you."

"We'll always be there for you," Charlie said.

"Yeah sure." Back hand wave. "Just like her father was. Just take her and leave me alone. You're both useless."

Lung cancer arrived with a fury six weeks later. Stage Four. No warning. They buried her two months before their wedding.

After college, Abby took a job with Marriott and quickly advanced as an event planner. She liked the job but soon realized that she would never be satisfied working for someone else's company. She was an entrepreneur.

A few years before Trista arrived, she opened her own business. She called it, Fairytale Wedding Planners, and she was doing very well with it. She had an office built out of about a third of their two-car garage. Hank wouldn't give up the rest of the space. He said he needed that for his sports stuff. She was making more money than Hank was making, and he resented this, but he rationalized that her money was *his* money anyway because she hadn't kept up her end of the marriage bargain by giving him his son. She owed him.

It was a crisp Saturday in late October and Abby was meeting a new client to discuss their fairytale wedding. The couple, Lisa and Anthony, arrived on time and Abby was making them each a cup of coffee with the Keurig.

"I love the name of your company," Lisa said. "It's what made us call you in the first place. And we loved your website. The photos are wonderful! Isn't that right, Anthony?"

Anthony smiled and nodded, but said nothing.

"The name came from my own marriage," Abby said, setting down the cups. "My husband and I were born on the same day and delivered by the same doctor. We were next to each other in the nursery, but we didn't meet until we were in high school."

"Really?" Lisa said. "That's amazing! Isn't that amazing, Anthony."

"What hospital?" Anthony asked.

"The one in Plainview," Abby said.

"Oh," Anthony said.

"That's like a real fairytale," Lisa said.

"Yes, I told my mother that it was like Hank and I had been married before, and when we got to heaven, we decided to come back and do it all over again."

"That is so sweet!" Lisa said.

"Thanks," Abby smiled. "Let's talk about *your* fairytale wedding. That's most important. What are your dreams?"

"I want everything white," Lisa said. "Anthony will wear a white suit to match my gown. The ushers and the bridesmaids will also wear white. I love white. It's so, oh, I don't know. Pure." Lisa giggled.

"Tell me about your budget," Abby said.

"We have up to $60,000 to spend," Lisa said.

"For how many people?"

"I can't say just yet," Lisa said. "But figure hundreds. I have sooo many friends. My Facebook posts get sooo many likes it's ridiculous." She smiled at Anthony. "Right, honey?"

"Uh, huh."

"And Anthony has a small family, and not many friends. He's giving me his numbers for the wedding. I just hate having to decide who my *bestest* best friends are. They're all going to want to be there. I'm so excited! Right, Anthony?"

The corners of Anthony's mouth twitched. He nodded.

"We want this to be very special, a wedding loaded with love," Lisa said and giggled. "Lots and lots of love!"

"If that's your dream, then that's what we'll make happen," Abby said.

"And I want white draperies all around the perimeter of the room. And I want it by the water. It has to be by the water? Right, Anthony? Water is pure."

"If that's what you want," Anthony said.

"Can we get a white horse-drawn carriage with a white horse?" Lisa asked. "That's always been my dream. I want to be like Cinderella."

"We can make that happen, too," Abby said.

"You really *can* make fairytales come true, can't you?" Lisa said.

"That's what a perfect marriage is all about," Abby said.

"You should know," Lisa said.

Abby smiled, but at that moment, Trista shrieked, which caught Lisa by surprise. Even Anthony turned to look at the closed door.

"Will you excuse me for a moment?" Abby asked. "I just want to see why my daughter is crying."

"Is she alone in there?" Lisa asked.

"Oh, no! Of course not. She's with my husband. Let me just check. I'll be back in a flash."

Abby quick-stepped into the living room, leaving the door to her office partly open. To shut it fully would have seemed rude.

Hank was watching a college football game. "Where's the baby?" Abby asked.

"I don't know. In her crib, I guess," Hank said, not looking up. "I can't hear the fucking game with all that screaming. *Do* something."

"I'm with a client," Abby said, racing to Trista's room to find her diaper full.

"She needs to be changed," Abby shouted.

"So change her," Hank screamed, still looking at the game. "And tell her to shut the fuck up! *Catch* that! *Catch* that! Ah, *FUCK!*" he yelled. "I can't fuckin' believe you *missed* that." Louder now. *"YOU ASSHOLE!* You gotta be able to catch those. You're useless! *Useless!*" Hank leaned forward and smashed his palm onto the coffee table.

"Will you help me, Hank? I'm with a client," Abby said.

"Fuck that. I don't do diapers," Hank spat. "Especially *hers*."

So Abby changed Trista's diaper and got her settled down. When she went back to her office, Lisa and Anthony were gone.

Charlie and Abby are walking on the beach at Tobay, down near the surf where the sand is flat and hard. Seagulls are hanging in the air like white, porcelain kites.

"Do you remember when you were very small and your mom told you never to turn your back on the ocean?" Charlie asks.

"She said that to me a lot," Abby says. "So did you. It sure seems appropriate with all that's happened, doesn't it? I turned my back on a lot of things, and I got knocked down pretty hard."

Charlie reaches for her hand. The waves are calm today and the piping plovers are scurrying in and out, never turning their backs on the ocean. The waves can't catch their tiny bird feet because these little ones can run faster than waves. And unlike the people who walk the sands of Tobay, the plovers are a protected species.

"She also told me again and again that you love me to the moon and back." She leans into him.

"That's still true," Charlie says. "More so than ever."

"And when I got older, Mom told me again and again that nature doesn't care about any of us. Only people care about us."

"Your mother is very wise, Abby. Nature is a powerful force, but it doesn't feel. It doesn't care. Only people care, and not enough of them."

"She always seems to know things somehow. She knew about the problems Hank and I were having. I never mentioned any of those things that were going on in our lives. In fact, I did my best to hide them, but somehow she knew."

Charlie stops to pick up a clam shell. He hands it to Abby. She puts it up to her ear and smiles. "Your mother is very perceptive, Abby."

"She's your best friend," Abby says.

Charlie squeezes her hand. "Her and you," he says. Abby smiles, puts the clamshell to her ear again.

"Does it still work?" Charlie asks.

"Yep."

"How do you think she does it?" Abby asks a while later. "I mean know things the way she does."

Charlie looks out at a big plane following the shoreline, heading toward JFK Airport. There's another not far behind it, and a third way off in the distance. So many lives. So many journeys.

I think there's magic in this world, Abby, and I know there's magic in your mother. I saw it for the first time on the day you were born. She changed on that day. Went from girl to woman right before my eyes. She gained something spiritual. She got tough, and very protective toward both of us. And the funny thing is, when she tunes in on something, I begin to sense the same thing she's sensing. It just comes out of her and into me, and without words. It's like radio. She thinks it, and somehow I know."

"So you suspected things weren't right between Hank and me?"

"I didn't suspect. I knew, and it was killing me. I hated him for what he was doing to you, but there was nothing I could do about it."

"Why?"

"Because you wanted to believe in your fairytale, Abby. You built your whole life around it. You built your business around it. It was sacred to you. I would have hurt you if I had said anything at all against him. You know that's true. And I can *never* hurt you, Abby. And the fairytales are my fault. Mine and your mother's. We raised you on tall tales."

Abby considers this. Squeezes his hand. "I know and you're right, Daddy. I would have denied it and fought you. I'm sorry. I love you, and I loved your tall tales. Still do."

"I love you more, Abby."

"Not possible," she says, and laughs. Got him that time.

They walk a while with only the lapping of the waves.

"So what makes it happen?" Abby asks. "I mean the psychic thing between you and Mom."

"I think it's the common memory. That's the greatest treasure of a long marriage. You're together so much, going through so much, the good times and the bad, the sickness and the health, the richer, the poorer. It's all there in the vows. Nothing about happy every day, just commitment. You learn to be selfless, and you learn to love unconditionally. It's very hard to do that because we're all born selfish. Look at the way babies and children are? What is maturity but learning *not* to be selfish, learning to love? And love is about giving unconditionally, not taking. That's what the common memory is. It's pure love, shared through time."

"It sounds magical," Abby says.

"It *is* magical," Charlie says.

They turn and head back. The breeze is behind them now and the autumn sun feels good on their backs.

"Hank chased something he couldn't have," Abby says. "He chased a promise made to his father after his father was dead. I don't know if it was guilt or if it was his image of love for that man, or just ego, but I think that if his father could have seen how it all turned out he would have acted differently toward Hank when Hank was a boy."

Quiet.

Quiet.

"There are people who can never get over a death in their family," Charlie says. "The dead travel with these people. It's not easy."

"That was Hank," Abby says.

"And others," Charlie says.

"I thought Hank would be like you, Daddy. People liked him in high school and in college. He was such a good athlete."

"They liked what he did, winning the games and all. He made them feel good about themselves, but because of the way his father raised him, he never really had a chance. And that's tragic. He missed so much."

"Yes, he did."

They walk.

"What makes people the way they are, Daddy?"

"Gosh, Abigail, I don't know."

"Can we fix people?" Abby asks. "Is there something I should have been doing that I didn't do with Hank?"

"Nobody can fix another person, Abby. We can be there for them, and you were always there for Hank, but each person has to fix themselves."

"You fixed *me*," Abby says.

"No, honey, I *loved* you. There's a difference. *You* fixed you."

"I love you, Daddy."

Charlie puts his arm around her, pulls her in close. The sun feels good.

35

"Saint Clare," Charlie says. "Have I ever told you about this little bar in New York City called, The Dubliner?"

"Nope. I would remember that, Charlie. I like Irish." Her brown hair is out of the ponytail today. Parted down the middle. Grey eyes gleaming.

"I visited there and saw a sign out front that read, Women and cats go where they will. Men and dogs go where they're told. What do you have to say about that?"

Clare considers this with that adorable face-scrunch that she does. "Okay, I'll go with that part-way. Cats and Dogs. Women and men. Yep, for some that's true. Some men are cats, though, Charlie. Grant me that. I've met 'em. What do you think, Donna?"

"I think you're wise beyond your years, Clare."

"Why thank you, young lady. What brings this up, Charlie?" Clare asks.

"Well, Lady Donna and I were out on our constitutional this morning so that we could drink wine with you this afternoon. The calories, you know. Anyway, we came upon a couple walking a baby in a carriage. The man had two old basset hounds on leather leashes. Not an easy thing for a man to handle: Two dogs, one baby, one wife."

"They're townies," Clare says. "I've seen them around. Cute baby. Pretty wife. Ragged dogs."

"I agree, but have you seen what the hounds do with each other?"

"Uh, they do doggie things?"

"Not what I meant, Clare, but thanks. No, they're both male dogs. Not that there's anything wrong with that. They're just friends. No, what they do is coordinate their poops."

Clare cracks up. Donna smiles. "Stop it!" Clare says.

"Lady Donna?" Charlie says. "Please confirm."

"For once in his life, Clare, what he's saying is God's truth."

"Thank you," Charlie says. "You see, that's the problem with this bar. You meet so many scoundrels, Saint Clare, that when a sincere, truth-telling gentleman such as yours truly arrives, no one knows how to deal with him."

"World-class," Clare says.

"None better," Donna agrees.

"Now, Clare, here's what happened and I saw this with me own eyes. The two hounds walk side by side. They stop and sniff. Not each other, but the ground beneath their ancient noses. Heads go back up, and they look at each other with those sad basset hound eyes. Then they nod. No, they really do! Don't laugh; I'm serious. And then each hound does one perfect pirouette, followed by a tired, face-to-face squat, and just like that, we witness syncopated pooping. It was like watching the Canine Singer Island Olympics."

"God's truth," Donna says.

"It was inspirational," Charlie says. "If Cliff was still in town, rather than in the frozen tundra of the North, I'd ask him to try it with me."

"Did you take a picture?" Clare asks. "Not of Cliff, the hounds."

"Yeah, I got down on the ground with them and took a selfie. It was a first for me. A bit messy, but worth it."

"*Now* he's bullshitting," Donna says.

"And you want to know the best part, Clare?" Charlie adds.

"I do."

"I was laughing with delight, and the guy pushing the carriage tells me that they do this *every* morning, and on the *exact* same spot."

"Men and dogs go where they're told," says Clare. "I get it."

"Unless the men are cats," Donna says.

"Exactly," says Clare.

An afternoon drinker down the bar raises a glass and beams a smile at Clare, and she is off.

"She's adorable," Donna says.

"Yes, but you're prettier," Charlie says.

"You need to get your eyes examined, buster."

So about Clare.

36

Clare was 35 years old that February on Singer Island when Donna and Charlie were drinking in the afternoon. She looked 15 years younger than that, especially when she was working the bar and wearing the shorts and the tee. The bar really was her gym, and she was born to this life.

She worked the early shift because that's when Chara was in her day program. Chara was born just before Christmas, when Clare was 25 years old.

Kiss me; I'm Irish.

She had met Kieran at the bar. He was over here in Florida from Dublin, Ireland on a work visa, and he said he had no plans to ever go back, even if he had to cheat. Guys who look like Kieran do well working in Irish-themed, American bars. And Kieran really liked America. No way was he going back.

So one thing led to another because sex is like a wasp in a jar, and Clare soon found herself in a family way, as they say. She told Kieran, and he seemed very pleased. He lifted his glass. "To you, dear Clare, and Céad Míle Fáilte to our child."

Clare lifted a glass of water. "Glasses up!" she said. "Sláinte."

"Indeed. May God bless us all with good health and plenty, now and forever."

And then came all those other words of love, and Clare wrapped them around herself like silk and linen. She had found he whom she thought of as her man forevermore, and he promised her love and fidelity for all the days of their lives, 'til death do they part. She was the sweetness of his life, and he would work hard for her and for their magical child to come.

And what of marriage, you ask, dear Clare? Why marriage is nothing compared to their love. 'Tis but a wee scrap of paper against such a powerful love. No, a paper marriage is for the old, who don't understand the ferocity of modern times and true, everlasting love. So, my dear, let us forget this paper business for now and just cuddle a bit like this. Yes. Just a wee bit. That's it, dear Clare. Like that. Paper cannot hold people together, dear Clare. Only love can hold people together. Let me touch you like this. I know, the child, the child. I'll be careful. Just like this, dear. That's it. Relax now. All will be well. You'll see. Trust in me, dear Clare. I will be here for you forever. But for now, this. That's it. *Ahh.*

Clapton was singing *Key to the Highway* on Clare's small CD player as they made careful love.

Oh, give me one more kiss, darlin'
Just before I go.
'Cos when I leave this time, little girl
I won't be back no more.

Kieran always liked that bluesy song. Said it was his favorite. He stayed two more weeks and then left for work one morning and never showed up there. He also took what money Clare had in her purse that day, along with the Clapton CD. He left no note.

Clare didn't bother looking for him. What was the point? He was a boy.

So she got up and went back to work at the Singer Island bar that tucks itself back into the building like a kid hiding under the bed. The people were good to her there, and they got even better as her belly grew. The workers and the drinkers all gathered around her and they protected her.

Some say that guys drink less when they're served by a woman who is in a family way because it makes them think of responsibility, but this wasn't a concern for the owner of this lovely bar, Mack McBride, an older man who loved life, and nor was it an issue for the drinkers. You know why? Because Clare boomed with life and bloomed with child. She loved people, and she made everyone feel better than they were, and she was tough and soft, and all at the same time. And she was very good with The Chat. And she was a friend to those who needed a friend, and she did not suffer fools. She could tell you to go to hell in a way that made you go looking for a GPS. She was born to this life, and she was then, as she is now, and forever will be, adorable.

And how about this? She even organized a pool around when the baby would arrive. During the months that she worked before Chara's birth, Clare was a one-woman Super Bowl with that pool. And she extended it to other bar games.

Guess the hour the baby will arrive.

Guess what minute.

Guess the baby's weight.

Guess the weather on that blessed day.

Put up your money, lads, and let's have some laughs. Take a chance on me. Take a chance on *life*. Grab the world by the balls and give it a squeeze, lads. C'mon, glasses up! Let's do this together. We can *do* this!

The whole place got behind her and she came out of it with a decent amount of cash. She was going to be okay. She was *Clare*. She would *always* be okay. She loved people, and she accepted life as it hit her, no matter how hard, no matter how fast. She understood the simple grace of acceptance. She took it all, and she would survive, for herself, and for her child.

Her labor wasn't long, and she cried when the doctor placed the infant in her arms. She was tiny, no bigger than a minute. Clare was alone, but never *really* alone, for there was the doctor, and the nurse, and her child, and the entire world waited for her and for her babe. She held her daughter close and thanked God for bringing them both through this safely. She cooed over her child and touched her face, and her hands, and her tiny feet. She kissed the top of her head, and it didn't matter to Clare that Chara had Down syndrome. What difference does an extra chromosome make, other than to make the dear child a child forever? A child is a gift from God, and this one is beautiful, and through the simple grace of acceptance, Clare felt peace like a river flowing through her, and through her helpless babe.

She called her Chara because Chara means joy, and there is nothing in this world more precious than a daughter. Nothing. "I am your Ma *and* your Da," she whispered to her baby. "And I will love you forever and protect you from all that is evil in this world. This I promise with all my heart, my precious little girl. I will *never* leave you alone. You are mine, and I am yours. *Forever.* I am strong, and I love you."

Clare's mother and father *did* plan her, just as Charlie knew they had, and Lime Day in New York City was lovely that year. A fine time for conception.

Both were Irish-American, second generation on this side of the pond, and they, too, had met in a bar. Seamus was the day bartender, and Mary was the waitress in that small Irish bar and grill in Woodside, Queens, not far from where the New York Mets play baseball. They understood love, and they gave to each other all that they had, this true man and this true woman.

They lived in a small apartment, one they could afford on their own two salaries, and Clare was to be their only child. Dermot, the owner of the bar liked Seamus and Mary for the hard way they worked, and for their honesty. He also loved watching them together, the way they looked at each other, always checking to see where the other was in the little bar during their shift. Are you okay? Yes, are you, dear? Yes. They were beautiful together, like two hands clasped in prayer.

Dermot was an old bachelor, with a wide, Irish face as flat as a pancake. He had come to America as a young man and none of his relatives in Ireland were alive. He had worked hard and made a good life for himself here. He went to work in the bar right after he arrived, and eventually bought the place, and the apartment building above it, from Hugh Clancy. Bought it over time, and paid it off in full. Clancy's name is still over the front door, may he rest in peace. No need to change it. Why mess with a good thing?

When Clare arrived, Dermot told Mary and Seamus that the bar could be their day care. "Just bring the darling in here, like at home. We'll set a wee crib for her in the corner over there. It's good for business. What drinker doesn't love a beautiful baby? And she has such a sweet cry. Reminds me of the pipes," he laughed. "And this place needs as much life as we can fit between its walls," he said with a wink.

And it was true. The afternoon drinkers fussed over Clare. The women cooed, and the men stuffed dollars into her infant seat when Seamus and Mary weren't looking. It was that sort of a place. Everyone kept their eyes on Clare as she grew, and before long, she was off to Catholic school.

They were a close family, these three. There were no aunts or uncles. Both Seamus and Mary had been only children, and both sets of Clare's grandparents had passed on. Cancer of the lungs took two of them, and heart attacks the other two. The Irish diseases. It was sad, but there were many good memories and no regrets. They had loved, and were loved.

Clare continued to be a jewel to all of them at the bar as the years went by. She was bright and tiny, and as Donna often said, she was adorable. She laughed all the time at the jokes, and helped her mother and father with the work. She did her homework each day at an empty table in the back, over there where her crib once stood. She was a very good student, especially with the math. She was a natural with the numbers, and she was never a problem to anyone.

She graduated from high school and thought about applying to Queens College, but the more she thought about it, the more she realized that the bar was her college, and the people in the bar were her courses, so she went to work for Dermot, as bar-back to her father. She kept the place neat and humming, and everyone loved her.

When she turned 21, and was legal to serve booze, she gave her father a break, and that was when she realized that she truly *was* born to this life. More and more people came in to chat with Clare, and life was good for everyone. The future looked as bright as a new penny.

She was in the apartment late one morning, making beds and cleaning up. The bar was just opening and she was going to head down there in a few minutes.

Mary and Seamus and Jesus, the cook, were making things ready for the lunch crowd. Dermot was sitting at the bar, reading the *New York Post*.

A twitchy kid walks in. He's about five feet tall and wearing an oversized black hoodie and jeans. Sneakers with untied laces.

"Gimme the fucking money!" he shouts, pointing to the cash register with his left hand. His right hand is in the front pocket of the hoodie. Dermot and Mary turn on their stools toward the kid. Jesus opens the swinging door to the kitchen and steps out. He's wiping his hands on a towel. "Qué mierda."

There's not much money in the register. Just enough to make change. The day is just starting for everyone. Dopey kid got his times all mixed up. He should come in later when there's money in the till. This makes no sense.

Seamus laughs at the absurdity of it all. "Fuck off, kid," he says. "Get outta here before I come around this bar and kick your skinny ass down the block."

The twitchy kid answers by moving his right hand out of the hoodie pocket. There's a Ruger 9mm in that hand, which he raises, holding it sideways, gangsta-style. He says nothing, just shoots Seamus right in the face. Dermot gets off his stool. Takes one step. The kid shoots him in the throat. Jesus is frozen in place, staring in horror. He's next.

Then the kid turns on Mary, whose last thought is of Clare, safe at home. Thank God for that.

The kid gets just over fifty bucks for his efforts. Mostly in singles. A few coins. Leaves his fingerprints all over the place. He has a long record of little crimes.

Clare finds them all 20 minutes later.

The cops know who he is within hours and they get an anonymous tip two days later. They corner him, but he's out of his mind. He screams and points the same gun at the cops. He fires wildly.

They shoot him dead. They shoot him until there are no more bullets left in New York City. They kill him as hard as they can, and they wish they could kill him again, and again, and again, and again, and bring back to life those four good people whose lives he took.

But that's not possible.

Never will be.

It makes the newspapers, of course. Why so many bullets?

Why?

Fury.

And Poor Clare, who now has nothing but the courage left to her by her Ma and her Da and poor Dermot, and a strength born from witnessing pure love throughout her young life, takes care of the funerals for all of them with what money she can gather from friends, and then she gets on a bus.

37

Charlie and Donna slept in one day and then decided to take a late-morning walk west across the big bridge that takes you over to the mainland. It's a good long climb up that bridge, and the view from the top is terrific. Charlie thought the walk down the other side was easy, but he remembered that they had to walk up again on their way back, so slow and steady. They had done this before.

They stopped to look at the boats when they were partway up. There were several yachts that neither of them would ever want to own, even if they could afford it, because there is always someone else with a bigger yacht, and that chase is as silly as a dog going after its tail.

There were also two charter fishing boats that would make Charlie seasick. Donna figured that if they wanted fish, they'd get it at the supermarket. Nature is just too scary to deal with, and it does not care about any of us.

"Look at those two guys down there," Charlie says, pointing to two men sitting on the curb. There were two sleeping bags balled up next to them, and a shopping cart filled with stuff.

"Homeless sweet homeless," Donna says.

"Not a bad place to settle," Charlie says. "If I was going to be homeless, I'd want to be homeless in the South. I never understood the attraction of being homeless in the North, especially in New York City. It's too cold there."

"Lots of potential donors, though," Donna says.

"That's true."

"Where in Florida would you be homeless?" Donna asks.

"I don't know. Probably Key West, I suppose? It's warmest there."

"Yeah, but it's also pricey," Donna says.

"But most everyone is drunk down there. Afternoon drinking is the national sport of the Conch Republic. Affluent drunks can be generous if you tap 'em properly."

"I suppose if you have the time, you could make the walk," Donna says. "Just keep heading south."

"I'm with you. If I was homeless in New York, I'd definitely walk a few miles south each day. Every journey begins with a first step."

"Remember that homeless guy in Key West? The one with the animals?"

"That guy was the best," Charlie says.

"Yeah, he had that old dog, and draped across the dog's back was an old cat. The dog was wearing that cat like a coat. The cat looked miserable. So much for women and cats going where they want to go."

"Yeah, but how about what the cat had on its head." Charlie says.

"A friggin' mouse!" Donna laughs.

"Such indignity. Do you remember what you asked the homeless guy?" Charlie says.

"Yeah. Hey, Mister, where do you *start*?" Donna cracks up. Charlie puts his arm around her.

"And he said?"

"Beats the *shit* out of me!"

"Who says the homeless have no sense of humor?" Charlie says.

"You know what we should do?" Donna says.

"What?"

"Let's go over to the store and get those guys some wine. They look like they'll have some good stories to tell."

"You serious?"

"Absolutely. Let's go make their day."

"How will we know what they drink?" Charlie wonders.

"Let's pretend we're homeless. What do we like to drink?"

"Box wine. Like the Pope."

"Yeah, quantity beats quality. C'mon," Donna says.

They head for the supermarket. Charlie gets a big box of cab sav and another of pinot grigio.

"That should do it," Charlie says.

"We need some plastic cups," Donna says.

"You're a classy broad."

"You better believe it. Should we get snacks?"

"Snickers," Charlie says.

"Anything else?"

"How about Twinkies?" Charlie says.

"Perfect!"

They head for the candy aisle, and then the cake aisle. Charlie picks up a 12-pack of Twinkies and stares at it. Donna waits.

"You okay?" she says.

"Yeah, I'm good."

"You used to like those," she says.

"I did," he says, still staring at the box.

"What?" Donna says.

"Nothing, I'm good. Let's get going."

"Hey, guys. You up for a chat?" Charlie asks. He puts the wine boxes down. Tosses the bag of mini-Snickers to the skinnier of the two men, and the Twinkies to the other guy. "We were out walking and saw you from the bridge. Figured we'd stop by and be neighborly. This is my wife Donna. We've been staying over there for a few weeks." Charlie points over his shoulder with his thumb. "It's good to get away from the cold for a while. I'm Charlie." He offers his hand. The two guys accept it. Who doesn't like Snickers and Twinkies? Oh, and box wine.

"I'm Lou," the skinny guy says. He's the younger of the two, probably early-40s, rumpled but not too dirty.

"And I'm Andy. How you doing?" Andy looks to be about Charlie's age. He has a grey beard and a bowling-ball belly. He also has a Mets baseball cap. Both guys look at the box wine.

"That for us?" Andy asks.

"That's for all of us," Donna says.

"Cool."

"You a Mets fan, Andy?" Charlie asks.

"Long as I can remember," Andy says. "I was born up there I think."

"How long you been down here?"

"I don't know. What do you think, Lou? How long we here?"

"I guess since summer. It was warmer then."

"Where were you guys before?" Donna asks.

"Here and there," Andy says. "We sort of followed the weather."

"Makes sense," Charlie says. "We were talking about that when we went for the wine." He points across the water to the supermarket. "I said to Donna, if I didn't have a place to stay and I was in New York, I'd definitely start walking south. Sure beats sitting on the sidewalk in Manhattan."

"Yeah, we've both done that," Lou says. "It got tough up there. They force you into the shelter when the temperature goes below freezing. It's not safe in those shelters. Somebody will knock you on the head when you're sleeping and steal all your stuff."

"Better here for you?" Charlie asks.

"Oh, yeah. It's peaceful here. Live and let live."

"That's the way to be," Donna says. "And to sort of quote Billy Joel, 'Box of red? Box of white?'" She holds them up. "What's your pleasure, gents?" Charlie passes around the Solo cups.

"You ever think about heading for Key West?" Charlie asks. "It's warmer there."

"The tourists are worse than the homeless down there," Andy says. "Those people are crazy. We know guys who tried it and came back up here. More civilized here."

"You reporters or something?" Lou asks.

"Nah," Charlie says. "We're retired. We just like to chat and drink wine in the afternoon."

"Who doesn't?" Lou says, raising his Solo cup.

"Don't you have anyone over there to chat with?" Andy asks, pointing to where Charlie said they were staying.

"Sure we do," Charlie says, "But if we stayed over there, we'd miss chatting with you gentlemen."

"Well, this is certainly a first," Andy says to Lou.

"You ain't kidding."

Drinks poured all around. Charlie raises his Solo cup. "Sláinte, lads. To your health."

"And to yours, sir," Andy says.

"Indeed," Lou says.

Charlie and Donna sit on the curb and wait for the stories to come. "Anyone gonna bother us here?" Charlie asks.

"Not if we're quiet and minding our own business," Andy says. He passes the mini-Snickers bag to Donna.

"Thanks," she says. Peels a wrapper.

"What did you have for breakfast?" Charlie asks.

"Box wine and mini-Snickers," Lou laughs. "Just now."

"Me, too," Andy adds. "And Twinkies."

"Breakfast of champions!" Charlie says.

"Yeah, we were just talking about what we should do about some food when you two showed up," Lou says. "It's an inertia thing, you know. The longer you sit in one place, the easier it gets to stay in that same place."

"It's sort of like having a job," Charlie says. "It's also how trees grow."

"Yeah, just like that."

"Where do you usually eat?" Donna asks.

"We'll go over to the Subway at the end of the day sometimes. They toss stuff out, but if we're there, they'll share it with us. Good people over there. But sometimes we're sleeping by then so we don't get to eat at all."

Donna fills the glasses. "You guys have family?" she asks.

"Sure," Andy says. "We both do. At least I think we still do. We haven't seen them for years."

"Why did you leave?" Charlie asks.

Andy and Lou look at each other. "You go first," Lou says.

"For me," Andy says, "it was the drink." He holds up his Solo cup. "I had a wife, no kids, and an okay job, but I loved the sports on the TV and you know how it goes when you're into a game and you keep sipping. She was a teetotaler and she wanted me to stop, but it was too much a part of my life. I love the games. They make me feel young again. I just couldn't stop the sipping. She got pissed off enough one day and walked out. I let her go. Stupidest thing I ever did in my whole life, letting her go. I should have listened. But you know how it is; you get caught up in the game. It owns you. And then there's the sipping. She never came back. I kept watching the sports, and with no one to tell me to stop, I kept at the sipping. I probably wouldn't have listened to anyone anyway. I sipped so much I forget to go to work, so they just let me go. That was depressing, so I sipped some more. There was no money coming in, so I couldn't pay the rent. The landlord threw me out, and there I was, out on the street. I met Lou and we've been moving around together ever since. We get along fine."

Donna poured more wine. "How about you, Lou?"

"Drugs. I had a great office job. Never married. No kids. The gang would all go out after work for drinks. One night, this hot gal I worked with brought out some cocaine. She talked me into taking a hit. Said it was great, which it was. Makes you feel bulletproof. And she was so hot, I just couldn't say no. One hit and that was it. I have an addictive personality. I went from coke to crack real fast, and that shit owns your soul. I lost everything I had. Nobody wanted anything to do with me."

"You hurt anyone?" Donna asks.

"Only myself."

"Still doing drugs?" Donna asks.

"No more. I drink now when I can get it. It's safer." He laughs. "Yeah, *safer*."

"You have a nice laugh, Lou," Donna says.

"So do you, lady."

"So when do you two head home?" Andy asks.

"In two days," Charlie says. "If you listen closely, you'll hear us screaming."

"Too bad you can't stay," Andy says. "Life's good here under the bridge."

"Always room for two more, eh?" Charlie says.

"If you're good people, yeah," Andy says.

"You think you'll ever go back inside?" Charlie asks.

"I don't know, Charlie. It's not that bad," Andy says. "I mean it's uncomfortable at times, but down here, if you mind your own business, and you don't look for trouble, it's not a bad life. Sometimes, we pretend we're like the Indians who used to live here. It's an easy life. We drink in the afternoon and do a bit of dumpster diving at night. We smoke when we can get 'em. We talk a lot. Share stories. It's not a bad life."

"Sounds like retirement," Charlie says.

"Yeah, just like retirement," Lou says. "And look at that view." He points at the boats on the water. "Imagine what it would cost to have a house here. We get the same view for free. And you know the funny thing about this life? People who are not in it think we're all nuts, but that's not always the case. Sure, some of the homeless *are* nuts, but then some of the people with houses are nuts, too. Look at Phil Spector. Rich and completely nuts, right?" Everyone nods.

"I met a woman who was homeless," Andy says. "This was when I was living in the shelter for a few days. She had been a college professor. Never married and she had no living relatives. This gal has a PhD. Imagine that?"

"How did she wind up in the shelter?" Charlie asks.

"She got diabetes. I don't know if it was her lifestyle or something from her family, but it doesn't really matter. She winds up losing her legs because of that lousy disease. Her job wasn't guaranteed at the college, so she loses her job because she can't get to work. Not the school's fault, right? Shit happens. But no job means no money coming in, so no more apartment, and just like that, she's in the shelter with rest of us lost souls."

"That's horrible," Donna says.

"Yeah, she fell right through the cracks, and there are a lot of cracks out there. But listen to this. I'm talking to her one day. She was very smart. Me, not so much. She'd listen to classical music on this little radio she had, and she'd read books I couldn't even pick up. One day, she asks me what I think is the difference between us and the rest of America. At first I didn't get it, but she says, 'You know, the average people with the ordinary houses, the people with the jobs. What's the difference between us and them?' I say I don't know. She tells me the only difference between us and them is about five paychecks and a credit card. That's it. She says that's how close most Americans are to the shelters, or to the underside of a bridge. I've been thinking about that for years. I think she was right. And we're not all nuts, Charlie; we just fell through the cracks. But what can you do? It is what it is. We accept that, Lou and me."

They drank more wine, and swapped more stories, and pissed away the afternoon and Charlie took all of this to heart. When it was time to part, Donna rose and handed each of the men twenty bucks.

"For breakfast," she said.

"Or for more wine," Charlie suggested.

"Or for more Snickers and Twinkies," Donna laughed.

When they had gone, Andy and Lou looked at each other. There was still wine in the boxes and mini-Snickers in the bag, and a few Twinkies.

"Angels," Lou said. "Sent from heaven."

"Probably," Andy agreed.

"We using these two twenties for food?"

"Fuck that," Lou said, and they both laughed.

Life is good.

38

The day before they have to head home, Donna and Charlie go back to drink in the afternoon with Clare.

"I'll miss you two maniacs," Clare says as she sets down their wine. Cab sav for Charlie, pinot grigio for Donna, as always

"We'll miss you, too, Saint Clare," Charlie says. "What will we do with our afternoons now?"

"Probably drink," Clare says.

"It's two o'clock somewhere," Charlie laughs.

Donna shakes her head, laughs. "But it won't be the same without you, Clare," she says.

"Aww, you're so nice, Donna."

"We drank with the homeless yesterday," Charlie said.

"What?"

"Andy and Lou. They live under the big bridge. Nice guys."

Clare stands there with her mouth open, her eyes wide. It's her WTF? face. She turns to Donna. "He's bullshitting, right?"

"Nope, I was with him all the way. In fact, it was my idea. We went to the supermarket, got a couple boxes of wine, a bag of mini-Snickers, and some Twinkies. We had quite a party."

"Why?"

"Stories," Charlie says.

"Yep, good ones," Donna adds. "And plenty of food for thought."

"What did they have to tell you?"

"It's a secret," Charlie says. "We promised not to tell."

"Please?"

Charlie looks at Donna, who shrugs. "What the hell. Tell her."

"Well, okay then." He looks around to make sure no one else can hear. "They're not really homeless," he whispers. "Those two guys? It's all an act. They're retired and living on a fixed income, just like us. Thing is, their income isn't that much, so they have to keep the rent low. They live together to keep it even lower. They share all expenses."

"But where is their house?" Clare asks.

"It's under the bridge," Charlie says.

"There's a house under the bridge?" Clare asks.

"Well, not a house with walls, but it's where they live. It's an alternative lifestyle. Very modern, and yet timeless. Great ventilation."

"We call that homeless," Clare says.

"Well, you *could* put it that way, sure, but consider all the people who are living in those tiny houses. There are shows on TV about them. Seen 'em?"

"Yes."

"Okay, so if you're living in a house that's, say, four-hundred square feet, or maybe even smaller, how much of a leap is it to just live under a bridge? Trolls have been doing it for ages."

"And you save the cost of the tiny house," Donna says. "Those things can get pretty pricey. What you save on the tiny house you can spend on the booze."

"I never thought about it that way," Clare says.

"All sorts of ways to think about things," Charlie says.

"But what do they do about bathing?" Clare asks.

"The showers by the beach," Charlie says. "They're free."

"But you can't get naked under those."

"You can if you stay up late enough, and if you're quick. And there's always the ocean. What did the Indians do?"

"Okay, but what about food? Where do they cook?"

"Leftovers from Subway," Charlie says.

"And the dumpsters," Donna adds. "Lots of good food gets tossed around here, and it's all free for the taking."

"Bathrooms?" Clare says.

"Public toilets by the beach," Charlie says.

"And a lot of people use the restrooms here at the bar. All those joggers who go by the back door. The restrooms are right there. You're aware that they use them, aren't you?"

"Sure. It's good for business. Let's them see the place. A lot of them stop by later on. You two have all this figured out, don't you?" Clare says.

"We're looking into it," Charlie says. "That way, we can see more of you. We won't have any rent, which means there will be more money for the afternoon drinking. We have to support our local bartender, right? What do you think?"

"I'm warming to the idea," Clare says.

"We have an appointment with an unreal-estate agent later on today," Charlie says. "She works for the Underbridge Agency. She gets a commission on every sale of every house without walls."

"But it doesn't cost anything to live under the bridge," Clare says.

"Yes, that's why her commission is 100 percent. It's sort of like free pie."

Clare rolls her eyes. She's heard the free-pie story. "I really am going to miss you two. You always make me smile."

"Hold that thought," Charlie says and slides off his stool.

"Flush once for me, too, hon," Donna says.

"Will do."

"He's quite a guy," Clare says.

"He is, and this trip has been so good for him. He needed to do some fixing after all that took place on his job.

He's not good with big changes, and that's what was going on. It was a major culture shift, and those people hurt him. You had just the right tools to help him, Clare. So did the guys under the bridge. Thanks for being there. Thanks for being *you*."

"My joy, Donna," Clare says, hands folded over her heart.

"May I ask you something?" Donna says.

"Sure."

"What's your daughter's name?"

Clare's eyes go wide. "How do you know I have a daughter?"

"I just do. Little tells. I get like that. You *do* have a daughter, don't you?"

"Well, yes, I do."

"What's her name?"

"Chara."

"That's a beautiful name," Donna says.

"It means joy."

"I love that. How old is she?"

"She's ten," Clare says.

"That's a fun age. Show me a picture."

Clare gets her iPhone from its spot by the cash register and shows Donna a picture of the two of them together.

"She's lovely," Donna says.

"She has Down syndrome," Clare says.

"I can see that. It means she has found the Fountain of Youth. I wish we had time to meet her."

"Would you like to?"

"You bet we would," Donna says. "She's a part of you."

"Okay, you and Charlie will come to my place for dinner tonight. I get off in an hour. You know that. You can come as you are; we'll have fun."

"Do you live close by? Funny I never asked."

"Not far. We have a house."

"Are you married, Clare? That's another thing I never asked you."

"Nope. Single mom. And dad, too, I suppose. No man in my life right now."

"I can't believe I never asked you about that, and so many other things. I've been sitting here talking for weeks, and mostly about myself and nonsense. You're such a good listener, Clare. I'm sorry I didn't ask more about your personal life. I guess I didn't want to pry, or seem nosey."

"That's okay, Donna. I'd rather learn about others than talk about myself anyway. It's my nature. I already know about myself. But thanks."

"Thank *you*, but now I have to be nosey. How the heck can you afford a house around here on a bartender's salary?" Donna asks.

"Oh, I own this place. I probably never mentioned that to you, did I?"

"This place? You mean your house?"

"Well, I own my house, yes, but I mean the bar. *This* bar. I own it." Sweet smile.

"Holy shit!"

Charlie comes back from the Men's. "Did I miss anything?"

"Uh, *yeah!*" Donna says.

Clare smiles. "Everything come out okay, Charlie?"

"'Twas the proper color and the stream was strong. All's well."

"TMI," Donna says.

"Don't tell him," Clare says to Donna.

"Your secret's safe with me, child."

"Don't tell me what?" Charlie asks.

"I'll tell you later. It's a story," Clare says. "A good one. And there's someone I want you to meet. You're coming to my house for dinner. You can take a cab. It will keep you out of the news, but I'm not done with you here yet." She fills their glasses.

"Well, that's certainly a fine way to end our sweet month on your small island," Charlie says.

"'Tis." Clare says.

39

Clare left a bit early to get Chara. A half-hour later, Charlie and Donna were in the cab.

"So what's the secret?" Charlie asks.

"You won't get it out of me," Donna says.

The house was near the water, about a half-mile from the bar. They had walked by it every morning for the past month. It was a ranch house, very well maintained, all white, with bougainvillea around the front door. It also had a pink flamingo mailbox.

"This is it? We could have walked here," Charlie says.

"She's watching out for us. We've had a few wines. That's why she got us the cab."

"How can she afford this place?" Charlie says.

"Wait."

Charlie rings the bell. Chara answers the door. She is short, like her mother, but stocky. "Hello!" Her tongue protrudes a bit, giving her voice a slurpy sound. "Mommy says you're *nice!*" Chara giggles and runs to Clare. She hugs her mother and gets shy.

"Nice job, honey," Clare says, hugging her back. "She asked to do that. I've been telling her about you two for weeks."

Charlie is delightfully dumbfounded. "Who is this?" he asks.

"This is Chara," Clare says. "And you're right, Charlie. There's nothing more precious than a daughter."

"*Daughter!*" Chara says. She has a round face, slightly slanted, almond-shaped, intensely blue eyes, brown hair in a bowl cut, and a smile that just won't quit. She laughs. "*Hello!*"

Donna and Charlie take two steps and join the hug.

"Mommy *likes* you," Chara says.

"And we like Mommy," Charlie says. "And you!"

Chara laughs. "Likes me!" Hugs.

"Let's sit," Clare says, leading them into the living room. Charlie takes it all in. Cozy couch, grandma blankets, beach-scene pictures on Easter-green walls, flowers in a vase, candle scent in the air, jars of seashells everywhere, light beige rug to tickle bare feet, stocked bookshelf, soft jazz playing. No TV.

Clare brings them wine. "What would you like for dinner? The bar is going to deliver."

"How did you arrange that?" Charlie asks.

"It was easy. I own the joint, Charlie."

"Now who's the bullshitter?" Charlie says.

"She's telling the truth," Donna says. "That's the other part of the surprise."

Again, Charlie is delightfully dumbfounded.

"Story to follow, Charlie," Clare says. "But first, if you were being executed, what would you want for your last meal? Anything at all, as long as it's on the bar's menu."

Chara is looking at Charlie, waiting for his answer. Sweetest smile in the world.

"I'll have what she's having," he says and smiles. Chara claps her hands and laughs.

"Pizza it is!" Clare says, and texts their order to the bar.

"Okay," Charlie says after more wine. "Story, please."

"Which one?" Clare asks.

"Chara first."

"Well, she was born just before Christmas, Charlie." Clare smiles, raises her thin eyebrows. "Remember? Kiss me; I'm Irish?"

"Gosh, I'm sorry I ever said that to you at the bar," Charlie says, now embarrassed.

"I'm not. You were spot-on in your observation, as you usually are."

"No offense," Charlie says.

"No regrets," Clare answers, and smiles.

"Gosh."

"No, really, Charlie. It's life. Want the story? I know you do."

"I do. I care about you, Clare."

"And I care about you, my friend."

"Okay, so he was a nice Irish boy. Loved me to the moon and back, until it counted. Then he got scared and took off. He always said he had the key to the highway. You know that Eric Clapton song? Well, I never believed him. I should have.

"But he missed something wonderful here, Charlie. I can't fix that." Clare hugs Chara, who giggles and hugs back. "His loss."

"Do you ever hear from him?"

"Not a word," Clare says. "And that's fine with me. He's a boy, and I'm done with boys."

"Wise beyond her years," Donna says.

"Thanks, Donna. Sometimes, people leave us for a reason, but we don't know what that reason is at the time. Everything happens for a reason. Everything. That is what I've learned."

Soft jazz. No words.

And then Clare smiles at Charlie.

"And, my dear friend, I'm not twenty-two anymore, but I love you for thinking that I am, and for saying that again and again."

"And I love you for being you, Clare. You brighten our days."

"And you mine. Glasses up!"

"Tell us about the bar," Donna says. "How did that happen?"

"Fate, I guess," Clare says. "It starts with me staying home in our apartment on the day that my mother and father, my friend, Jesus, and old Dermot, one of the best men I have ever known, got gunned down by a drugged-up kid."

"Oh, my god. Where?" Donna asks.

"Woodside, Queens. Where I grew up."

"That's close to where we live," Charlie says.

"I know."

She tells them the story. No tears, just acceptance. She brings them though the joy and the horror of those days, stringing events together like the words of a poem she has lived.

"Horrible," Charlie says.

"Not all of it, Charlie. There was also great love there to go with the great sorrow, but if events hadn't played out as they did, Chara never would have been born, and I never would have been here to meet you two. Everything happens for a reason."

Charlie thinks of his prayer.

Thank you, Lord, for all that you've given me by your grace and generosity.

Thank you for all that you've taken away from me through your wisdom, for you know what's best for me. Always.

Thank you for all that remains, for it is far more than enough.

Amen.

"Yes," he says. "I get that."

The pizza arrives.

"Dermot Muldoon was the name of the man who owned the bar and the apartment building the bar was in. He was an old Irish bachelor. First generation in America and no living relatives anywhere. He loved my parents and me, and he treated us like family. As I said, I literally grew up in a bar.

"I left soon after the murders. I just had to get out of New York and away from all that had happened. I was twenty-two years old then, Charlie, and I had no one, and I had very little money left after the funerals. I got on a bus and headed here. I don't know why. I guess it was because of the weather. I figured that if I was going to be on the streets I might as well be warm.

"But I didn't have to live on the streets. I just walked into the bar one day and asked for a job. Mack McBride, the owner, asked me if I had any experience."

"As if," Charlie says.

"Yeah, I showed him."

Chara laughs. "Showed him!"

"She's adorable," Donna says. They all smile at the little girl with the round face and the intense blue eyes.

"Anyway, those were the lonely times. I had a furnished room, and was alone with my thoughts when I wasn't working. That's when I fell under the spell of the sweet-talking Irish boy, but no regrets. If not for him, such as he was, I would not have this one." She hugs Chara.

"This one!" Chara says.

"How did you buy the bar?" Charlie asks.

"When I left New York, I didn't know that my parents were Dermot's heirs. He had no one else in the world, so he put them in his will. They would have owned the bar and the building the bar was in, as well as all of Dermot's other assets, which were considerable. I don't think my parents knew they were his heirs. Dermot loved surprises."

"So how did they find you?" Donna asks.

"The lawyer who held the will hired an investigator to find me. It took a while, but he did. Next thing you know, I'm a rich lady.

"Mack, the old fellow who owned the bar was looking to get out of the business and take it easy for a change. I knew that, so I made him an offer. He accepted, and that's the story."

"And you like working there," Donna says.

"I love working there," Clare says. "It's so filled with life."

"It is."

"How did you manage to survive all of that tragedy, all that terrible sadness?" Charlie asks.

"I just accepted it, Charlie. I couldn't change anything, so I accepted it. Do you know the Aesop fable about the oak tree and the reed? My Ma and my Da told it to me many times when I was growing up."

"Not sure. Tell me."

"There's a big oak tree near a stream and a small reed takes root at its base. The tree laughs at the reed because the reed's roots are so shallow. The tree tells the reed that it would be so easy for someone to come along and just pluck it from the ground. The tree laughs at the reed's seeming weakness.

"But then a hurricane arrives and uproots the tree. Knocks it right down. Dead. But during the fury of the storm, the reed just bends against the wind and survives. When the storm passes, the little reed stands tall again and continues to grow. It survives because it's able to bend with the circumstances and accept whatever comes at it. It knows how to let go just let it be, whatever it is."

"I see," says Charlie.

"The tree died because it wasn't capable of bending, Charlie. It was trying to change nature, but nature doesn't change. I suppose the moral of the tale is that it is better to yield when it is folly to resist."

"The simple grace of acceptance," Charlie says. "I used to know more about that. I lost track of it in recent years."

"Yes, what you can't fix, just accept and move on. Live life as best you can with what you've got."

"Yes," Charlie says.

Clare looks at Donna? Tilts her head. Christmas-morning eyes.

"Yes," Donna finally says. "Everything happens for a reason. Even the death of those we love so deeply."

"Yes," Clare says.

"Donna?" Chara says, breaking the spell. "Donna, *Donna?*"

"Yes, darling."

"On the beach, you get sand in your *legpits.*" She points to the back of Donna's bare knees. Laughs.

"Yes, I do, my love. I always brush my legpits *and* my armpits." She pantomimes.

"I brush too!" Chara says, touching Donna in the same places. It tickles. They both laugh.

"You're pretty!" Chara says.

"You're perfect," Donna says. "*Perfect.*"

Clare is watching and smiling. "Well done, Clare," Donna says. "Well done all around."

Clare raises her glass. "Thanks."

"You're welcome. I don't know how you do all of this alone."

Clare leans back. Sips her wine. "When I was growing up I used to love to watch the pigeons. People said they were dirty, that they were rats with wings, but I loved the sounds they made and the way they walked with that head bob of theirs." She imitates this, which, of course, is adorable.

"They are such messy birds," Charlie says.

"Well, yes, if you call them pigeons they are. But their proper name is rock dove. Did you know that? Isn't that a lovely name? Rock dove?"

"I didn't know," Charlie says. Donna shakes her head.

"Don't they sound better now?" Clare asks

"Better, but not cleaner," Charlie laughs.

"Have you watched them fly, Charlie?" Clare asks. "They fly together, like geese, but not in a chevron; they fly in a bunch, like grey skyrocket explosions, waltzing. They move in gorgeous ovals, this way and then that way. One two three. One two three. A waltz. And they always return to the same place. It's like they're conducting a symphony with their bodies, one only they can hear."

"I never noticed that," Donna says.

"Oh, they all do it," Clare says. "They do it when they're scared, but it's still so lovely. And where we lived, they would all come to land on this one stretch of electric line. They'd sit next to one another, like beads on a rosary. My father told me that's how they pray; that if I listened carefully I could hear all those Hail Marys and Our Fathers in the cooing. He said they were praying for a safe place."

"That's a beautiful thought," Charlie says.

"My father saw things other people missed. He had a poet's soul."

"You must miss him so much," Donna says. "Him and your mother and the others."

"I do, but they are still with me. They always will be with me." She smiles.

Charlie looks at Donna. Looks.

Looks.

"Yes," Donna says.

"There was a fall when the leaves had gone and the pigeons were waltzing in the sky," Clare says. "When they came to light on the wire, one sat on another wire below where the rest were saying the rosary. He was the loan pigeon. He was different. He had more white than grey; the only one that was like that. The only one that was different. My father told me to watch closely as they all flew, because they always flew together, but the white pigeon flew alone. He wasn't allowed in. They'd bump him out. So he flew the exact same patterns as the group, but in another part of the sky. Alone. And he perched alone. And my father said that there are people like that. People who can be near the group, but who will always be somewhat different and not accepted by the group. They'll always be alone, even in a crowd. He told me that there is nothing sadder than that. To be truly alone."

Quiet.

Quiet.

"We're never *really* alone, are we?" Donna asks.

"Not if we love," Clare says.

"Or *once* loved."

"Yes."

Quiet.

"Love!" Chara shouts, claps, breaks the spell and they all laugh.

"Do you think you'll work again when you get back?" Clare asks.

"I don't know," Donna says. "I'm getting used to this retirement thing. We'll see."

"It was a tough job you had, wasn't it?"

"It was," Donna says. "And I don't think I could do that again. It was brutal, working for that law firm. Most of the clients I spoke to were poor and uneducated. They were all Southern folk in dire straits. They felt they were being taken for a ride. I had to assuage their fears and talk them through the convoluted process from filing their claim against the company to getting the check in hand. We're talking years for the whole process to play out."

"That's rough. It was a medical situation, right?"

"Yes."

"Tell me about some of the people."

Donna smiles. "Gosh, there were so many, and most of them were wonderful. The first time I spoke with Alvis, I couldn't understand a word of his frustrated rant. My brain struggled to translate what sounded like a foreign language. The harder I tried to parse out a word, the more tangled it all seemed. Finally, seeing no alternative, I leaned back in my chair to wait out his rant. I thought when he finally wound down, I would say, Uh, huh, and write him a letter explaining the current state of his case, and hope for the best. But as I sat there, Alvis' words tumbled around and around and bumped into one another until they became a melody, and unbelievably I could finally hear the words, the sentences, his meaning. I think he was as shocked as I was when I began to respond to what he was saying. We both laughed. He said his mamma had been Louisiana Creole and that she could see into people's hearts and that she had passed on that gift to him. He said I didn't have to put any stock into any of that, but he would call me Angel just the same. Angel. Any time I'd come into work to find a note in my email that let me know an unintelligible man with an Alabama area code called, I'd pick up the phone and return Alvis' call."

"I had a tough time understanding a lot of the people when I first got down here," Clare said. "Fortunately, many of them are New Yorkers, and that helped."

Donna smiled and said, "Often, when I'd call a client and announce who I was, I'd get, 'Suga', I know who you are the first word that pops out of your mouth. I don't have any other Yankees ringing me up.'"

"You slide in and out of the Irish thing yourself," Charlie says, laughing. "I love it when you say 'tis."

"Do I do that?" Clare laughs. "Must be me Ma and Da talking through me." She raises her glass to heaven. "Tell me more Donna. I love your stories. You tell about people *so* well."

"Tell more, Donna!" Chara giggles. "I like the peoples!"

"Okay, I will, darling. I'll tell about Mellon. He is very sweet and gentle, just like you."

"Mellon is a *nice* name!"

"It is," Donna says.

"'Tis," Clare says with a wink.

"Well, Mellon would share stories with me about the plays that he was in," Donna continues. "These were all townie plays. He said a while back, the director had noticed him at every performance, absently mouthing the actor's parts with such joy. So he asked Mellon to audition. That means to try, Chara. Mellon was so happy every time he told me about his good luck at being chosen for big parts to play. Whenever I had to leave Mellon a voicemail, he would return my call with sincere apologies and explain that he was over helping his lady friend with her car, her faucet, her heating, all sorts of stuff. Or he was picking up the neighbor kids from school, because they had a half day and their mother couldn't get off from her job at the Piggly Wiggly to fetch them."

"Piggly Wiggly!" Chara laughs.

"Yes, that's a nice name, too. And, of course, he would've called me as soon as he'd gotten home, but he had to fix them some lunch. Mellon was always doing for his neighbors, and acting like he was blessed to be allowed to serve them. When Thanksgiving rolled around, I asked Mellon who he'd spent it with, and he said he just made himself some ham and some sweet potatoes. When I asked about his 'lady friend,' he replied pleasantly that she had dinner with her kids and they hadn't invited him. It didn't seem to cross his mind that any of all those neighbors he was always helping might've invited him for holiday dinner."

"That's so sad," Clare says.

"Yes, but he is a pure spirit," Donna says. "He gives without expecting anything in return."

Charlie is looking at the pool of wine in his glass, remembering something. Clare glances at him but he doesn't look up. "Tell more," Clare says.

"This is the best one," Donna says. "Her name is Rose. She called me as a last ditch effort to come up with money she needed to pay off a lien on her home from a loan one of her sons had secured for himself and defaulted on. She needed to pay off the lien and sell her home so she could move 'up the road into the old folks' home' because she felt she wouldn't be able manage things on her own much longer. Rose had pretty much come to believe that the lawsuit was a hoax, and that the joke was on her. After her call, I looked into it, and the court appointed middle-meddlers had indeed dropped the ball on her payment two years before. It was going nowhere."

"Horrible," Clare says.

"For sure," Donna says. "But on that first phone call with Rose, once she realized that I was actually going to look into this for her, she and her 'gorgeous poodle' - It's not often they come in brown and white, you know! she tells me – settled onto her sofa for a nice long chat about collards her neighbor had just given her, and why on earth was I calling them collard *greens*. Of course they are *greens*. What else would collards be! And the fact that she could drive to the prettiest beach from her house if she wanted in just two hours. She didn't happen to want to; because, well, it took two hours, what with traffic what it was these days and all. But she could if she wanted to, and her late husband who looked like Clark Gable - honestly, it was such a pain when they had to go to the next town over where no one knew them. The women would swoon and act downright ridiculous, certain they were in the presence of Hollywood royalty."

"But Rose was no slouch herself," Donna continued. "She told me on that first call, 'Honey, I'm nigh 80 years old, but I look GOOOOD! I pee myself sometimes. But I look GOOOOD!'

"From that first call forward, Rose would call me every other week to chat. I would call Rose anytime I'd had an especially bad day, to get what I came to call a Rose-ism to brighten my day and restore my faith in humanity. She never disappointed." Donna turns to Charlie. "She's my Thomas Hardy, Charlie. I never told you that. I miss her."

Charlie peeks up from out of his thoughts and his wine, his eyes bright. He smiles. "Yes."

"What happened with that great lady?" Clare asks. Chara leans forward, waiting.

"Rose finally ended up getting her settlement check," Donna says. "She called me a couple weeks later. She felt she needed to confess to me that she had used a chunk of the money for something other than her intended goal of resettling in the old folks' home. Turns out that as soon as Rose's family got word of her settlement money, they all came out of the woodwork with their hands out. Well, that pissed her off real good, and she handled it in classic-Rose style. She drove herself down to the car lot and bought herself 'a brand spankin' new, sassy, silver Lincoln with everthin' on it, everthin' 'ceptin' a commode!" Donna says in Rose's voice.

"And that was probably the one thing dear Rose could've used in a car," Charlie says.

Laughter all around and one more glass for the road.

"So we'll never really know what happened next, will we?" Clare says.

"Some stories have no ending," Donna says.

"So then that's it," Clare says.

"Dathsit," Donna says.

Clare smiles, "There's such beauty in people."

"Some people," Donna says.

And Charlie smiles.

"People!" Chara laughs.

"What will you do when you go home?" Clare says.

"I don't know yet," Donna says, thinking about home. "Something."

40

"I like your friends," Chara says.

Clare tucks the blanket under her chin. "They're your friends, too, sweetie."

"Donna is *pretty*. She tells good stories!"

"She is, and she does, and Charlie is handsome."

"Yes!" Chara laughs.

"Did you enjoy the pizza?"

"Yes!"

"Do you want me to tell you a story tonight?"

"Yes, please!"

"Which story?" Clare asks.

"About the nice man who loved you."

"Okay, I like that one."

"Me too!"

Clare sits on the edge of Chara's bed and smoothes the blanket, and in a voice as soft as summer dawn she begins a story told many times.

"When I was born, I was tiny, so tiny that I could fit into a teacup," Clare says as Chara begins to giggle.

"Teacup!" Chara says.

"It's true!" Clare laughs. "My Ma said that was why I was so sweet, because people put sugar into teacups."

"And sometimes milk," Chara says.

"Yes. And sometimes lemon, but lemon makes you make this face," Clare scrunches her face and Chara does the same. They both laugh and hug each other.

"So, there I was, sleeping in a teacup all day long because I was a babe and that's what babes do. They sleep all day long. It's true!"

"Tell about the color of the teacup."

"Oh, it was blue like your eyes and white like your teeth and beautiful, just like you, the most delicate teacup in the whole world. It was lovely, just like you. And it had a tiny handle, made for tiny fingers, just like yours." Clare reaches for Chara's fingers.

Chara is expecting this part, longing for it, giggling. Clare counts each of her daughter's fingers. "One, two, three. Yes, these are *lovely* fingers. Four, five. Oh!" Eyes wide, grabs for the other hand. Sweet, shared laughter. "Six, seven, eight, nine, ten!" Chara still laughing. "Yes!" Clare tickles her with her other hand. So much beautiful laughter. "*Any* of these lovely fingers would be *just* right for my teacup crib. You could rock me back and forth and help me to sleep."

"Mommy?"

"Yes, my love?"

"I like to sleep."

"I know you do, darling."

"Tell about the man who loved you," Chara says.

"Oh, he loved me so, the man. His name was Dermot and he was as old as the big trees in our backyard, as old as the Indians who used to live in our bar a long, long time ago. They drank milkshakes!"

"*Chocolate* milkshakes!"

"Yes, and my Ma and my Da worked for him, that sweet old man, and he was like a granda to me. Loved me to the moon and back, and again and again. He owned a bar, just like the one we own, but not as large, and it was in a big city that got cold in the winter. We'd have to bundle up with lots of clothes when we went outside."

"And there was snow!"

"Yes, lots of delicious snow. I would eat it and it made my tongue happy."

"I like that."

"Yes, it was lovely, but oh so cold. It made me giggle."

"Tell about your other bed," Chara says, knowing the story, and loving it even more because she did know it.

"That's the best part, Chara. When I grew too big to fit into the wee teacup, my Ma and my Da put me into a shoebox to sleep. They lined it with cotton and used a washcloth for my blanket. and a pair of old stinky socks for my pillow. I slept so soundly on those socks, but they were soooo smelly." Clare holds her nose. Chara holds her nose and laughs.

"I like that part, Mommy."

"Me, too!"

"Where did the shoebox come from?" Chara asks, knowing the answer.

"Why it was from old Dermot, the man who was like my Granda. He saved it from when he was a little boy, when he got his first pair of new shoes. He was so excited about those shoes, and who wouldn't be? They were his very first pair of new shoes. Before that, all his shoes had holes in them and his feet were always cold from the snow in the winter.

"He saved that box for years and years and years, and when I outgrew the teacup and needed a wee crib, he made one for me from that old shoebox that he had saved for so very long. He knew that the old shoebox would always keep me warm. Oh, he loved me so."

"And then what happened?"

"I ate all my vegetables and I grew even bigger. I grew and I grew, and I needed a bigger bed, and I went to school, just like you do."

"So what did he do?"

"Oh, Dermot built me a crib from love and hope. He shined up all the pretty love and hope parts, and held them together with strings of caring, and turned them all into a lovely crib that shined like the sun and the stars and the full moon. It held me and filled me with pure light. It was the sweetest bed ever made, my love. He placed it near the back of the bar, in the same place where I would later sit with my schoolbooks and learn how to be smart and strong, just like you. And in that bed I always had sweet dreams. I would dream of *you*."

"I like this part!"

"And I love to tell this part because each day, they would set me in my wee crib made of love and hope, and held together by strings of caring, and all the men and all the woman who visited the bar for a drink and a chat would stop by to talk to me and to coo over me, and to tell me stories in their sweet, soft voices. Oh, endless stories. They told me about how some day you would come to make my life even sweeter. And here you are!"

Clare touches her daughter's face and smiles. Chara takes her hand. Kisses it. Giggles.

"And that is how I learned about The Chat, my love. It is the best thing in the world, except for you."

"And what happened to everybody? Tell that. I like that part."

"Oh, one day, God reached down and carried them all to heaven, where there is always good weather and nothing but love and pure light and grand times. God has such big, lovely and gentle hands, and they hold the whole world, and all at the same time.

"But when he really, really loves someone, he reaches down for a hug, and then that person goes to heaven with Him, no matter how young or old they are, and that's where they all are now, my Ma and my Da and my Granda Dermot, and my friend Jesus. They smile down on us every day, and if we ever get sad, we just have to look up and tell them that we love them, and that we need their love, and their help, and their prayers. It works every time, Chara. Every time. It does. They answer. I promise. They always do." She bends and kisses her daughter on the forehead.

"You need only to ask for help."

"Does Charlie help?"

"Yes, he does, my love. And we help him, too."

"Why does Charlie need help, Mommy?"

"Oh, Charlie carries a sadness that most people can't see because it hides deep in his heart."

"Why is Charlie sad?"

"Because he is afraid."

"Why is he afraid?"

"Because he has seen much of life, and the things he loves best have changed. He can't catch up with it all. It all goes by too fast for him. You know how that is, when you can't catch up, and the whole world seems to move by you, and you don't understand it? It's all so fast. It makes your head hurt."

"It makes me sad," Chara says.

"I know it does, darling, and Charlie is like you in that way. He is not always sad, but many times he is, and when he is, he is very, *very* sad, even though he's smiling, even though he's laughing. And he's not sure why he's sad. He doesn't know what to do."

"Is that why he talks to you, Mommy?"

"Yes, it is."

"Can you fix him?"

"No, I can't fix him, dear. He must fix himself. Everyone must fix themselves. But I can help him find the tools he needs."

"Tools!"

"Love, my dear. Love as pure as sunshine, and as giggly as green grass in the summertime. And slower times. Those are the proper tools that Charlie needs right now. Love and slower times."

"Is Charlie a Granda?"

"Yes and a very good one. That's one of the reasons why I love him so. My Granda Dermot taught me about The Chat, and Charlie also taught me about The Chat. They are both good men, and they are in both heaven with God, and on earth with us. They are two sides of a scale, Chara, and I am their fulcrum. That's a big word. Fulcrum. It means balance, like when I stand on my tiptoes to reach the glasses above the bar." Clare raises her hands high. Smiles at her daughter.

"Full *crumb*!"

"Yes, dear, like crumb buns. Yummy!" Clare laughs.

"Can I help fix Charlie, Mommy?"

"Yes, I believe that you will."

"I love you, Mommy."

"And I love you, my angel. Are you ready to close your eyes now and have sweet dreams?"

"Yes." She snuggles into the pillow. Clare kisses her on her forehead and tucks her in.

"Sweet dreams indeed, my daughter. Don't let the bedbugs bite!"

"If they do, him 'em with a *shoe!*" Chara says and, giggles. Clare kisses her again, pads out of the room, closes the door softly, except for a crack. Never shut a door fully.

Clare pours herself vodka on the rocks. Hangar One. She sits alone, but never *really* alone, in her stuffed chair. Puts her little feet up on the ottoman. Wiggles red toes. Holds the glass near her ear and swirls the ice. Listens to the soft-bells sound of the ice against the crystal. Runs her free hand through her brown hair. "Ma, Da, dearest Dermot, Jesus. I love you all, and I miss you so," she whispers. "Thank you for all that you did for me."

The ice tinkles against the silence of her home. She twirls a strand of hair.

"And sweet Charlie, may you find peace," she whispers. "Glasses up." she raises the crystal glass like a chalice as high as she can reach toward heaven. Brings it back down to her lips, takes a long cool pull on the chilled vodka, lays her head back softly, breathes out deeply and smiles at the ceiling, listens to the peace. A small tear appears, but it's a happy tear.

"I love you all, dear ones," she whispers. "Please continue to pray for me. Please and thank you."

"And thank you, God, for life, and for love, and for this precious day. Glasses up!"

41

They took three days to drive back, stopping in the same places, eating at the same restaurants, laughing at the memories, and making new ones. Sadly, Tom wasn't their waiter in Richmond. He was off that night. And it wasn't Wednesday, so no free pie, regardless of the cost.

When they got home, Trista was waiting for them in the driveway. She was shaking with excitement. Charlie stepped out of the car and she jumped into his arms. "Did you bring my seashells, Grandpa?"

"I did!" Let's go inside and I'll show you. She's bundled up for early-March, wearing one of those green puffy jackets that make kids look like hand grenades. Her blonde hair is in a braid with a red ribbon. Pink leggings. Neon orange sneakers with lights that come on when she runs. Charlie wishes they made those sneakers for grown-ups.

Abby hugs him and kisses him on the cheek. "Welcome home, Daddy. After you called from the car, she insisted on waiting out here so she could look up the street. The fresh air did us all good."

"Did she happen to see the *Daily Pop* mermaid," Charlie asks.

"No, Daddy. We're still looking for her, though."

"That's good. Never stop looking."

"Promise." Abby crosses her heart.

"It's good to be home. I missed you both so much."

Charlie puts Trista down so he can get the bags out of the trunk. Trista claps her hands. "Which one is it?"

"This one here," he says. "The green one. It's an Irish suitcase. It never shuts up. Let's take it inside and put some cotton in its mouth."

They go into the house and Charlie lays his Irish suitcase on the floor and opens it. Trista goes down on her knees. He loves the way her hair smells, fresh, like summer. He unwraps the pink, heart-shaped plastic bucket from its plastic grocery bag and presents it to her. "All for you," he says. Her smile makes him forget everything that was ever wrong with his life. "How did I do?" Charlie asks.

"I *love* them, Grandpa!" She hugs him. "Will you play with me?"

"I will play with you forever," Charlie says. "Promise."

"Will you play beach with me now?"

"Sure," Charlie says. "Were should we go?"

"My room."

"Go, go," Abby says. "Mom and I will take care of the rest."

"Okay."

They climb the 13 steps and count each one together. They always count steps when they're together, no matter where they are. Trista loves this. She's in a big-girl bed now. It's white and has low sides to keep her from rolling out in her sleep, but she can easily get in and out on her own. Her blanket is red. The walls are a light blue to match the sky on a good beach day. Charlie had painted it that color for her before they left for Florida. It's her favorite color. He also sponged in some white clouds. Not bad. When Charlie was painting, he thought of how Abby once listened to the sky by holding a gold, star-shaped balloon to her ear. Bits of childhood can bounce like echoes through an old man's mind.

There's a rocking chair, where they read bedtime stories. There's a white dresser, filled with clothes she will soon outgrow. There are stuffed animals and toys for the imagination, and there is a white-noise machine to help her sleep, and a baby monitor so they can watch over her when she does sleep. There's a changing table they don't need as much anymore because Trista is trying to use the potty. She doesn't always make it, but no worries; she'll get there. There's an A-B-C rug with animals in the center of the polished wooden floor.

"Where should we be?" Charlie asks.

"On the rug with the animals," Trista says. "They like the beach."

"Can you take this out?" she asks, pulling on her braid. Charlie undoes it and runs his hand through her hair, remembering Abby at this age. Trista's hair now looks like it just came out of the clothes dryer. She sits and takes off her shoes and socks. She shows Charlie where to sit. "Take off your shoes and socks," she says. "We're at the beach. These are my feet." She points. He does. "These are your feet," she says, touching them. "They're handsome."

"Why thank you, young lady, say my feets." She upends the bucket and the shells make the slot-machine sound as they fall onto each other. "What should we do?" he asks.

"We should line them up," she says, and so they do. "Let's make a big square."

"Okay, which way should we go?"

"Let's go this way, and then that way." She points to where she wants them on the A-B-C rug. Together, they place the shells.

"They look like they're having a shell meeting," Charlie says.

"No, they're guarding the animals," Trista says. "There's a big fish that wants to eat the animals, and the shells are the fence that protects them."

"Can the big fish swim over them?" Charlie asks.

"No, there's no water over them, silly. Fish need water."

"Can it swim under them?"

"No, it can't. There's sand there. Fish need water."

"So the shells are on the beach?"

"The fish can't get the animals because the shells are protecting them. I *told* you that, Grandpa."

"Okay, sorry."

"You're being silly, Grandpa."

"What color is the big fish?"

"I think he's red."

"You're not sure?"

"Sometimes he's green," Trista says. "Like your Irish suitcase." She moves six of the shells aside.

"Is that a gate?"

"Yes, to let the big fish in. Once he goes in, we'll close the gate and he'll drown on the sand. Watch."

Charlie sits and watches her imaginary fish swim in. She moves her hand across the rug, making a swooshing sound as she does. Then she quickly puts the six shells back where they were and says, "Now you're trapped!"

"Can the big fish ever get out?"

"No. Not ever. He's trapped."

"What will happen now?"

"He'll drown. Watch."

They sit together and look at the rug. "There," Trista says. "He's dead. See?" She points at a spot.

"I can see him. Dead as Kelsey's nuts."

"Now he can't eat the animals."

"These are very magical shells," Charlie says.

"*Very* magical," Trista agrees.

"I think you would like the beach where they used to live?" Charlie says.

"Is it magical there?"

"It is, and the people are very nice."

"Tell me about the people, Grandpa?"

"Well, they have funny names."

"Like what?"

"Like Hot Dogs and Meatballs and Spaghetti," Charlie says. "And Bacon Cheeseburger."

"Really? What do they look like?"

"Well they look just like the food in their names. The Meatballs and Spaghetti man had long hair like yours, but it was red, like spaghetti with sauce. And his eyes were brown like meatballs and they bulged out like this." Charlie opens his eyes wide and puffs out his cheeks.

"Really?"

"Absolutely."

She laughs. "What did the hot dogs man look like?"

"He had a very long nose. It looked just like a hot dog. It was the same color, and it smelled just like a hot dog, too. Your grandma got mixed up one day and bit it."

"Really?"

"Yep, she was hungry."

"What did the hot dog man say?"

"Well, first he sneezed because of the mustard, but then he said this." Charlie pinches his nose and nasals, "What did you do *that* for?" Trista laughs so hard she rolls over on the floor. Charlie lies down with her. Puts his arm around her. "Do you know how much I love you, big girl?"

"How much?"

"More than all the water in the oceans and all the sand on all the beaches and all the seashells in the whole world and all the fishies, big and small."

"Even the fishies that eat animals?"

"*Especially* the fishies that eat animals."

"I love you, Grandpa." She hugs him. Wraps herself around him, arms and legs, and hugs. Won't let go.

"And I love you, big girl." He lies there, smiling at the ceiling. "Thank you, God," he whispers.

"Where is God, Grandpa?"

"He's everywhere, honey."

"Can we put him inside the seashell fence and keep him there with us forever?"

Charlie holds her. "Sure," he says. "I think God would like that a lot. So would I."

"How's he doing?" Abby asked Donna.

"He's okay. It was a bit rough in the beginning. He was very antsy. But he settled into the easy pace of the place and it got better day by day. We met some wonderful people down there and one in particular. Her name is Clare. She was our afternoon bartender in this terrific bar that's tucked back into a building. She's small, like me, so your father took to her right away. And she's as good at The Chat as he is, so they really hit it off. Oh, and the best part was, she owns the bar. That came as a total surprise, and we didn't find that out until the last night we were there. Here we were thinking she just worked the afternoons there. You never know with people."

"I'm glad you found her."

"Your father did. I was at the beach a lot. He was out making new friends. He needed that time to fix himself. She helped him a lot. He needed to talk and be silly. Those young engineers and that new boss made him feel like an old fool whose time has passed. Clare listens as well as your father does, and they are beautiful together. And she's a single mom, Abby. Her daughter is ten and has Down syndrome."

"Wow. How is she doing with that?"

"She's great. It's wonderful to watch the love between them. She reminds me so much of you and Trista. Clare's two years older than you, but she looks like she's in her early-20s. You'd like her. She's a woman in full."

"How the heck did she come to own the bar?"

Clare tells her the story, which adds sadness to the day, but then Donna tells about how accepting Clare is of whatever comes her way, and how she manages to cause good to bloom out of bad. "She's pretty special."

"I'd like to meet her someday."

"I wish we all lived in the same neighborhood," Donna said.

42

"Do you know where he's living now?" Donna asks.

"Just somewhere in New Jersey," Charlie says. "He never gave me the address. He's with a friend, I think, but I don't know the person."

"And he hasn't answered any of your texts?"

"Or any of my emails."

"Did you try calling him?" Donna asks.

"Yes, but I just get voicemail."

"That's strange. Why wouldn't he keep up with his messages?"

"I don't know. Maybe he was trying to cut ties with Bertha?"

"Try Googling him. See if anything comes up. Maybe there was an accident or something." So Charlie Googles, and up comes the *Newsday* story.

"Oh, no," he says.

"What?"

He shows her.

"Oh, shit," she says.

"I can't believe this," Charlie says. "I should have talked to him more. I made him wait before I answered his texts. I couldn't be bothered because we were having such a good time down there. This is horrible, Donna. I feel responsible."

"Don't put this on yourself, Charlie. You *did* answer him. Every time. You did. You were there for him. He just went over the edge. You can't be responsible for what other people choose to do."

"But I should have been there for him more than I was."

"Charlie, he flew down to talk to you and you were there for him. You constantly told him that we were both there for him. You offered help again and again. I think he just snapped."

"What's wrong?" Abby asks. She's holding hands with Trista, just back from the food store. Donna tells her.

"I saw that story in the paper when it happened. I had no idea you knew him. That's so sad!"

"We never talked about him to you, Abby. You couldn't have known."

Charlie chokes back a sob. Abby goes to him, as does Donna. They hold each other. Trista looks scared.

"We're scaring her," Charlie sobs.

Trista starts to cry.

"It's okay, honey," Charlie says, picking her up. "Don't cry. Everything is okay. Do you want to play with the seashells with me?" She stops crying, nods yes. "C'mon, let's do that. Which room?"

"Bedroom."

"Let's go. We'll see you later, Grandma and Mommy."

"Why do big people cry, Grandpa?"

"Because they're either happy or they're sad, Trista."

"That's silly."

"I know."

"Which one are you, Grandpa?"

"That was a sad cry. A small one. I'm sorry I scared you."

"Why are you sad, Grandpa?"

"Someone that I know did something bad, and that made me sad."

"Was it a man or a lady?"

"It was a man."

"Was he big like you?"

"Yes."

"Why did he do the bad thing, Grandpa?"

"I think because he was also sad, and that made him angry."

"Why was he sad?"

"Because he couldn't have what he wanted."

"What did he want?"

"He wasn't sure."

"That's silly, Grandpa."

"I know. It really is silly."

"Did his mommy give him a time-out?"

"No, his mommy wasn't there to do that, Trista. I wish she was."

"Where was his mommy?"

"Far away. She couldn't do anything to fix him."

"Could you fix him, Grandpa?"

"I tried. I tried by listening, but it didn't work. That's why I was sad. I thought I could help, but it didn't work."

"Mommy says that if you try, that's what matters, even if you don't get what you want right away."

"I did try, Trista."

"Then don't be sad, Grandpa."

"Okay, honey."

"Do you want to play with the Little People with me?"

"Instead of the shells?"

"Yes, the shells are sad today."

"Why are they sad?"

"Because the man did something bad."

Trista gets her plastic bucket filled with Little People and dumps them onto the floor. "I love you, Grandpa."

"And I love you, big girl."

"You're crying again, Grandpa."

"This is a happy cry, big girl. Thank you for always making me so happy."

"You're silly, Grandpa."

"No, I'm just a Little People, Trista. That's all," he sobs. "Just a Little People."

"No, Grandpa, you're *big*. Like *me*." She hugs him. "Let's play."

43

Charlie rolls over and puts his arm around Donna. "Your hair smells good."

"You looking for something, mister?"

"Always."

"Before I have my morning coffee? I'll have more energy after coffee. And I think I hear Trista."

"Did I ever tell you about that couple I met in a bar?"

"In a bar? Go figure."

"Yeah, he told me that he got the urge one day when his wife was bending over and getting something out of the freezer. It was an overwhelming urge. He just couldn't help himself." Charlie moves his hand. Donna pushes it back.

"*Trista*, mister."

"Sorry, it's your hair. Just smells so good. *You* smell so good."

"I'll smell better later. Calm down."

Charlie starts singing Carly Simon's 1971 hit, *Anticipation.*

"Yeah, me too. So tell me what happened with the couple. Did the wife let him do the deed?"

"She sure did, and right there over the freezer."

"Well, that's romantic," Donna says. "Sort of."

"Yeah, but now they're not allowed back in that supermarket ever again."

"And that actually happened, right?" She pokes him in the ribs.

"How could you possibly doubt me?"

She kisses him on the mouth. Pushes him away. "I'm getting coffee."

"I guess I am, too."

The four of them are having breakfast. Microwave oatmeal for Charlie and Donna. Cheerios for Abby and Trista. Three coffees, one milk.

"I'm thinking about joining one of those coot clubs," Charlie says. "You know the ones where old guys meet every morning and sit in the same place, order the same food, and complain about the world."

"Why?" Donna asks.

"It's what coots do," Charlie shrugs his shoulders. "I'm a retired coot now. I'm supposed to have a club. I'll get myself some sweatpants and tee shirts with pockets so I'll have a place to keep my coupons. And I'll need some black socks to go with my sandals. Summer is coming."

"You'll also need a hat," Donna says.

"I'll wear my Mets cap and leave it on when I'm indoors."

"Would you be a diner coot?" Abby asks.

"Probably not. Diner coots usually have canes and walkers and oxygen tanks. Ever notice that? They come in like a parade and bang their way across the diner with their medical equipment. And they always seem to have a table way in the back."

"That's true," Abby says. "Why is that?"

"I think it's so they can crash into as many people as possible. It gives them something to talk about when they sit down. How nobody gets out of their way. No respect for the seniors and all that."

"And diner coots always get separate checks," Donna says. "That's a pain in the ass for the waitress."

"*Ass*," Trista repeats.

"No, Trista," Donna recovers. "I said *ask*. They *ask* for the checks when they're done eating."

"Pain in the *ask*," Trista says.

"That's it," Donna says. "Pain in the ask."

"Yeah, and they don't tip well," Charlie adds. "I've been watching them as I do my research."

"You're researching?" Abby says.

"You bet I am. I'm not joining just *any* coot club. We have to be compatible. I don't want to be with guys who go scrounging through brown change purses for pennies. You know you're a coot circling the drain if you carry a brown change purse."

"Unless you're of the female persuasion," Donna says.

"Well, yeah, I'll give you that," Charlie says. "There are lady coot clubs, too, but most of them do lunch, not breakfast. They wear red hats and sit with their purses on their laps, holding onto them with both hands, like they're driving a bus. When they eat, they still hold the purses, but with just one hand. They take quick bites and then go back to two-handed holding of the purses. And each one of them has at least a thousand photos of grandkids and great-grandkids in their purse.

"Oh, and they talk loud and all at the same time, and each group has a cackler. I can't stand the cacklers. One coot says the tuna fish is good and that sets off a cackler. What's so funny about good tuna fish?"

"Beats me," Donna says.

"And there's always at least one smacker in the group," Charlie adds.

"Smacker?" Donna says.

"Yeah, you know the one who smacks you on the arm every time you finish a story? She'll say, 'Oh, that is sooo funny!' and then she smacks you on the arm. Sit next to a smacker at a female coot lunch and you're coming away black and blue. I saw a smacker the other day in a diner. This one had a receding hairline, so you know what she did?"

"What?" Donna asks.

"She shaved off her eyebrows. You could see the stubble where they used to be. To replace them, she drew make-believe eyebrows about two inches above where her real eyebrows used to be. It looked like she used a brown Sharpie to do the job. I guess she figured it made her receding hairline look more natural, but it scared the crap out of me. And she was a smacker. I hate smackers."

"Diner coots are strange in general, no matter the gender," Donna says.

"Yeah," Charlie says, but especially when it comes to the money. I was in a diner on one of my trips. This place advertised a Two Times breakfast special. It was two eggs, two pieces of bacon, two slices of toast, and coffee. Two bucks. Get it? Two times. Anyway, these two coots walk in. Two. Go figure."

"We talkin' guy coots?" Abby asks.

"Of course. It's breakfast," Charlie says. "Anyway, they come in and one of them orders the special, with a black coffee. The other coot says he's good. Doesn't need a thing. He's just going to sit there and keep his buddy company."

"Two bucks is cheap for all that," Abby says.

"It is, but wait. Here comes the best part. The breakfast arrives. The coffee is in a cup on a saucer. The coot who ordered the food slides one fried egg, one piece of bacon, and one slice of toast from his plate onto the saucer and gives it to the other coot. That guy reaches into his pocket and comes out with a plastic fork and a napkin from McDonald's. He brought his own fork and napkin. Imagine that. They both eat. The first coot drinks the coffee and asks for a free refill. He gets it because it's a Two Times special. Get it? Well, the waitress fills his cup, and the first coot asks for cream. The waitress says, 'I thought you were drinking black coffee.' The coot says, 'I changed my mind.

I need cream.' Milk won't do. So she goes and gets him some cream, and guess what? The second coot drinks *that* cup of coffee - the one with the cream.

"Then, when the waitress isn't looking, they each grab the sugar packets and the Sweet'N Low packets, and pocket them for home, wherever that is. The first coot takes out two plastic baggies and empties the salt shaker into one and the pepper shaker into the other. Then he palms the butter knife. Sticks it up his sleeve. His watch strap holds it in place. I watched all of this happen from the next table. They knew I was watching. They didn't care."

"So what happened next?" Donna asks.

"The waitress brings the bill. It's two bucks, plus sixteen-cents tax. The coots split that."

"Did they leave a tip?" Abby asks.

"Ten cents," Charlie says. "In pennies."

"Nine-point-nine on the Cheapskate Scale," Donna says.

"And they banged into people on their way out. And then they got into cars. *Cars!*"

"So what are your other options?" Abby asks.

"Okay," Charlie says. "First, I thought of Starbucks because I like their coffee, but that won't work because coots don't go to Starbucks in groups. You'll see a stray coot in there every now and then, and he's always reading *The New York Times* and shaking his head sadly. He'll lick his fingers before he turns each page. And he'll be wearing sneakers with black socks, or in the summer, sandals with black socks. I have to get some of those socks."

"Why don't coot clubs go to Starbucks?" Abby asks.

"They don't go because there are too many young people in there looking at their screens. Not enough places for a coot group to sit together. It's the free Wi-Fi that attracts the young people.

"And then you have your business people who don't have offices. They use Starbucks as their office. They spread out all over the place and loud-talk on their cell phones. Coots loud-talk, too, but not into their phones. They usually don't have phones. They just loud-talk.

"And to make it worse, Starbucks is always playing music that gives coots bowel problems. Backs them right up. You can Google that. It's true. Oh, and Starbucks food is pretty pricey and often too fru fru to be coot food."

"But the baristas are sexy," Donna says.

"Yes, they are, and that's another reason why coot clubs don't gather there. Too many tattoos and piercings on the baristas. Coots can't shake the tattoos and the nose rings out of their heads, or their conversation. Look at that one, they say. And, what's the matter with kids these days? Meanwhile, there's lust in their hearts for the baristas, but not much in their pants to back it up, so they get even more frustrated and aggravated and they never get to complaining about the politicians, which is the purpose of any coot club. Sexy baristas take their minds off of Fox News, and you just can't have that."

"So Starbucks is out," Abby says.

"Yeah."

"And that brings us to Dunkin' Donuts." Charlie continues. "This is a very good option. Most of the people who go there get their coffee and food to go, so there are always tables available. The prices are reasonable, and you can help yourself to the free napkins and straws. That cuts down on what you have to buy for your own use at home. Just be sure to arrive with lots of pockets."

"You've given this a lot of thought, haven't you?" Donna says.

"I have, and the other thing Dunkin' Donuts has going for it is that most of the franchises are owned by the sons and daughters of India, who have that delightful sing-song bounce in their voices. They remind me very much of Mr. Patel and handicapped toilets. They are very accommodating, in their own special way. Very, very accommodating. And very clean. Very, very clean."

Abby looks at Donna. "That's a story for another day," Donna says. Abby nods.

"Yes, D.D. is definitely an option. You pay before you sit, and you don't have to tip unless you want to. There's always a cup on the counter for tips, but most people pretend they can't see it. It contains a few pennies. Maybe a nickel. That's it. Oh, and there are clean bathrooms in D.D. That's important."

"Do they have handicapped toilets?" Donna asks.

"In some cases, yes," Charlie says. "I'll avoid those places. I'm still in the investigative phase here, my love."

"What about McDonald's?" Abby asks. "Lots of coots in there."

"Yes, that's true, and that brings me to my next option. You can sit in McDonald's for the rest of your life and beyond. If you die there, it will take them several hours to notice your corpse, so that's a plus. The bathrooms are not as clean as D.D. because everyone who drives a car uses McDonald's as their public toilet. That's a minus. The food is cheap. Plus. The coffee is good. Plus again. You pay before eating, and you don't tip. Plus, plus. The cash registers have pictures of food instead of numbers, so the kids make fewer mistakes. If they sold cantaloupe you'd never get a coconut instead. Big plus there.

"Lots of kids, though. It's the Happy Meal thing and the indoor-playground thing. But when coots start talking politics, there's a good chance the F-bomb is going to get dropped. Some coots have no check valve between their brain and their mouth, so that's a concern. We can't be wrecking children with the F-bomb."

"F-bomb!" Trista shouts.

"Speaking of check valves," Donna smirks.

"I said *Ref*-bomb, Trista. Like in soccer? You know, the referee? When the ref gets mad, he drops the *bomb* on the players."

"Nice try, Grandpa," Donna says.

"What about Burger King?" Abby asks.

"Coot clubs *never* go to Burger King," Charlie says.

"Why not?"

"It's that scary Burger King mascot they use in their commercials. You know the big king with the plastic head and the maniacal smile? Looks too much like a waxy corpse to the coots, and corpses are foremost in the mind of your average coot, so no B.K."

"That mascot really is creepy," Abby says. "I'm surprised Stephen King hasn't used it in one of his books."

"Yeah, that would be a *whopper* of a story," Charlie says.

"Ouch," Abby says.

"So what's it gonna be, Grandpa Charlie?" Donna asks.

"I don't know yet. Maybe I'll just join the coots that walk the mall in the mornings. Do they talk while walking? Gotta have The Chat."

"From what I've seen, they never shut up," Donna says.

"And some of those old ladies are pretty hot," Abby adds.

"Lot to be said for mall walking," Donna says.

"Burns calories," Charlie says.

"Which makes room for afternoon drinking," Donna says.

"I'm sensing a plan here," Charlie says.

"Man plans," Donna says.

Charlie smirks.

Lime Day on Long Island arrived on April 23 that year. Well, at least according to Charlie. Trista wasn't calling it yet, so naturally, Charlie and Donna thought of Clare.

"I miss her," Donna says.

"I miss her, too," Charlie says.

"Let's call her tonight and wish her a Happy Conception Day."

"Okay. Hey, speaking of Conception Day, I came across something interesting."

"What's that?"

"Well, the other day, I stopped at Saint Charles Cemetery to say a prayer for my folks."

"Seriously?"

"Yeah, I figured they needed them."

"Where *they* are?" Donna said.

"*Anyway*, while I was there, I took a walk around, just looking at the names and the dates on the stones. Birthdays, Death Days. I started doing the Conception Day translation, counting forward three months from the birthdays. What was interesting was how many of the death days came very close to the conception days."

"You have way too much time on your hands these days, Charlie." Donna says.

"No, wait. This gets better. I was wondering if there's a pattern to it all. Think about this. Each year we live, we celebrate our birthdays, and you and I also celebrate our conception days because that's another reason to have fun."

"And to drink wine in the afternoon," Donna adds.

"As if we needed a reason. But think of this. Each year we live, we tiptoe through our death day. We just don't know which day it is."

"Only God knows," Donna says.

"Right, but listen to this because this is very intriguing. I went online and got a list of all 40 U.S. Presidents who are currently on the other side of the lawn. I looked up their birthdays and their death days. I converted the birthdays to conception days for all of them by counting forward three months, and then I looked at their death days. Out of the 40 dead presidents, 17 of them died during their conception month. And seven others died within one month either way of their conception day. Add it together and you have forty-six percent of all the former Presidents of the United States of America dying within 30 days of the date they were conceived. Isn't that amazing? And the same happened with twelve of the first ladies."

"I'm listening," Donna says.

"And beyond presidents, how about this short list? This took me like five minutes to put together." He reads from a yellow pad. "Okay, random famous dead people. We have Patty Duke, Joan Rivers, Fred Thompson, 'Rowdy' Roddy Piper, Jack LaLanne, Omar Sharif, Beau Biden, Ed McMahon, Betty Ford, Oscar de la Renta, Osama bin Laden, Muammar Gaddafi. Well, both of those guys had help. Al Davis, owner of the Oakland Raiders. I'll have to tell Jimmy Hot Dogs about that one. Anna Nicole Smith." Charlie pauses here, places his hand over his heart. Sighs.

Donna smacks him in that hand. "Oh, and Josef Stalin. All of their conception days match their death days, within a month."

"I'm speechless," Donna says.

"And are you ready for this? Geologists say that, according to excavations, and the New Testament, Jesus died on April 3 in the year 33. So He is within a *week* of being on that list as well. I would love to see a wider study on this, wouldn't you? Imagine if nearly half of the people in the world are destined to die right around the same date that they were conceived."

"It's sort of like having your warranty run out, I suppose," Donna says.

"Yeah, and it sure would help you plan your vacations."

"For sure."

"Do you think this has anything to do with Obamacare?" Charlie asks.

"Probably not." Donna says, "But if you decide to join a coot club, ask them. I'm sure they'll be able to somehow make that connection for you."

Clare answers the phone and is delighted to hear from them. They have her on speaker.

"Happy Conception Day!" Charlie says.

"And Happy Long Island Lime Day!" Donna adds.

"Ah, Lime Day! Happy, happy to you two, too!" Clare says. They can hear her smile. "How *are* you? I miss you so much. Afternoon drinking just isn't the same down here without you two maniacs."

"We're grand," Charlie says. "How's Chara?"

"She's happy, but she also misses you both. She can't stop talking about your visit, and how pretty Donna is."

"What am I, chopped liver?" Charlie laughs.

"Well, she thinks you're very handsome, too, Granda Charlie."

"Tell her I miss her."

"You tell her. Here."

"Hello?" Chara slurps.

"Hello!" Charlie and Donna say at the same time.

"What are you doing?" Chara asks.

"We're talking to you on the phone," Charlie says.

"Me?"

"Yes, *you!* We miss you, Chara."

"Miss me!"

"We do."

"Come see me?"

"We'd like that," Donna says.

"Come now!"

Clare is back on. "You *should* come see us. Bring Abby and Trista. We'll have a ball. We really miss you."

Charlie looks at Donna. "We will. For sure," she says.

"Hey, I went to see the guys who live under the bridge. I brought them some leftovers. You were right. They're good people."

"Andy and Lou?" Charlie says.

"Yep. I told them to stop by the bar if they were hungry, or if they needed some honest work."

"Did you go by yourself?"

"No, I brought Chara with me, and Brady and his son came along as a favor. Chara likes to look at the boats. I also told her about houses that have no walls and the people who live in them. She was very excited."

"I'm glad you had Brady with you," Donna says. "Andy and Lou I trust, but they could have been others there who are not so nice."

"Yeah, I thought about that. Nobody's going to mess with a bouncer Brady's size. He's a gentle giant. Anyway, all was fine and we had a good chat. I hope they stop by. We always have food to spare, and I can always use help cleaning up."

"You're pretty special," Donna says.

"Me? You're the one who told me about them, Donna. Thanks for that."

"And you know they're not really homeless," Charlie says. "Just a couple of retired guys on a *very* fixed income."

"He never changes, does he?"

"No, he doesn't," Donna laughs.

"Thank God for that," Clare says. "Do you think you'll come back?"

"We'd really like to," Donna says.

"Try, okay?"

"We will."

"Do you miss the work, Charlie?" Donna asks. They're in bed and she's snuggled up against him, tiny and warm.

"I miss some of it, but I was missing it for years. It all changed. I miss the relationships, the casualness of the visits to my customers years ago. Getting to know people, caring about them, listening to them. *Really* listening to them. It all changed in the final years. It got so serious, and so cutthroat. I think it was the recession. That's when people stopped laughing."

Her head is on his chest and she listens to his heartbeat. He's stroking her hair.

"Do you miss the travel?"

"I miss the stories, and the airport bars. But Singer Island reminded me that the stories are everywhere. I've always known that, but I had forgotten. That island was like a refresher course in life for me, Donna. I needed it, especially after all that happened with Abby and Trista. Singer Island slowed me down. And Clare reminded me about acceptance and moving on. And I haven't had that bad dream in months. That's a blessing in itself. I loved the slow pace of that island. It was a good place, like no other I've ever been."

"I know."

"And it was so good to be with you for all that time. I'm really enjoying these days. I just hope we'll be okay. I just hope."

"We will be. I promise."

"I'm fixing myself, Donna."

"I know, Charlie. I love you so much."

"Those are my tools, your love."

"I know."

He smiles in the dark. Holds her close.

"Curtis Hayden," Charlie says 10 minutes later.

"Who?" Donna asks, blinking out of a twilight sleep.

"Curtis Hayden, one of the young engineers. He was the one who asked me questions about the old times, and about my sales techniques, especially about how I kept the maps of where my customers sat, and about the pastries they liked, their kids' names, all of what I was good at doing with people. The Chat."

"Was he that interested?"

"I thought he was. He'd always take the time to ask and he was a good listener."

Charlie went still and Donna listened to him breath in the dark. He pulled her closer, pressed her head to his chest.

"On my last day, when I was cleaning out my desk, he came into my cubicle to say goodbye."

"You never told me about that," Donna says. "That must have been nice. What did he have to say?"

"He brought me a box of Twinkies. He knew they were my favorite because when I told him about my customers and the pastries he asked me what I liked best. I laughed when he asked that because it's what I would have done, had we reversed positions. He laughed when I said Twinkies. He said he liked those when he was a kid."

"That's nice, Charlie."

"There were 12 in the box that he brought."

"Yes? Like the box we brought when we drank with Lou and Andy."

"Yes, just like that box. Curtis Hayden also brought paper towels."

"So you had a little party?"

"We did. Curtis Hayden covered half of my desk with the paper towels and laid out the Twinkies, end to end. The stuff I was packing up was on the other side of my desk."

"That's so nice," Donna said. She could feel his breathing quicken.

"He put six unwrapped Twinkies this way, end to end," Charlie says, tracing his index finger vertically down Donna's spine. "And then he put the other six Twinkies this way." Charlie turns his finger horizontally from the base of Donna's spine toward her right hip.

"Oh, my god."

"Yep, a big capital L. For me, Donna. *Loser*. That's what I was."

"Oh, Charlie," Donna sobs.

"And then the rest of them came in. They'd been watching from around the corner. Each grabbed a Twinkie, laughed, and left me there alone. Curtis Hayden was the last to leave. 'We won't miss you, old fool,' he said. He took a bite of his Twinkie and spit it into the garbage pail. Tossed the rest onto my desk and laughed. 'Have a

Twinkie, Loser,' he said. And that was my last day at the company. My retirement party."

"He was wrong. *So* wrong," Donna sobs. "And so cruel."

"He was. I know that now. I'm not a loser, Donna. I have you, and Abby, and Trista. I'm *not* a loser. I did the best I could for all those years with what I had to work with, and I'm *nobody's* fool. I know that now."

"Oh, I love you, I love you, *I love you*," Donna sobs as she holds him close in the darkness, adding this moment to their common memory, and embracing it.

44

Memorial Day.

It's the official start day of summer on Long Island. This year, it arrived softly and with the promise of good weather throughout the whole weekend, warm and sunny. It's supposed to be a day to remember those who died in our wars and to decorate their graves. Charlie knew that Americans used to call it Decoration Day for that reason, but it had morphed into something else in recent years - a three-day weekend.

Charlie remembered marching in the Memorial Day parade in his hometown when he was in Little League, and then later when he was a Boy Scout.

Mario Pistori, who was in his troop, and three years older than he was, told him about the mechanics of how babies got made. This was after one of their weekly troop meetings in the basement of the Catholic church that sponsored the troop. Charlie was shocked at first by this news. Grossed out, really, and he kept the knowledge to himself. He wondered if his father or mother was going to tell him about this baby business at some point, but they never did. He had to take the word of Mario Pistori, Life Scout, and as it turned out, Mario was right about most of it, especially the Be Prepared part.

Charlie was also a member of the Junior High School marching band for a while. He played the bass drum. They chose him for that task because he was big enough to carry the damn thing. It was an easy instrument to learn. He would have preferred the snare drum, but his rhythm was never good enough for that. You can still see that lack of rhythm in his dancing. Donna once told him that when it comes to dancing, he's a very good drinker.

Charlie remembered that between the Little League, Boy Scouts, and Junior High School band, only the band was organized when it came to parades, and even there, not so much. They practiced for weeks on the wide side streets by the Junior High School before each Memorial Day. It must have made the neighbors crazy, all that drumming and the not-so-good music, but hey, they were Junior High School kids, so what would you expect?

The baton girls in their short skirts kept dropping their batons during those practice marches, and bending at the waist to pick them up, which made Charlie wish that he played the piccolo instead of the bass drum. The piccolo kids marched up front. He was in the back row where the view wasn't as good.

The band leader, Mr. Cleary, had wanted to be a Marine, but he couldn't qualify because of a heart murmur.

Nevertheless, he was a stickler for order. His face glowed a plump, inflamed, blood-pressure pink on most days as he fast-walked alongside the kids while they marched and played off-key and dropped batons. He shouted like a Drill Instructor. God help any kid who was out of step.

Mr. Cleary died when Charlie was in his first year of high school and out of the band for good. He dropped dead out there in the street, right in the middle of a scream about keeping cadence. The band was doing their best with the Marine Corp Hymn at the time. He went down like a cut puppet, and the whole band marched another five blocks before one of the neighbors ran up front to stop them and give them the sad news. They all walked back, but not in formation. They stood around, watching the police and the EMTs. One of the trumpet kids played *Taps*, which was nice. Mr. Clearly would have liked it, but Charlie was sure he would have liked it better had it come, say, fifty years later.

No parade for the band that year. The school wasn't able to hire anyone to take Mr. Cleary's place. Instead, the band played at Mr. Cleary's funeral, right there beside his fresh grave. They played Amazing Grace, and the Marine Corp Hymn, which seemed appropriate. Everyone enjoyed it. When they were done, they marched off in perfect cadence. It was quite ironic.

The earlier parades in Charlie's life, the ones where he marched with his baseball team, such as it was, or the

Boy Scouts, such as they were, were much easier. No one expected anything more than him showing up wearing his uniform. Oh, and he wasn't supposed to scratch himself while marching. Other than that, it was just a chaotic romp down the avenue while parents and kids sat on the curb and watched.

Sometimes, kids would get up off the curb and romp with them for a block or so before filtering back to their parents. When it was over, his parents always took him for butter pecan ice cream at the Sweet Shoppe.

They'd go home, and if things weren't just so, he'd hit her and leave for a few hours.

And when he was gone, she'd hit Charlie with the strap. "Don't' you be like him," she hissed. "You *hear* me? Don't you be like *him*."

"I *won't*, Mommy. I *won't*."

Life.

Charlie looked through *Newsday* for a parade. He thought Trista, who was three-and-a-half now, might like a good parade. He found one in Levittown that started at 10 in the morning, so the four of them drove over there early to get a good spot on the curb. They brought folding chairs.

The parade was going to be a half-mile long and parking wasn't a problem since the parade worked its way straight up Hempstead Turnpike, and there were plenty of stores with big parking lots along the way. Charlie chose a parking lot about halfway into the parade route. They parked, walked a few hundred feet, and set up their lawn chairs curbside. Other parents and grandparents were gathering and the mood was good. Happy Memorial Day!

The parade started sort of on time a quarter-mile down Hempstead Turnpike, but nothing was happening where they were sitting, and Trista was getting antsy.

"I want to go *hoooome*," she whined.

"But the parade hasn't started yet," Charlie said. "It will be here soon. You'll see. It's going to be nice."

"Why are we sitting on the *sidewalk*, Grandpa?"

"Because we're going to watch the parade."

"Where will the parade *beeee*?"

"In the street. Right here in front of us."

"But won't the cars run over the parade?"

"No, the police stop the cars from moving during the parade so everyone can march and we can watch."

"But how will people get to the stores then?"

"They'll have to wait to go to the stores."

"That's not fair. What if they need stuff?"

"They can go to a store that doesn't have a parade."

"Can *we* go to the store that doesn't have a parade?"

"Maybe later."

"Okay. Can it be a *toy* store?"

"If you're good."

"Okay."

"You know, Trista, I used to march in a parade just like this one," Charlie said a few minutes later.

"But where *is* it?"

"It's coming soon. You'll see."

"This is *boring*."

"It will be good. You'll see." Abby and Donna were having their own conversation.

A guy pushing a supermarket shopping cart with a big pegboard filled with small American flags, balloons, and toys on sticks designed to take out eyeballs is walking up the other side of Hempstead Turnpike. "Souvenirs! Getcha souvenirs! Happy Memorial Day, everybody! Getcha souvenirs! Wave a flag! Best way to honor our country! "

"Who is that man?" Trista asks.

"That's the man who sells parade stuff."

"I want parade stuff."

"We'll see if he comes over here."

"But I want him to come over here *now!*" Trista pouts.

"Trista," Abby says. "Be nice to your Grandpa."

"But I want the parade-stuff man to come here *now*."

Charlie waves at the guy. He ignores him and keeps going up the other side of the street.

"He'll come to us later," Charlie says. "Or another parade-stuff man will come to this side. You'll see."

"I want a *toy*."

They hear the music before they see the band, but now the drummers are drumming and the rest of the band isn't playing. They march right by.

"This is the parade, Trista!" Charlie says.

"Will they play the music for us?"

Charlie realizes that he picked a parade dead spot. They're sitting in the parade's commercial.

"I want the *music!*" Trista shouts.

"Nice spot, Grandpa Charlie," Donna says.

Charlie gives her a look, but she's smiling sweetly.

"Yeah, I sure know how to pick 'em." he says.

"I want *music!*" Trista whines.

"The drums are lovely, honey" Donna says. "Especially the *bass* drum. Right, Grandpa Charlie? Isn't the *bass* drum just the best instrument in the whole wide world?"

Abby laughs.

"Yeah," Charlie says. "Lovely."

Charlie watches them drum by and notices that none of the kids in the band are marching in step, and they're not wearing sharp uniforms like he used to wear when he carried the bass drum. They just have matching shirts over khaki shorts of all sorts. Each kid is wearing sneakers but none are alike. And all different colored socks. Some pulled up, some slouched, some not even matching. Charlie thinks about the long-dead Mr. Cleary, and how this band would probably have killed him twice.

Next came the old veterans and their grandkids. The veterans carried flags and plugged rifles. Each vet had a belly the size of a college fridge. They were huffing and sweating.

Behind the vets were the politicians. They waved small American flags, probably made in China because you can't beat the price, and they wove from side to side along the parade route, waving to the people in their lawn chairs, and trying their best not to shake hands with anyone because there was no telling which political party any of the parade watchers favored. Waving was safer. Politicians hate being refused a handshake, or worse, being called an asshole while weaving like town drunks from one side of Hempstead Turnpike to the other. They were all sweating in their suits, which pleased Charlie, and their frozen smiles made them look like the plastic-headed, Burger King mascot.

"Hello, beautiful!" one of the politicians, who has chins like a stack of pancakes, says to Trista. She retreats back into her lawn chair, gives him the stink-eye, and his smile freezes even more in place.

He moves on. "Hey, how you doing, fella? Good to see you! Hey, guy! How *you* doing? Hello, young man, young lady!" And he's gone.

"That's my girl," Charlie says to Trista.

Next in line were a bunch of emergency-services vehicles, moving at parade pace, with lights flashing.

Charlie thought this was appropriate since they were following the sweating politicians in their suits and the huffing vets with their impressive bellies. Better safe than sorry, right?

Then came the Girl Scouts. The Boy Scouts were right behind them, checking them out. None of the scouts, boys or girls, marched in step. The Scout Masters sported cummerbunds of blubber under their taut Boy Scout uniform shirts, whose khaki buttons were screaming like rock climbers about to fall. The Scout Masters are yakking with each other as they slog by. No shout-outs to the parade watchers. They're like a coot club with the food already eaten.

"Those guys should be wearing Wide-Load signs on their fat butts," Donna says. "For safety's sake."

"Yeah, be prepared," Charlie says.

Little League came behind the scouts. Baseball always plays second-fiddle to scouts in any townie parade, mainly because it's total chaos with the Little Leaguers. Those kids move like the balls in a Lotto machine. Thankfully, they don't carry bats. They run and jump and scream. They push each other and punch each other and have the best times of all just being crazy kids. It's Memorial Day on Long Island and they are all young and healthy. So just get the hell outta their way.

A fife-and-drum band approaches. They stop blowing and go drums-only as they're within 200 feet of Charlie. He looks over at Donna, who smirks.

"Why did they stop playing *music*, Grandpa?" Trista asks. Abby smirks.

"They ran out of breath," Charlie says. "It's not easy blowing and walking."

"That's silly, Grandpa. I want the music!"

"I know. I know." Charlie cranes his neck to look down the turnpike. What's next?

Volunteer firefighters carrying flags and axes and wearing uniforms and white gloves are next, and here we have rows of bellies that will make any cardiologist who might be in the crowd smile and think about buying that gold Rolex.

It seems like every fire truck within 30 miles slowly follows, and then one lonely ice-cream truck.

Dathsit.

"Can we get ice cream?" Trista says.

Charlie stands up, whistles loud with two fingers, and waves for the driver to stop. The guy sneers at Charlie and just keeps driving.

"*Prick*," Charlie says under his breath.

"What is a prick?" Trista asks.

"No, I said *pick!*" Charlie says. "*Pick.* I wanted you to *pick* your flavor, but he didn't hear me. Did you like the parade?"

"No!" Trista shouts, stomps her foot. "I *hated* it. It was stupid and ugly. Can we go to the toy store now?"

"How about if we go to the cemetery first and decorate the graves of those who gave their lives so that we might be free?" Charlie suggests to his beloved grandgirl.

"Grandma!" Trista shrieks. "I want to go to the *TOY STORE!*"

So guess what?

They go to Target for more Little People, and to show Trista the true purpose of Memorial Day in modern America, which is to go to the beach if it's warm enough, to hang out with friends and get pie-eyed if it's not warm enough, or to go shopping if it's raining. They chose shopping because, well, you know.

Target is open on Memorial Day, and every other day of the year, except for Christmas Day and Easter Sunday, regardless of the weather. Charlie thinks this is a lovely nod to Jesus. Sure, they're not in the same Jesus league as Chick-fil-A, but Christmas and Easter are nice days to close. Chick-fil-A, that delicious business with the funny billboards all across America (who doesn't love cows on ladders with paintbrushes?), has closed every Sunday since they first opened in 1946. They do this so that their employees can have time to spend with friends and family, or to worship God, should they choose to do so.

Or, Charlie supposed, to go to Target and buy stuff.

Trista has her eye on Little People Discovery Airport. It comes with a plane, a helicopter, a taxi cab, a windsock, a control tower, a radar dish, a restaurant area, a binocular stand, two vehicles and two little people. Thirty bucks.

"Can you buy me an airport, Grandpa?"

"Ask Grandma."

"Can you buy me an airport, Grandma?"

"How much is it?"

"Thirty bucks," Charlie says.

"How about if we just get some Little People," Donna says.

"But I want an *airport*," Trista says.

"This airport is broken, though," Charlie says.

"Why is it broken, Grandpa?"

"Look here. See? The bar is missing." He points at the picture on the box. "It's not a good airport if it doesn't have a nice bar. The Little People will be very sad if they have to go sit in the gate area during a storm. It's too crowded in the gate area, even for Little People. They'll cry all day long. Let's just get two Little People and make believe they're happy at home already, okay?"

"Okay," Trista says.

"I can't believe he got away with that," Abby whispers to Donna.

"You and me both."

They spend the rest of the afternoon relaxing in the backyard, eating burgers and drinking wine. Glasses up to those who died to make us free.

Happy Memorial Day indeed.

Charlie and Donna, being lovers of summer and haters of winter, always thought of Memorial Day as a trigger. Touch it, and the next day is the Fourth of July. The warm months move that quickly. Winter creeps like a coot club in a diner. And the day after the Fourth of July is Labor Day, of course, the official end of summer, and the psychological beginning of the cold weather to come. Fewer and fewer people on the beach and school starts once again. Charlie and Donna both get sad when they see the Back to School display go up in Target. That seems to happen about two weeks after Memorial Day.

But about the Fourth of July.

Thousands of Long Islanders had driven to Pennsylvania last winter and returned with enough fireworks to get on the Terrorist Watch List. They do this every year. You just have to dip your toe into the state of Pennsylvania from the Western edge of New Jersey to find the fireworks stores. Their billboards are bigger than Chick-fil-A's.

Snowbirds stopped in South Carolina on their way home in the spring to buy *their* weapons of mass annoyance. They, too, do this every year. Their kids gave them lists of which holiday ordnance to choose. Snowbird grandpas and grandmas bought everything on those lists because they love their kids, and they love America.

Long Islanders start lighting the fuses on their rockets and bombs around the second week in June each summer, and they don't stop until they run out of everything, which is usually around August 1. Dogs are peeing on themselves whenever the sun goes down. Kids are screaming and shaking. Coot-club guys are looking to see if someone is at the door every time an M-80 goes off. It's the Fourth of July on Long Island, and no one is safe.

And of course there's afternoon drinking. There's also evening drinking. There's boating drinking, and driving drinking, and beach drinking, and park drinking, and the lawyers are looking at second homes in the Hamptons because business has never been better for them.

The big day arrives and Charlie shows up with a box of sparklers late in the afternoon, just before they put the burgers on the grill. Abby isn't sure if Trista is old enough for sparklers, and Donna is watching closely. The bombs are going off. The skyrockets are flying, even though it's not yet dark. The dogs are yelping and peeing on the rugs.

"This is a sparkler," Charlie tells Trista. "It sparkles. Watch." He lights it and she recoils. Screeches! Throws herself at Abby. Shrieks! She does this because little kids have a way of pissing in every well-meaning old guy's punchbowl.

"Nice going there, Sparky," Donna smirks.

Charlie sticks the sparkler into the lawn, hot end first, and goes inside to get a glass of wine. The radio's on low. The Mets are still losing.

Oh, and the lawn is now on fire.

Happy frickin' birthday, America.

On August 25, Trista reaches the ripe young age of four. The Weather Channel guy predicts thunderstorms, which is okay since her party is going to be a family affair at Chuck E. Cheese, a business whose registered trademark is:

Where A Kid Can Be A Kid! ®

Which means that the grown-ups are pretty much screwed.

But that's a choice. You can't even get into this place unless you bring a kid. They stamp your hand and the kid's hand when you enter and then they watch you like you're Number 1 on the National Sex Offender Register. Don't try to leave with a kid whose stamped hand doesn't match yours.

Charlie looks around and figures out that he has to stick money into a machine to get tokens. "How many should we get?" He asks Donna.

"Let's get twenty bucks worth," she says, and hands him a twenty. "Abby and I will go order the pizza."

"Okay," Charlie says. He puts the twenty into the machine and the tokens clatter down, which makes him think of the seashells. He scoops them into a plastic bucket as Trista watches. "Are those the monies?" she asks.

"Yes."

"How many monies do we have?"

"Enough to start. We'll see how much fun we want to have, okay?"

"Okay."

They walk around a bit, checking out the place. Trista is looking at the games. Most are designed for older kids, but there's still enough there to grab her interest. She's in no hurry.

"What do you want to do first?" Charlie asks. Donna and Abby are over there at a table. There's a plastic sign with the number 21 in front of them. The staff will bring the pizza to them whenever it's ready. Behind them, scary animatronics animals on a stage are jerky-moving and singing scratchy songs.

Somewhere, Stephen King is smiling.

"The *truck*," Trista shouts, jumps and points. "I want to go on the *truck*."

It's a small replica of a monster truck, the sort that climbs over other trucks. Charlie helps her get into the thing and she grabs the wheel. Charlie inserts four tokens, trying to figure out how much this one ride is costing him. It starts with a recorded roar, rises up quickly and starts shaking from side to side, and up and down. Trista's smile turns to terror. *"Out! Out!"* she screams. Charlie reaches up and yanks her out. Then they stand there and watch the damn thing going berserk.

"You didn't like it," Charlie says

"I hate it!" she shouts. *"Bad!"*

"But you picked it."

She kicks it.

"Okay," Charlie says, picking up his plastic bucket of tokens. "Kick it again."

She does.

"How about Skee-Ball?" Charlie suggests. Charlie has always liked Skee-Ball. It's such a fluid sport. Trista scowls at him. "Skee-Ball? It's nice."

"Do we have to go in the snow?" she asks.

"No, it's not that kind of skiing, and there's no snow now. It's your birthday. It's summer." Charlie says. "Skee-Ball is a game where you roll balls."

"Why do they call it that if there's no snow?"

"I don't know."

"Why don't you know?"

"I just don't."

"You're supposed to *know*. You're Grandpa."

"Well, I don't. C'mon, I'll show you. Showing is better than telling anyway. It's that way." He points.

They walk over that way and she watches the other kids toss the balls underhanded. She sees the tickets come out of the game when they're done.

"What are those?" Trista asks, pointing at the tickets.

"You win tickets when you play this game," Charlie explains.

"What do tickets do?" she asks.

"You use them to get prizes."

"Where are the prizes?"

"I'll show you." Charlie walks her back to the front of the place and her eyes go wide when she sees the possibilities. There are colored pencils, plastic figures, balls, yo-yos, tiny monster trucks, all sorts of junk. Charlie remembers when he was a kid and you could win Chinese handcuffs, which were these woven tubes made of palm fronds or something like that. You stuck your two index fingers into the thing and pulled backwards. The tube would tighten on both fingers and you were trapped forever. What this had to do with China, other that it was probably made in China, Charlie didn't know, but there were none of those in the glass case. Probably not politically correct these days.

Trista spots a doll and smiles. It's going for 1,000 tickets, which is a lot in real-people money. "I want *that*," she points.

"We have to win the tickets first," Charlie explains.

"I want it *now*," she says, stamping her right foot.

"It doesn't work that way. I'll show you. Let's go play Skee-Ball and we'll win some tickets. Then we can come back here and see about the doll."

"NO!'

"Please?"

Pout. Crossed arms. Stomped feet. Again.

"Pretty please? We'll come back with the tickets. I promise."

"I want the doll!"

"We'll get it. I promise."

Trista stares at him hard. Charlie smiles. "I promise. I cross my heart two times." He does.

"I want the doll."

"I know. Let's go play the game and get the tickets."

Charlie sticks a bunch of tokens into the machine and nine wooden balls roll down. He hands one to Trista and tells her to roll it gently up the ramp and over the hump to score points. Trista takes the ball and flings it overhand at a Skee-Ball machine eight feet away. The older kid who is playing that machine looks at her. He makes that *Asshole!* face that older kids aim at younger kids when the wee ones do jerky things.

Charlie walks over and apologizes to the kid. He retrieves the ball and turns to see Trista walking up the ramp with a wooden ball in each hand. She's under the net now and stuffing both balls into the 10-points hole. Now she's sitting on the holes. Charlie tells her to come down this instant. She folds her arms and gives him the stink-eye. He looks around for help, but there is none. So he climbs onto the sloped and slippery runway to go get her, being careful not to throw out his back.

A stringy teenage boy with an acre of acne and an oversized Chuck E. Cheese shirt that engulfs him in red cotton appears out of nowhere to explain the rules to Charlie.

"Sorry," Charlie says. "This is her first time here. She's never played Skee-Ball before."

"Have *you* played Skee-Ball before?" the teen asks.

"Of course I have. I'm a grown-up."

"Well, then you know that climbing is *not* allowed in Skee-Ball. It's the rule. Please explain that to your daughter." Charlie is still standing on the machine. Trista is scowling.

"She's my granddaughter."

"Whatever. *Explain!*"

"I want my doll," Trista tells the kid.

"Whatever," he says.

Charlie pries her off the machine and they try again, this time by the rules.

Charlie's iPhone chirps a text. It's Donna. The pizza is ready. Trista doesn't want pizza. She wants to play Skee-Ball and win tickets. Charlie texts back and she tells him to take his time. This is not a gourmet meal.

So they play five more games, but now Trista is bored and wants to move on. She's won about 40 tickets because every ball that didn't go onto the floor went into the 10-points hole, or the no-points hole.

"Do you want to eat pizza now?"

"No," Trista says.

"What do you want to do?"

"I want to get my doll with my tickets."

"But we don't have enough tickets yet."

Trista starts to cry.

"Let's get pizza and ask your grandma if she can do something about the doll. I hear the pizza is delicious. And you can have a Coke, too. And your Grandma is smarter than me. She can help."

Trista's lower lip is still out, but she agrees.

Happy frickin' birthday.

It truly is the worst pizza in the world, and it exists on Long Island, a land that is home to some of the finest pizza on earth. Charlie takes one bite and drops the slice. "This is horrible," he says.

"The worst," Donna agrees. She ditched her slice a while ago.

"It tastes like ketchup on white toast, with a bit of string cheese tossed in," Donna says. "And maybe some vomit? How can they call this pizza?"

Trista loves it.

"Grandma," she says through her last mouthful of that soggy, spongy pizza pulp. "Grandpa said you will get my doll with my tickets."

"He did, did he?" Donna says.

"Yes, he said you are smarter. Will you take me now?"

"Sure," she says, holding out her hand for the tickets. "How many does she need?"

"I don't recall," Charlie lies, handing her the 40 tickets.

Donna and Trista walk to the counter. Trista shows her the 1,000-ticket doll.

"I don't think we have enough tickets, sweetie."

"Make some more," Trista says.

"Make some more? Do you want to play more games?"

"No! Just make some more."

"Okay."

Donna smiles at the gangly teenage boy who is working the counter. Donna has a *very* nice smile, especially right now. The kid starts hearing Beach Boys songs in his head.

"Hello?" Donna purrs.

"Hello?" he sputters, collapsing into her green eyes.

"I'm thinking about applying for a job *here*? You know, after *thchool*? Is it a nithe place to *work*? Are the people *nithe*? Are *you nithe*?"

Donna attaches a spring to end of each sentence, which causes bunches of decades to drop off her age. She's suddenly an irresistible teenager again. No one can explain how this happens, but it does. Dathsit.

She smiles again. He gulps.

"Is it nithe working *here*?" she lisps.

"It's . . . okay, I *guess*?" The words are clumsy in his throat, tripping all over each other.

"How much do they pay *you*?" she whispers, looking around.

"Minimum *wage*?" he admits, embarrassed.

"Oh, daths not *much*? How do you get *by*?"

"It's *okay*? I *guess*? I don't *know*? I go to *school*? *Um*? *Huh*?"

"Hey, disth isth my little thister, *Trista*?" Donna whispers, leaning in. She points at Trista, who also smiles. None of this makes chronological sense, or any sense, but the kid's brain is just drowning in Donna's eyes and voice, and is currently on vacation in Sexy Girl Land.

"She jusths loveths that *doll*? Donna points at it. The kid starts to look at the doll. "Don't look *away*?" she coos. "Look at *meeee*?" He does. He has to. She smiles and holds out her hand, like she wants to shake his. He takes it nervously. It pulses with softness and warmth. There's a folded ten in there. He feels it, heated by her skin, but he doesn't look, nor does he think. He can't think.

"Dis is for you from my little thister and me because we think you are so cute, and soooo *nithe*? Please give her the doll *now*?" She hangs onto his hand for a few seconds more. Green eyes blaze. She lets go of his hand but keeps looking at him. Dreamy smile. "*Now?*" she purrs.

He's shaking as he hands Trista the doll. "Um? Um? *Thanks*?" he stammers. He's trying to understand why he just did what he did, but his brain just crested the first hill on the Sexy Girl Land roller coaster and it's all downhill from there.

"No problem," Donna says and walks away, holding Trista's hand.

"I hope you get the *job*?" he calls after her as he rides up the second hill. Why did he just say that? He's trying to remember his name. Donna is holding Trista's hand. She wiggles two fingers of her other hand over her shoulder at him without looking back. He backs up. Trips over his chair. Lands on his keister.

Trista is laughing and skipping when they get back to the table. She shows the doll to Charlie. "*Grandma* got it for me!" she says. "I *love* my doll!"

Charlie looks at Donna. Smiles. "Just like that, eh?"

"Yep. Dathsit," she says.

"You know, you're one of the reasons why they don't allow grown-ups in here on their own," Charlie says.

"What?" Wide-eyed innocence. *"Me?"*

"You."

The following day is Labor Day, of course. Reality has nothing to do with any of this. Memorial Day was the trigger. The day after that was the Fourth of July. That was yesterday. Today is Labor Day. Bang, bang, bang. And so goes summer.

Charlie figures another parade would be good, in spite of how Memorial Day went. He sits with Trista and tells her about how this parade is sort of like the one on Memorial Day, but much better because there will be even more volunteer firefighters at this one, and they have a big tournament at the end.

"What's a turnyymint?" Trista asks. "Is that like candy?"

"No, it's a place where they race big fire trucks, and climb ladders really fast, and hook up water hoses to the trucks and shoot the water at targets. It's very exciting, but a little noisy. Want to go?"

"Will the parade-stuff man with the toys be there?"

"Probably," Charlie says.

"Can we sit on the side of the street that's he's on?" Trista asks.

"I'll do my best."

"Okay, then. We can go."

Charlie always liked the Labor Day parade because it involves a large amount of afternoon drinking. Long Island's volunteer firefighters are famous for that. They have firehouses with bars that rival any big-belly bar in America. The Labor Day tournament features food tents and beer tents and everyone is as happy as can be. It's not the best day to have a fire in your house if you're planning on having one, though.

So Trista, Abby, Donna and Charlie drive to a parking lot, arriving there early enough to set up on what they all hope is a good spot at the curb this time, one with actual band music. Trista now understands that there's a certain amount of waiting involved with any parade, and she's okay with that. The parade-stuff man with the toys shows up early and, thankfully, on their side of the street. Charlie helps Trista pick a toy, a stuffed monkey, hanging from a string off a long stick. Donna pays for it. What monkeys have to do with Labor Day is anyone's guess, but Trista is happy and all's well with the world.

So they're sitting on their lawn chairs, waiting. Charlie leans back to look at the sky, which is as clear as grace with a caressing breeze, summer's traditional last gasp. He notices a grey squirrel balancing on the wire just over their heads.

"Look up, Trista," he says. "It's a circus squirrel!"

She leans back in her chair, as does Abby and Donna. People sitting around them also lean back to look because there's not much of anything else going on right now, and the squirrel's really cute. He's dancing on the wire, like Philippe Petit moving between the twin towers of the World Trade Center.

"I like him," Trista says. "He's funny."

The squirrel can't decide what to do. He keeps switching directions, this way and that way on the thick black wire. Should I stay, or should I go?

Finally, he decides. He steps between two wires that have a ceramic insulator separating them. He spots a bump in the wire that looks tasty, so he takes a deep bite with his sharp squirrely teeth and thus turns himself into a furry conduit, which instantly brings back the Fourth of July for an instant.

There's a flash of pure-white light, a ZZZZZZZTT, and the squirrel freezes in place and glows red for a few exquisite moments before falling crispy and smoking to the asphalt. Trista watches, fascinated.

"What happened to the squirrel?" she asks.

The round transformer on that wooden pole over there catches fire in a spectacular electrical outburst. Lots of hot stuff arching down onto the parade route. A bunch of wires snap and go down, sparking and writhing like death snakes in the street. A breaker somewhere in the system trips and shuts off the power to, well, everything. No traffic lights. The crunchy sounds of cars hitting each other. No band music coming down the street. The parade-stuff man with the toys looks up and says, "Shit!"

But at least there are plenty of fire engines available.

Donna looks at Charlie. "Ready to go, parade boy?" Sweet smile.

"Yep." He stands and folds chairs.

"Where are we going?" Trista asks. "Can we help the squirrel?"

"Oh, he'll be fine," Donna says. "He's just sunbathing. We're going to Target, honey. It's toy time. But only if they have power."

Happy frickin' Labor Day.

Next up? Halloween. These days, people decorate their homes for Halloween like they used to decorate them only for Christmas. The stores get busy in August, selling blow-up ghouls and gory, Made-in-China mannequins for a lot of money. Large, empty stores in the malls open as temporary Halloween stores to sell more ghoulish crap. There's a major competition to see who can best scare the children.

It didn't used to be this way, Charlie thinks. When he was a kid, the only decorating for Halloween involved taping a few white-cardboard ghosts, or orange-cardboard jack-o'-lanterns in the front window. You would reuse them each year, so there were raw grey-cardboard spaces, like torn-off scabs, along the edges from last year's tape removal.

If you felt like wasting a perfectly good pumpkin, you could carve a face into it, stick a candle inside, and place it on your front stoop. The candle would summon the neighborhood's feral teenagers, and two minutes later, your jack-o'-lantern would be pumpkin pulp in the road. Cars would be squishing its sorry remains for the next week.

His mother would give him some of his father's old clothes and a beat-up fedora to wear. She'd blacken a wine cork with a match and smear the burnt part on his face, even though the cork was still hot. If he cried, she told him to shut up and stand still. His father would give him the remains of one of his nasty cigars to carry. "You're a bum," his mother would say, and that was the classic kid costume.

He was a bum every Halloween, and so were all of his friends, both boys and girls. It didn't cost anything to be a bum. Nowadays, kids have to have store-bought costumes that cost more than his father used to make in a week, and you can't wear the same costume next year.

The only other thing Charlie needed on Halloween when he was a bum was an old sock filled with flour. Some of his friends copped their father's shaving cream, but there would be hell to pay if Charlie got caught doing that. Worse than normal. So Charlie stuck to the flour sock. Smack your buddy with that sock and he'd look even more like a bum. White flour everywhere. And it hurt like hell to get hit with that sock, which made it even more fun.

They'd knock on doors and people would *always* answer, except for a few grouchy old bastards. That's what the shaving cream was for. Oh, and the eggs, if you could get them.

"Trick or Treat!"

Charlie loved the people that gave out Lemonheads and Now & Later candy. He hated the people who gave him apples, but what can you do? He'd toss those in the street with the smashed pumpkins when he got around the corner. One time, he found a long sewing needle in an apple he had smashed. That was the year he figured out that tricks work both ways.

Trista wanted to be Elsa from the Disney film, *Frozen*, as did just about every other little girl on Long Island. The streets in their neighborhood looked like an Elsa casting call, but it made her happy, so there they were. The four of them walked the neighborhood and knocked on doors. Charlie had decided to blacken his face with a cab sav cork at the last minute. He turned his coat inside-out and did the same with his NY Mets cap. He looked like he could live under a bridge. Donna wouldn't let him take the flour sock, though. Boo.

Trista said he was embarrassing her. "You look like a dirty man," she said.

Perfect!

The counterweight to Lime Day is Blow Day, and this is the day when the prettiness of autumn has passed and the remaining brown leaves are hanging on the trees, as crispy as the Labor Day squirrel. They're waiting for the Nor'easter that will always arrive to slash them from their trees and send them swirling. Blow Day is winter's true front door. But before that day arrives on Long Island, we first have to deal with Thanksgiving, a day that can either warm your heart or break it, depending on what you chose to remember.

It was coming tomorrow and the weather forecast was good. Chilly with no rain, and the winds were supposed to be light. That would make it a good day for the big balloons at the Macy's parade. Charlie suggested that they get up early and drive into the city. He and Donna used to take Abby when she was small, but they had never taken Trista.

"Haven't you had enough parades for this year?" Donna asked.

"There's no better parade than this one," Charlie said. "I want it to be like it used to be. Let's go, okay?"

So they went.

Charlie has a special way of getting to the Macy's Thanksgiving Day Parade. It starts at 9 am from West 77th Street and Central Park West. They blow up the big, character balloons the night before just around the corner from there. They would leave their house at 6 am and drive the Long Island Expressway through the Queens-Midtown Tunnel. No traffic at all on Thanksgiving morning. Once out of the tunnel, Charlie would head North and then West across Manhattan. He'd look for a free-parking spot on the street near East 72nd Street and Fifth Avenue. Good luck getting a spot there during the week, but it's easy on Thanksgiving because so many people left town yesterday.

Get out of the car and head for the park. It's a crisp and gorgeous walk across Central Park, and you come out on West 72nd Street, right across the street from The Dakota, built in 1884 by Edward Clark and Isaac Merritt Singer, father of Paris Singer, who developed Singer Island. It would be nice way to close the circle that had opened last February.

Charlie knew that the best part about watching the parade from this spot was that there was music, and when Santa finally rode by, just ahead of the sanitation trucks, they could walk across the park, drive home, and the parade would still be on the TV, which was a magical thing for any little kid.

Trista was so fascinated by the big balloons that she never once asked where the parade-stuff guy with the toys was.

It was an old-school Thanksgiving, the best one ever.

"What are you most thankful for this year?" Donna asked him in the dark when they were in bed that night.

"You."

"Aww thanks. What else?"

"Abby and Trista."

"What else?"

"Clare and Chara, and those wonderful memories."

"And what else?"

"Um, afternoon drinking?" he said.

Donna giggled like a little girl. Poked him in the ribs. He smiled in the dark and reached for her.

She reached back.

Daddy.

Abby's Christmas gift to them that year was another vacation on Singer Island. Charlie and Donna were gobsmacked. "It's going to be different this time, though," Abby said

"How so?" Donna asked.

"I didn't rent an apartment this time. I rented a house, and not for a month. For two, and starting on January 15th."

"Why?"

"So we can all be there for Clare's 36th birthday on January 27. Trista and I are going with you. We have beautiful seashells to find, and new friends to make. And Clare knows we're all coming. She helped me find the place. It's very close to her house. We'll fly down this time. I've taken care of everything."

And so they returned.

45

"This is a pretty one, Grandpa," Trista said, brushing the sand from the shell. "Let's keep it."

"Yes, that's a nice one." He holds out the pink, heart-shaped bucket and she drops the shell into it.

"Are there any red ones?" she asks.

"The red ones come when you're older," Charlie says. "They'll appear by magic. You'll see."

"Okay, let's look for more pinks," she says.

"Lots of pinks. Here's one." Charlie bends, being careful of his back. He picks up the shell and examines it. "I don't know. What do you think?" He hands it to her.

She looks. "Do you like it?" Trista asks.

"I'm not sure."

"Then let's put it back. We have to be *sure*. We *both* have to like it," Trista says.

"And if we don't, it's not bucket-worthy, right?" Charlie says.

"What's wordy?"

"*Worthy*. It means it deserves being in the bucket with the other pretty shells.

"Oh. Okay." She stoops and picks up another. "This one is wordy."

Charlie doesn't correct her. He likes bucket-wordy better. It makes it sound like the shells will be talking to each other. Chatty shells. Nice.

"Yes, that one looks very wordy," he says. "Into the bucket she goes."

"How do you know it's a she, Grandpa?"

"I can tell."

"Is it magic?" Trista asks.

"Yes, it's magic."

"Will you teach me how to tell?"

"I will. Pick up another one you like."

Trista looks around, trying to decide. Finally, she does. She picks it up and hands it to Charlie. "Okay," he says, brushing off the sand. "Look at it and tell me if it's a girl shell or a boy shell."

"How will I know?"

"Ask it." Charlie hands it back to her.

Trista take the shell, holds it to her mouth and whispers, "Are you a boy shell or a girl shell?" She looks at Charlie.

"Now hold it to your ear," he says. She does. "Listen carefully," Charlie says.

Trista does. Her eyes go wide. "It's a *girl!*" she says.

"And that's how the magic works," Charlie says. "You just have to ask the right questions. Do you know what we call that magic?"

"What, Grandpa?"

"We call that The Chat."

"I like The Chat," she says.

"That's good, sweetheart. It will serve you well in life."

The breeze is light on Singer Island right now. Seventy-three degrees with a robin's egg sky. Snowing and windy on Long Island.

Who cares?

"I'd say it's a shame you have to work on your birthday, if I didn't know any better," Charlie says.

Clare laughs. "What better place to be on my birthday?" she asks. "The work is a joy, and I am with dear friends."

"Amen," Donna says. She and Charlie are sitting at the bar. Just behind them, at a table, are Abby, Trista and Chara. They're sharing a large plate of chicken fingers and an even bigger plate of fries. Donna turns to check on them. "All okay?"

"Oh, yeah," Abby says. "I am the Mother of the Year, committed to feeding the children healthy food." She pops a fry into her mouth. Smiles.

"That's my girl," Donna says. "Thanks for sitting at the kiddy table."

"Hey, don't thank me. I'm very happy here." She lifts her margarita.

"You're *pretty*," Chara says to Trista.

"You're pretty, *too*," Trista says. "Do you like seashells?"

"Yes!" Chara laughs. "And birds. Birds *fly*."

"I wish *I* could fly," Trista says. "I would go all the way up to the top of a tree."

"What would you see there?" Chara asks.

"I would see the ocean and the fishies, and more seashells."

"That's nice," Chara says. "Do you like French fries? I like French fries."

"I like French fries, and . . . ketchup!" Trista lifts a fry up high and zooms it down into the ketchup, like a seagull stealing a sandwich. Chara laughs so hard that tears form in her eyes. "You're *funny!*" Chara says.

"Those are happy tears, Chara," Trista says. "Grandpa taught me about happy tears. They're nice."

Donna is watching all of this from her stool. Clare is off taking care of Drink Sync. Charlie is shedding another tear for Ireland.

"Where is home?" Donna whispers to no one but herself, so no one answers.

"And *what* is home?"

"We once went to mass down here," Donna says. "It wasn't on Singer Island, and it was a while ago. Another place, but like this one."

"Is there another place quite like this one?" Clare asks.

"Good point. Not really, but the mailboxes were similar." Donna says, which makes Clare, she of the flamingo mailbox, laugh. "Thing I remember most about that mass was the old priest. He was filling in that day for the pastor, who was away on a retreat. The old priest lived in Virginia and he had a drawl that sounded like velvet feels. He talked about how some people spend money they don't have, to buy things they don't need, to impress people they don't like. Isn't that poetic?"

"'Tis," says Clare.

"Look at those two," Donna says, pointing at Trista and Chara, who are eating fries and chicken, laughing, and just loving the day. "And look at my daughter, who is back from the dead. What more could I want?"

"Yes," Clare says.

"And look at us," Donna says, reaching over to take Clare's hand. "How far we've both come."

"Yes." Clare squeezes Donna's hand. Soft smile and that wonderfully crooked cuspid. "*Yes.*"

"Where is *home*, Clare?"

"It's here, Donna. You *sense* that, don't you?"

"I *do.*"

"Good. Good."

"And *what* is home, Clare?"

Clare squeezes her hand again. Smiles again. "You *know*. You do."

"I *do.*"

"We should move here," Donna says to Charlie in the dark. She's tucked up against him, listening to his heartbeat.

"Is that possible?"

"I don't know. With Abby and Trista living with us, it would be a huge decision. We'd have to split up, unless. . ."

"Unless they moved with us," Charlie says.

"Yes."

They lay like that in the dark for a while, breathing softly. "Is that possible?" Donna asks.

"You tell me. I don't do money," Charlie says.

"It would be difficult, even if the four of us moved together. I won't depend on Abby for money. We just *can't*. Taking vacation money from her is one thing, but depending on her for day-to-day expenses, I just can't. She and Trista are fine now, financially. We can't cut into that. I won't do it."

"But there's nothing holding any of us on Long Island anymore," Charlie says.

"Well, there's Abby's business," Donna says. "But she's doing more and more work online now, so I don't know."

"So do you think there's a way?"

"I don't know. Let's sleep on it," Donna says.

"Okay. I love you."

"And I love you."

Long, deep kiss.

Charlie is filling the gas tank. Donna is in the passenger seat. Charlie always drives.

Donna is looking at the small convenience store attached to the gas-pump aisles. Used to be you could get a flat tire fixed at a gas station. Now you get energy drinks and bad hot dogs, Donna thinks. Good luck with that flat.

She's remembering their first car and how it had a hole in the floor from rust. It was on Charlie's side. He put a rubber floor mat over the hole to keep the rain from splashing up onto his legs when he was driving. She smiles, thinking about how that never bothered either of them. It seemed normal to fix the rust hole like that. And if some kid snapped off your radio antenna, you just replaced it with a wire clothes hanger. A cracked windshield was also normal. A pain in the ass if it was on the driver's side, sure, but it was one of those things you just lived with.

And make sure you have a few gallons of water in the trunk. Who needed antifreeze during the summer? And be sure to let the radiator cool before you pop that cap.

So many things they thought were both normal, and expected.

Donna keeps looking at the convenience store as Charlie waits for the tank to fill. There's a neon sign for the Florida Lottery in the window. It has a pink flamingo. She smiles at the image of that beautiful bird as Charlie pumps the gas. Her eyes half close and go dreamy. The neon bird goes out of focus.

Suddenly, she's out of the car and walking fast in her white flip-flops. "What's up?" Charlie asks, still holding the nozzle.

"I'll be right back," she barks over her shoulder, and heads for the store. "Stay there."

Two people are ahead of her on the line. The guy wants to get twenty bucks on Pump 4. He pays and leaves. Donna's tapping her foot, folding her arms, again and again, like she's waiting for a restroom. Hurry!

The woman needs a box of Marlboro Lights. "Got any matches?" she asks.

"No, we don't give matches with the cigarettes anymore. You want to buy a lighter?" He points at them.

"Nah, just looking for extra matches."

"Sorry."

She's gone.

"Help you?"

Donna is staring at the scratch-off Lotto tickets. She doesn't answer him. She has a look of furious concentration. She's quivering. He waits a moment and then helps the woman behind her. Diet Coke and a bag of Doritos.

Donna's eyes are practically closed. She's swaying.

"Are you okay, miss?"

Her eyes are closed now. She puts her left hand on the counter. Sways.

"Miss? You been drinking? You okay?"

Her eyes open and get wider. They're impossibly green. He's staring at them, shocked by them, but she's not looking at him. She's looking at the tickets. Her legs suddenly stomp apart, like a Flamenco dancer's. Her right hand comes up fast. A red fingernail points.

"No, I have *not* been drinking," Donna says. "I want *that* scratch-off ticket. *That* one." He turns to look. "Right *there*. No, the roll *next* to it. Dathsit. Five-thousand dollars a week for life."

He points. Raises an eyebrow. "Yes, *that* one. No, don't give me the one on the bottom of the roll. I want two up from there. The *third* one. Tear off that one for me. That's the one I need."

"I'm supposed to take the one that's lowest on the roll," he says. "It's company policy. I can't break the roll. I'll get fired. Sorry."

Donna is staring at the third one. "Fine!" she shouts. Give me all three. Quick! *That one*, the one that I need, and the two below it on the roll." She points. "One, two three. Quickly. Please." She blazes at him.

"Yes, sure. Okay," he says, shaking a bit, glancing at the security camera mounted on the ceiling. "You're a serious gambler, aren't you?" he laughs. "These are ten-dollar tickets, you know." He tears all three and hands them to her. His hand is shaking.

"I know," Donna says, handing him two twenties. He makes change quickly, glances toward the camera, hands her back a ten. She waves it off. "Keep it. Keep it."

"Really?"

"Yes, keep it." She staggers toward the door.

He looks up at the camera again. "Hey, thanks. You okay?" he asks, relieved that she's leaving, but still, those *eyes*.

She grabs the door handle. Pauses. Waits for her balance to return. "Yeth, I'm fine," she lisps, and turns. "Thankths."

She blasts her smile at him.

He gasps.

Donna turns and leaves.

Charlie is behind the wheel and waiting.

"You okay?" he asks. She's sweating and very pale now.

"I'm fine," she pants. Puff. Blow. "Just drive. Please. Just *drive*."

Charlie puts the car in gear. "Did something happen in there? What did you do in there? What *happened*?"

"I'm *fine*. I just bought a scratch-off ticket. Drive. That's all. Bought three, but you need just one of them. Drive. Three up from the bottom. I had a feeling. *Drive*."

"Where?"

Donna looks at the back of the third ticket. The odds of winning five thousand dollars a week for life are 1-in-6,060,000.

She smiles.

"Drive to Clare's house," Donna says.

"She's probably giving Chara dinner right now," Charlie says.

"That's okay. She'll be happy to see us. Trust me."

Clare answers the door. "Hello, strangers!" she says. "What's going on?"

"Charlie needs Chara's help," Donna says, brushing by her.

"Help with what?" Clare asks, concerned.

"With this?" Donna holds up the Lotto ticket, keeps walking. "He needs her to scratch it. Only *she* can scratch it. No one else."

"Why?" Clare looks at Charlie, who shakes his head and shrugs. Concerned.

"I don't know *why*," Donna laughs. "I just *know*."

Chara is eating Kraft mac and cheese. "Hi, Donna!" she says with her thick tongue, mouth full. "Hi, Charlie!"

"Hi, sweetheart!" Charlie says.

Donna slows; sits down next to her. Puts her arm around her. "Hi, honey," she says. "I need you to help Charlie."

"Help Charlie! Mommy, I help Charlie!"

"Yes, sweetheart. I need you to scratch this ticket for Charlie. I know you like to do this. It will really help him."

"Help *Charlie*!" Chara laughs and claps her hands.

Donna hands her the ticket and a quarter. "Go ahead, my love," she says. "Scratch away."

"Want some wine?" Clare asks, confused, but trusting.

"In a minute," Donna says. "We'll all have a drink in a minute. Thanks. Scratch, honey."

Chara's tongue sticks out a bit as she carefully scratches each dot with the quarter. She's meticulous, making sure all the covering is off each dot before she moves on to the next. Donna sits back and waits. No hurry anymore. She doesn't need to watch. Somehow, she knows.

"All done!" Chara says. "I hope you win, Charlie!" She hands the ticket to Donna, who hands it to Charlie and Clare without looking at it.

"Sweet Jesus," Charlie says.

"Oh, my god," Clare adds.

1-in-6,060,000.

Finally done.

Glasses up!

"You knew, *didn't* you?" Clare asks Donna the next afternoon. They're at her bar and the weather is just right. Charlie is gone for a moment, shedding a tear for Ireland, yet again, and without a care in the world. Not anymore.

"I had a very strong feeling, and then somehow I knew, yes."

"How?"

"I don't know. Something just made me get out of the car and go look at the Lotto tickets. I don't know why. I mean why do people choose a certain slot machine? Why this one and not that one? We've both heard stories about people hitting big. Why them? And why *that* machine?"

"I don't know," Clare says.

"How do you instantly know when you meet someone that this is the person you'll marry? That happens, too, and I'm sure all the time. I don't know how it happens, or why; it just does. This feeling with the ticket was so strong that I thought I was going to pass out. I just *knew*. Isn't that weird?"

"Wonderfully weird," Clare says.

"I was swaying and the guy at the register thought I was drunk, but I hadn't had a drink for hours."

"Could be a miracle?" Clare says.

"Could be. I don't understand."

"Don't try to understand, Donna. Just accept it." Clare smiles. "Be the reed."

"Always," Donna smiles back. "*Always*."

"So when will you cash it in?"

"We cashed it this morning. I listed myself as the owner. I'm better with money than he is. He knows that."

"I'm so happy for you both."

"I'm happy for *all* of us, Clare."

"You know, when I rented this place," Abby says, "the woman told me there was an option to buy if we liked it."

"What brought that up?" Donna asks.

"I don't know," Abby said. "She just mentioned it. She's a realtor. That's what they do."

"So what do you think?"

"Well, I love this place and there's really nothing keeping any of us on Long Island anymore," Abby says.

"What about your business?"

"I've been running that online for the past few years. You know that. I can be anywhere. People love doing things online these days."

Donna smiles at that, thinking about Charlie.

"And I would love for Trista to grow up with Chara. They're becoming such good friends. It would break both of their hearts if we had to leave."

"It broke your father's heart and my heart when we left last year. The only thing that saved us was that we were going home to you and Trista. There's really nothing else there for us anymore."

"Home is *here*," Abby says. "Here, where we're together. *All* of us. Palm Beach is a great place for weddings, and kindergarten starts this year."

"Yes," Donna says, "It's perfect, as it once was. People take the time to talk here, and to really listen to each other, and not talk over each other, and to share their stories. And to love. *Here*."

"I think Daddy's going to like being a townie," Abby smiles. "I think he's going to like it a *lot*."

Donna smiles.

46

"So now that you're set for life and in the perfect place, what are you going to do with yourself, Charlie?" Clare is wearing a pink bar tee and white shorts today. She sets another cab sav in front of him.

"Thank you very much, Saint Clare."

"My pleasure, young man. So what's it going to be? How will you fill your days?"

"Besides drinking with you, you mean?"

"That goes without saying."

"I was thinking of writing a book," Charlie says.

"Nice! You ever write a book before?"

"No, but there can't be much to it. Hey, it's nothing more than chatting on paper, right?"

"What will your book be about, Charlie?"

"I'd like to tell about all of this." Sweeping gesture. "All that's happened."

"You think people would believe it?"

"I don't know. If I told it right I think they might."

"Will I be in your book?"

"Absolutely."

"I'd like that. Is Donna coming by?"

"Later. She's taking her rays. That woman loves the sun."

"I know. We need to get her in here to appreciate some of this moody darkness and nice music."

The Beach Boys. Good Vibrations.

Perfect.

"Life is good," Clare says.

"It is, and now it's perfect. We want for nothing. My ladies are at peace. The stress is out of my life. We have our health. We're in the perfect place, and we have you and Chara as our dear friends. God's is in His heaven. All's right with the world."

"I'm so happy for all of you," Clare says. "For us."

That smile. He'll never have enough of that smile.

Chirp!

Can you order me a turkey club? No fries.

"See? We talk about her and she shows up. Well, at least on my phone. She's probably on her way over. She needs one of your famous turkey clubs."

"I like 'needs'," Clare says. "So much better than *'wants.'*"

"Well, it is one of your greatest creations," Charlie says.

"Yeah, we have a special recipe back there," Clare laughs, pointing a thumb at the kitchen. "We put the turkey on the top. No one else in the world does that." She smiles and puts the order into the computer. "Ready in a flash."

Chirp!

I forgot to ask if you could bring it over here. It's so lovely right now. I want to sit in the sun a while longer.

Tap, Tap, Tap.

Will do.

Clare is back with the turkey club. "She coming?"

"Change of plans," Charlie says. "I'm going to deliver it to the Sun Queen of the Beach."

"Nice. Just take it like that. She can bring the plate back later."

"Okay. Back in a few." Charlie puts the paper napkin over the plate and heads out the door. The sunlight hits him like God's Searchlight. He's had five wines but will tell anyone who asks that he's had two.

Irish division.

He starts across the street, humming Good Vibrations and happy he's not driving. He's holding the plate with the turkey club. A light breeze tugs at the napkin and he slows to secure it.

There's a turtle in the road. Charlie looks down at it.

"Why did the turtle cross the road?" he asks and waits for an answer, but the little guy's not interested in Charlie's question, or in Charlie. It just keeps plodding along.

Charlie turns and walks backward across the road, waving the plate with both hands in turtle encouragement. "C'mon, Speedy! You can do it!"

The turtle ignores him.

A black Camaro makes the turn from around the corner. Wheels squeal. Way too fast. The kid at the wheel spots the turtle and swerves to miss it, but he swerves *at* Charlie who is still in the road. That makes no sense at all.

The kid hits the horn but doesn't slow. Charlie jumps back and out of his way. The kid keeps going.

"Asshole!" Charlie shouts after him, waving the plate with one hand. The turtle keeps walking. Couldn't care less about any of this nonsense.

A seagull zooms in from behind Charlie and hits the sandwich hard .

Charlie shouts and takes a step backward. The sandwich is gone. The plate's in pieces in the road. White on black. God's Searchlight beats on the white shards. It doesn't care either.

Charlie backs up onto the sidewalk.

Six years ago, this tall palm started lifting the sidewalk just behind where Charlie is now standing. It had worked on that sidewalk with quiet determination and it didn't care what the Public Works Department thought about this. It was nature at work; and nature doesn't care about any of us.

The palm tree just did what palm trees do.

As did the seagull.

As did the turtle.

None of them gave a damn about Charlie, or anyone else.

Charlie, still shouting at the now-gone kid in the Camaro, takes one more scared step backward. His right heel hits the lifted edge of the sidewalk and he goes down, five-wines hard. The back of his head connects with the low brick wall that separates the sidewalk from the swings and slides.

Thump.

47

"I have to find her," Charlie slurs. "She'll know what to do." He's walking the beach. Trying to find balance on the warm sand.

The sand.

"Where does she sit? Where? Can't remember. Head hurts. *Hurts.* Donna?"

The shells are everywhere, spinning in the blurred blizzard of his sight. She'll know what to do. Always does.

No red ones. Trista is too small for red ones. They'll come later. When she's older.

Later.

But is that one? He bends. Reaches. The rest of his body follows his reach and he thumps face-first into the sand.

The *sand.*

It's in his mouth now. He pushes it out with his tongue. Tries to spit but there's no spit, just dryness and a real bad taste. He closes his eyes. Sand in his eyes. Blinks. Reaches for her warm hand. Squeezes. Her hand falls through his fingers.

The sand.

She'll put baby oil on my back in a little while, he thinks. She always does. And then we can go in the water to wash off the sand. I'll hold her. Can't let the undertow take her. I'll hold her. Hold her forever. Never let go. Not like I did with Abby. *Never*.

"I'm sorry, Donna," he whispers. "I'm sorry."

Quiet.

"Head hurts, Donna. Hurts. *Hur. . .*"

The sand doesn't care.

The gull, the largest of the flock, is bold from hunger. He has gray feathers on his breast, which makes him look dirty. His eyes are black buttons. He opens his beak wide and laughs.

Shrieks.

Steps forward and pokes Charlie's neck.

No movement. Nothing thrown. Nothing.

Pokes. Pokes.

SHRIEKS!

The others step up.

Poke.

Never *really* alone.

Made in the USA
Columbia, SC
06 May 2018